The Shape of Fear

of Fear

Also by Nan Hamilton

Killer's Rights

The Shape of Fear

Nan Hamilton

Dodd, Mead & Company
New York

Published by Dodd, Mead & Company, Inc.
79 Madison Avenue, New York, N.Y. 10016
Distributed in Canada by
McClelland and Stewart Limited, Toronto
Manufactured in the United States of America
Designed by Erich Hobbing

First Edition

1   2   3   4   5   6   7   8   9   10

Library of Congress Cataloging-in-Publication Data

Hamilton, Nan.
    The shape of fear.

    (A Red badge novel of suspense)
    I. Title.
PS3558.A4434S5   1986   813'.54   86-6227
ISBN 0-396-08838-4

For my son, John, and his wife, Kesang, whose loving support and unbounded confidence have meant so much.

The Shape
of Fear

Chapter One

Joe Flynn served the three men at the end of the bar, then walked back to the cash register near the door. Normally he would have stayed talking with them, cracking a few jokes, but not that day. Any time now Tak Shimizu would be coming for his money, as he'd done once a month for two years. Joe could see no end to it. Every so often Shimizu raised the ante; if he did it again, Joe knew he could not pay. It made his gut ache just thinking about it.

His eyes slid to the gun he kept for protection on the shelf below the register and he dropped his hand over it, smoothing the hard outlines. If he had any balls, he'd use it.

But he didn't need a gun. He clenched his massive fists and stared down at them. How easily he could batter Shimizu to death in an alley some dark night. Then his fingers uncurled and he let his hands drop. That way was closed to him, too, because of Mary.

Sighing, he rang up a No Sale on the old-fashioned register. When the drawer slid open with a dull, metallic ping, he took out an envelope stuffed with several large bills and laid it beside the gun.

As always when he was upset, Joe reached for a soft cloth and began polishing nonexistent smudges from the rich mahogany surface of the bar. It comforted him to feel the enduring wood beneath his hands. The long, old-fashioned bar with its brass footrail had been the glory of Flynn's Pub

1

since his father, Michael J., had first opened for business fifty years ago. The neighborhood was nothing much then: a few houses, gas station, diner, and market, but it at least rubbed elbows with sprawling Los Angeles. It always amused Joe to think how shrewd old Dad had been, shrewd and blessed with Irish luck. The small neighborhood had grown with increasing numbers of Irish, Poles, and Italians, all of whom had healthy thirsts. Flynn's Pub had prospered.

Michael J. had fondly imagined he was building a business for his son Joseph, but when the time came the boy had wanted none of it. He'd joined the navy, done his stint, then dashed his father's hopes again by turning pro wrestler. A black-haired, blue-eyed Irishman, young Joe had built a promising career as the Mighty Flynn. Broad of shoulder, narrow of hip, with muscles to spare, he'd made an imposing figure marching into the ring wearing a green cape and brandishing a shillelagh. He'd been a pretty good wrestler, too. So the old man had made the best of it, and proudly displayed pictures of the Mighty Flynn on every wall of the pub.

Joe smiled, remembering as he polished in wide soothing circles. As always, his thoughts turned to his wife, Mary. Her brother, a wrestler too, had brought her to see the fights one night. Joe had asked her out to be polite, and before he knew it, the Mighty Flynn had gone down for the count. Pretty Mary, with her red hair and green eyes, fun to be with, gentle and womanly . . . all he knew was that he felt like a king with her and was miserable without her. He'd suddenly realized how tired he was of the wrestling game. For too many nights, he'd sat alone in impersonal hotel bedrooms nursing his bruised and aching body, aware that as long as somebody got stomped, nobody in the screaming crowds really gave a damn whether he won or lost—nobody but Mary.

2

So they'd married, and Joe had taken over the pub, giving Michael J. his long-dreamed-of trip back to Ireland. The famous shillelagh now hung behind the bar, together with autographed pictures of the ring stars of his day: Gorgeous George, Lou Thesz, the great Rocco, and others. The pub became a mecca for ex-wrestlers and fans who wanted to "remember when."

He joked with them and listened, but the wrestling talk woke no longing for the old days. His happiness lay in his two kids, and Mary. Even now, paralyzed and in a wheelchair, she was the darling of his heart. He'd give her the world, if he could.

Half ashamed of his fit of nostalgia, Joe shook out his cloth, folded it, then continued to polish his way down the bar in long, sweeping strokes. His present customers were old-timers from the automotive plant nearby. It had contributed its share to Flynn's prosperity. So had the new apartments and businesses that had grown up around it. Joe felt as if time were catching up with him as he thought about the changes in the old neighborhood. Only Maple Street where he and Mary still lived had stayed the same, but even there most of the original families had gone.

One change had been the increasing number of hard-working Japanese-Americans who'd moved into the community. Joe recalled all the grousing that had gone on at the time. People worried over property values; some of them sold their homes. Gradually, however, the newcomers had melded into the neighborhood, making it better than they'd found it. The fine big community center they'd built was open to everyone, as was the recent low-rent senior-citizen apartment complex.

Before Mary's stroke, the Flynns had been closely involved with all the center's activities, as had their children. The Japanese friends they'd made there still came to see Mary regularly. Fred Hata, a retired gardener and their close friend, insisted on looking after Mary's small garden that she'd loved so much. He brushed aside any offer of payment.

That was why the anti-Japanese talk Joe heard in the bar these days worried him. Guys like Bill Stack, now drinking at the end of the bar, were always sounding off about what "Japs" and "Chinks" and the "rest of their yellow buddies" were doing to the country. Somebody nearly always added, "And look how they've taken over Maple Street."

It was ugly talk, and Joe never let it pass, though it cost him some customers. This faceless "they" being talked about were good friends and neighbors. He had never been one to evaluate things in general terms. For Joe, people came one by one; he liked or disliked them that way.

Bill had once threatened to beat up any Japanese that came into the bar. Joe had taken down the shillelagh and said, "Not while I'm running Flynn's." Bill had backed down; big as he was, he didn't want to tangle with Joe.

The big old-fashioned clock over the bar said it was six-thirty, a slack period before the evening rush. Joe put away his cloth and sat down on a stool, glad that Barry would soon come in to relieve him. Maybe Shimizu wouldn't come in today. He'd go home and get Mary's dinner, maybe spend a little extra time with her.

The evening news was on the TV. Bill and his friends nursed their drinks and stared at the screen. At heart they weren't bad guys, Joe reflected. In the old days when the automotive plant first opened, they'd always come in for a drink on the way home. They'd been real likable guys, always laughing and kidding around.

That had changed, too. Since they and a lot of others had been laid off at the plant, they'd grown sullen and morose. The only thing on their minds these days was the damn Japanese imports that they swore had cost them their jobs. Most of the guys who came into the pub, including occasional blacks and Chicanos, felt the same. They blamed the "gooks" for everything from unemployment to bad weather.

The hell of it was that Joe sympathized with their side of it, too. When a man works hard and does a good job, he doesn't expect to get laid off. At first there'd been a lot of talk about moving on, but where could they move to? There were unemployed autoworkers all over the country. He could understand their bitterness and their need for a scapegoat. God knows he had no answer to their problems.

"Hey, Joe, you asleep?" Bill thumped on the bar for service. "Give us 'nother drink." Bill's big voice and heavy fist commanded compliance, if not respect.

Joe hurried over. "What'll it be, the same?"

Bill grunted assent and rubbed his hand over his face. Belching, he put down some bills. "My buddies, too," he mumbled. He'd just cashed his unemployment check and was feeling flush.

"Thanks, ol' buddy!" Benny Polser tried to throw a comradely arm across Bill's shoulders, but was shrugged off with a sour look.

Polser was a skinny little guy with big ears and not much between them. Bill treated him like dirt, but Benny still kept trying to make an impression.

"Same for me, Joe." Erne Smith was black and had been foreman of their crew. He was rangy and rawboned without much to say; mean as hell, though, if he was crossed.

The TV announcer was intoning, "We'll bring you the latest news on the Victor Chin case after the station break."

Bill shushed everyone to silence. "Listen to this, Joe. They're trying to put two good guys in jail, guys just like us, for beatin' up some damn Jap. Can you believe it? So they got a little carried away . . . he had it comin'!"

5

"Did us all a favor, them guys," Benny chimed in. "I'd do the same thing, you bet." As usual, he was sucking up to Stack, saying what he hoped would please him. Joe could have predicted what he'd say next. "Look how the Japs took my pop's store from me!"

Everybody knew Benny had run his father's store into the ground after his dad had died. He'd been damn lucky the Watanabe family had bought it and taken it off his hands.

"Shut up, Polser," Bill growled. "I'm sick of hearin' about your damn store. Piss off! I'm through buyin'."

Erne was amused, but Benny wilted. His mouth worked for a moment; then he put down his half-empty glass. "Maybe I should go see how my ma's doing," he said, trying for some shreds of dignity. Benny's half-blind, senile old mother was his usual ploy for sympathy.

"Shut up! I wanna hear this." Bill made a swipe at Benny, who took off out the door without another word.

"Pretty hard on him, weren't you, Bill?" Joe had seen the shamed look on Benny's face, and felt sorry for him.

"He'll get over it. Now shut up and listen."

Against a background of an artist's drawings of the courtroom scene, the announcer brought viewers up to date. "The victim, Victor Chin, went to a bar to celebrate his upcoming marriage. A waitress gave evidence that two autoworkers, Ronald Ebens and his stepson, Michael Nitz, made racially denigrating remarks to Chin. A brawl started and they were all ordered outside. The two autoworkers armed themselves with a baseball bat, followed Chin, and attacked him in front of witnesses. He was beaten so badly he died three days later." Shots of the bar and the place where Chin had been beaten flashed on the screen.

"I wouldn't of needed no bat," Bill muttered, flexing his big hands.

Joe looked at him with disgust as the announcer continued. "It is tragic that Chin, who was Chinese-American, was mistaken for Japanese. Feeling runs high in Detroit, since many residents attribute the hard times in the auto industry to Japanese imports."

"You got that right!" Erne Smith was stirred to comment, subsiding as the announcer continued.

"The prosecutors dropped the murder charge, allowing the defendants to plead no contest to manslaughter. They were given a fine and three years' probation. However, due to an overwhelming tide of protests from Asians across the country, the autoworkers were indicted and brought to trial on the charge of violating Chin's civil rights."

"Rights!" Bill shouted. "Bull! The blacks got rights, the Japs and Chinks got rights, even the damn South Americans got 'em. What about us white guys? Ain't we got any?" He shut up only to hear what the announcer was saying.

"When the case went to trial, Ebens was found guilty, but his stepson, Michael Nitz, was acquitted. Today a United States district judge sentenced Ebens to twenty-five years in prison. The case will be appealed."

There was a close-up shot of the two defendants. Joe thought they looked quiet, decent types, like his own customers. Yet they'd killed a man in a crazy rage, the same kind of rage that was simmering in a lot of the decent, ordinary guys who sat at his bar.

"That's justice?" Bill shouted. "There's no justice for us guys anymore. We gotta make our own. Damn the bastards!" He went into a paroxysm of coughing, his face red and congested. Erne pounded him on the back, and Joe brought water.

No one heard the door open, but a new voice cut across Bill's spasm of coughing. "Hey, Joe, picked up my Nissan today. Gotta celebrate!'' Tak Shimizu's whinnying laugh filled the room.

Joe turned, his mouth going dry. Any Japanese coming into the bar at that moment would have been like a match to tinder, but in Bill's outraged mood, this plump, cocky little bastard was like dynamite.

Joe hurried toward him, hoping to give him the envelope and get him out, but Shimizu kept yammering about his wonderful new Japanese car as he settled himself on the barstool. He seemed oblivious to the tension in the room, carelessly opening the jacket of his three-hundred-dollar suit to pull out a gold cigarette case. ''Cigarette, anyone?'' he offered.

When no one answered, he took out a cigarette for himself and lit it with a monogrammed gold lighter.

''You know me, Joe,'' he said. ''Always buy the best. That's why I bought a Japanese car.'' Shimizu was enjoying himself. He knew most of Flynn's patrons were from the automotive plant, so he got a kick out of needling them. ''Don't take it personal, boys.'' He gave his short bray of a laugh. ''I'll buy everybody a drink to toast my new Nissan.''

''Another time,'' Joe snapped. He picked up the stashed envelope and shoved it in Shimizu's hand. ''Here's the insurance payment.'' He stressed the word *insurance* for Bill and Erne's benefit.

Tak put the envelope in the pocket of his expensive raw silk jacket and smiled. ''What's the hurry? I offered to buy drinks all around.'' He leaned on the bar, grinning.

Bill got slowly to his feet, then shoved Benny's half-filled glass down the bar. Before Joe could catch it, the glass fell over, spilling beer on Shimizu's sleeve.

''I don't drink with Japs,'' Bill shouted, his shoulders bunching. Shimizu's expression hardened and his hand went inside his coat. Joe tensed, knowing Shimizu carried a gun.

"Hi, folks!" Barry, Joe's relief, came in. "Sorry to be late." Shimizu took his hand out of his pocket and Joe let his breath ease out.

Erne got a grip on Bill. "Hey, buddy, cool it!" Erne knew Barry was an ex-cop, and he wanted no trouble with him.

Bill tried to shake loose. "I'm gonna get that dirty Jap," he yelled, then doubled over, choking on his own rage. Erne lost no time dragging him to the door and shoving him outside.

Joe turned to Barry. "Take over now. I'm going home."

"Not yet," Shimizu cut in. "Got some business to discuss." He got off the barstool and went over to one of the booths, where he sat down. "I'll have that drink now, Joe. Bring me a gin and tonic."

Joe stared at Shimizu. It was a hell of a thing when a creep like that could order an Irishman around. Joe fought down the desire to crack his fist across that smug face. With hands that shook, he mixed the drink and took it over to the booth.

"Sit down, Joe," Shimizu said genially. He tasted the drink, then remarked, "A touch more gin next time." Picking up one of the green shamrock matchbooks, he looked at it, then dropped it into his pocket. He stared at Barry, who self-consciously busied himself farther down the bar. Then he leaned toward Joe and began to talk. Barry could hear nothing of what was said until Joe's voice suddenly rose.

". . . but I can't pay it," Joe said.

Then Shimizu pulled an envelope out of his pocket and shoved it in front of Joe. Barry watched Joe look at something inside, but Joe's broad back hid whatever it was from view.

After a few moments Shimizu stood up, smiling. "All understood, Joe?"

Joe didn't answer. But apparently Shimizu was satisfied, since he left the pub whistling.

Barry moved closer. "Anything wrong, Joe?"

"No," Joe answered in a low, flat voice. As he stood up and turned around, his face was gray. "I'm going home, Barry," he said. "If I don't get back, close up as usual."

Chapter Two

"I'm goin' back in and fix that Jap bastard!"

It took all Erne's strength to hang on to Bill and keep him from kicking in the closed door of the pub.

"Where's your brain, man? You clobber the Jap in front of Joe and that ex-cop Barry and you're goin' to jail. Take him when no one's lookin'."

That got Bill's attention. "Yeah," he said, and turned his back on the pub. "When he's alone." Then he saw the car parked at the curb.

If Bill loved anything in this world it was cars, and this one drew him like a magnet. Even in the fading light he could see its sleek, beautiful lines, sense the hidden power, the smooth, intricate functioning of inanimate parts that gave it life. Gently he ran his hand over the shining blackness of the hood, then peered in at a computerized instrument panel worthy of an aircraft.

"Looks like it cost a mint." Erne's voice was bitter.

Bill straightened, ashamed to have been seduced by the very thing he hated. With a soft sound of pain, he raised his fists and slammed them on the hood, again and again. "Whore!" he muttered. "Dirty Jap whore!"

Erne grabbed at his arm. "Come on, let's get away from here."

Bill shook him off. "Leave me be."

One look at Bill's face and Erne knew he was wasting his breath. "See you around, then," he muttered, and turned away. He passed Benny Polser standing in the shadows of a nearby storefront. No matter how many times Bill kicked his ass, the stupid bastard always came back for more.

Bill just stood and stared at the car, rage burning in him. It was a symbol of everything that had gone wrong with his life, the frustration that haunted his dreams and poisoned his waking hours. Suddenly he wanted to smash it, punish it, reduce it to the nothing he'd become. His body began to shake, overpowered by a dizzying weakness.

When the moment passed, he pulled himself together and went across the street to his old blue Chevy, got in, and slammed the door. He searched for the bottle hidden beneath the seat and with trembling fingers opened it and put it to his mouth. The liquid heat joined and blended with the fire inside him.

The drink made him feel better, stopped the trembling. He looked over at Shimizu's car, but his rage no longer shook him. Now it shot through his brain, making him feel strong and righteous, demanding action. He drank again, then capped the bottle and dropped it on the floor of the back seat. It clinked against his old metal toolbox. Suddenly he began to laugh as a plan took shape in his mind. He wanted another drink, but decided against it and settled back to wait until Shimizu appeared. His eyes on the pub door, he didn't even notice Benny Polser coming across the street.

"Hey, Bill," Benny said, and paused, uncertain of his welcome.

Startled, Bill cursed, then said, "Get lost, jerk! Can't you see I'm thinkin'?"

Benny stared at him, his face clouding with disappointment. Then he trudged back toward his own beat-up old van with its faded lettering that said "Polser's Groceries."

It wasn't long before Shimizu came out and got into his car. The engine roared arrogantly to life, and the Nissan sped smoothly away.

Bill started the Chevy and U-turned to follow, catching up at a long red light. His quarry turned right and spurted ahead. Bill idled along, his eyes on the Nissan's taillights. Soon he saw Shimizu turn into the drive of a new apartment complex on the outskirts of the Maple Street neighborhood. Its modern, white, Mediterranean-style design looked out of place beside the older homes and apartments of the neighborhood, but there was a long waiting list of would-be tenants for its luxury units backed by open garage stalls. The kind of people who could afford its rents didn't like to park their expensive cars on the street.

As Bill drove slowly past, he watched the Nissan head into the first bank of garages on the left. By the time he had turned and pulled up to the curb, Shimizu was disappearing into one of the apartments on the right.

There was no one about. It was dinner and TV time. Bill knew he'd never have a better chance. He reached into his toolbox for what he wanted, then got out of his car, being careful to close the door quietly. Running up the drive to the left-hand bank of garages, he looked for Shimizu's car. The first stall was empty; the car was in the second.

A small scrape of sound made his heart leap, but he could see nothing, no one. His breath coming short and fast, he turned back to the car and stood looking at it, feeling a strange reluctance for what he was about to do. Angrily he shook off the momentary weakness and considered how he should begin. He realized that smashing the windows would be too noisy, so he knelt down beside the rear tire, let the air out, then cut and slashed it with savage strokes. He did the same to the others.

Pocketing the knife, he went to the front of the car and forced open the hood. He allowed his fingers to caress the beautiful complexity of the engine, but only for a moment. Then savagely his skilled hands began to disembowel it. As he smashed each intricate part, he felt an almost orgasmic pleasure.

But his compulsion to destroy was not sated. He took his heavy wrench and began to gouge the car's sleek black sides. Suddenly a shout jerked him around.

"You . . . get out of there with your hands up!" Shimizu's voice was ugly, like the small black gun in his hand.

Bill stood frozen, unable to move. It had seemed so simple to smash the car and slip away. Now he was caught. The gun made a clicking sound; the Jap was going to shoot! In desperate panic, he threw the wrench.

Bull's-eye! It struck Shimizu between the eyes. The Japanese fell backward, arms flailing. The gun fired as it dropped from his hand. Something red hot seared into Bill's right arm. He jerked and grabbed at it, doubling over in pain. The sound of the shot still rang in his head like a cannon. Someone must have heard! Shimizu lay on his back, eyes closed, hands outflung.

Terror blotted out the pain as Bill ran past the Japanese, clutching at his arm, trying to stop the blood. Somehow he reached his car. Once inside, he fumbled the key into the lock, started up, and sped away. He never noticed that the door to one of the apartments had opened and a woman looked curiously after the old blue Chevy.

The woman stood in the doorway looking into the street, but the blue Chevy pulling away was not the car she'd been expecting. She went inside again and closed the door, glad her husband had not come home earlier. The very thought that he might have walked in while Tak Shimizu was in the apartment made her feel ill.

14

The acrid smell of burning reminded her of the vegetables she had charred in the agitation of Shimizu's visit. Leaving the pan to soak, she cleaned some more vegetables and set them to cook. Then she finished icing the cake, which he'd interrupted. Duke should surely be home soon. She opened the apartment door and looked out, then went to stand on the short flight of steps that led to the sidewalk. The fresh air seemed to cool her burning cheeks. A motorcyclist and a van passed down the street, but there was no sign of Duke.

Tears of despair pushed at her eyelids, but she held them back. Her Duke must find her smiling, with no trace of tears. Then he would say, "My Midori," and kiss her, his lips gentle, his mustache tickling just a little. He would hold her in his arms and she would feel safe again. But she must be patient! The men in the carpool had probably stopped at Flynn's for a beer.

Sometimes they came in the back way, depending on who was driving. She went to look down the alley. Just then the automatic timer turned on the few lights between the stalls so that a huddled lump lying half in the shadows caught her eye. Maybe it was an animal, maybe hurt! She hurried toward it.

When she saw what the lump was, she almost screamed, but cut it off and dropped to her knees beside the body. It was Shimizu! There was a bloody gouge between his eyes, the side of his face was badly battered, and his neck was bent to one side. His jacket had bunched up and lay open, exposing his bloodstained shirt.

A sharp pain in her knee made her look down and reach under her skirt to see what was digging into her. It was a heavy wrench, and as she pulled it out she saw that one end was covered with blood. She dropped it beside the body and frantically wiped her hand on her skirt.

15

Was he dead? He must be! The thought of what that could mean to her was electric. No need to be afraid anymore! Fighting back the desire to retch, she tried to feel the pulse in his neck, but couldn't find it. What if he wasn't dead?

She knew what she should do, but could she? Bending over him, she forced her mind to the task. Being safe again was all that mattered.

The picture! She had to get it! When she saw the open wallet beside Shimizu, she picked it up and checked inside. But it was empty. Frantically she began to search his jacket pockets. It had to be there. Then she saw a thin edge of stiff paper outlining the pocket of his shirt. Before she could pull the picture out, Duke spoke from behind her.

"Hey, Midori, what are you doing?" He was standing just a few feet away. Shoving the picture deeper into the pocket, she stood up to face him. "Oh, Duke, I so glad you come." Her carefully practiced English almost deserted her.

Duke stared down at her, unsmiling. She hurried to explain. "I go outside, wait for you. Then I hear noise and come see what is. I find him."

Duke put his lunchbox down and knelt beside the body. "Who is he?"

"Not know," Midori blurted. "Maybe he live here."

"What were you doing to him just now?"

"Nothing," she stammered. "I try to feel heartbeat."

Duke turned back to the man on the ground. One arm was flung out, the hand with its heavy gold ring grasping at nothing. The little finger was missing down to the first joint. "He looks dead to me, but maybe he isn't. Go call an ambulance and the police."

Midori stood, unmoving. She'd thought Tak was finally dead and she was free. A new fear squeezed her heart.

16

"What are you waiting for?" Duke's voice jolted her. "Get a move on." He was staring at her as if he'd never seen her before. Timidly she reached a hand toward him, but he seemed not to see it. As her eyes blurred with tears, she turned and ran back to the apartment.

Duke had been shocked when he'd seen Midori bending over the body, going through the man's pockets and his wallet. None of it made any sense.

He picked the wallet up; it was empty. Had she taken the money? He dropped the wallet, rejecting the ugly thoughts in his mind. He'd ask her and she'd explain everything. But the thoughts persisted. If it was nothing, why had she looked so guilty, so terrified?

An old suspicion gripped him. He'd picked Midori out of a marriage broker's magazine, brought her over from Japan, and married her. What did he really know about her, anyway?

He couldn't forget how she'd searched the man's pockets. Looking down at the body, he saw a white edge of what looked like cardboard half pulled out of the shirt pocket. He eased it out. For a long moment he stared down at a small color photograph. His insides felt as though they had turned to water.

It was a photograph of two men and a girl standing at a bar. A long cascade of black hair framed the girl's face, the same silky hair he loved to stroke. Midori's beautiful eyes stared up at him.

All she wore was a short transparent apron, her naked breasts barely concealed by the tray of drinks she held. The man on her right seemed familiar. On one finger of the hand caressing Midori's bare shoulder, he wore a heavy gold ring; the finger next to it was missing. Duke looked down at the body. It was the same man. He clenched his hands

17

against the pain that shook him, not wanting to believe the truth even now.

He stared stupidly at the body. The thought of that maimed hand touching Midori was maddening. Then another, more terrible thought struck him. Had Midori killed him to get the picture? He looked around for a weapon and saw the bloodied wrench. Her fingerprints would be on it!

Not letting himself think, he picked up the wrench, and pulling out the white handkerchief Midori had tucked into his pocket just that morning, he wiped the wrench and threw it as hard as he could down the alley. It slid under a car several garages down. He crushed the picture into his pocket, then, looking around in desperation, saw the refuse bin beside the first garage. Running over to it, he stuffed the bloody handkerchief deep down into one of the bags. It was the best he could do.

He barely got back to the body before Midori came back down the alley. "Police come," she said. "Is . . . is he alive?"

"No." He looked up at her, his face savage. "He's dead. Now get out of here before someone comes. And change your dress; it's covered with blood."

She looked down at her bloodstained skirt, then back at him. "Duke . . ." She pleaded with her eyes, her voice. "Please, my husband, listen . . ."

He turned his head away. "Get away from me."

Sobbing, she turned and ran back to the apartment. He waited for the police alone.

Chapter Three

"Take it easy," Ohara muttered, torn between pleasure and pain as his wife's strong fingers kneaded his aching back.

"It's good for you," Peggy replied, smiling as she leaned her slight weight onto her thumbs, slowly working down either side of his spine.

Ohara sighed. Peggy could be ruthlessly single-minded at times, such as now when she was intent on giving him a yoga body alignment. He thought longingly about a soothing massage with fragrant oils, but knew this way was better. His recent undercover stint as a Japanese gardener had left him sore from top to bottom.

It had been a rough assignment, not so much because it had been difficult and dangerous, but because he hated gardening chores, as his own yard testified. After two weeks of mowing, weeding, digging, and trash-toting he'd caught his villains, but his garden-loving Japanese soul now cringed at the sight of anything green and growing.

Peggy ran her fingers down his muscular back, lightly smacked his rear, and told him to turn over. He obliged, groaning for sympathy, which did not stop her from pulling on his neck. When he had had enough of that, he caught her hands in his own. "Thank you," he said solemnly. "You are a satisfactory Japanese wife."

It was an old joke between them to which Peggy responded by bowing with exaggerated politeness and murmuring demurely, "I am grateful for your kind words, mighty *dannasama*."

As she leaned over him, he pulled her down for a kiss, which she returned with interest. He reached up to run his finger along the soft curve of her cheek, marveling at how little she'd changed over the years. Her skin was smooth and unlined, and her dark, curly hair a soft frame for her pretty face. As became the mother of two almost-grown children, her figure had acquired the rich curves of maturity in all the right places, with no unwanted pounds anywhere.

"Isamu," she said, "why do you stare at my face? Do you count all the wrinkles?"

He rolled over on his stomach and took her face between his hands. "I like to look at your face; it's beautiful."

"As beautiful as those glamour girls you meet?"

Peggy was convinced his work was peopled with a series of glamorous, beautiful women. There had been one or two, of course, but Peggy needn't have worried. Still, he liked to tease her, so he looked thoughtful. "Well, let me see . . ."

She looked startled until she saw the laughter in his eyes. Then she pushed him none too gently onto his back again. "I'll fix you," she said, and went vigorously to work on his shoulder joints, smiling as he pretended to groan in pain.

Relenting, she began to work the back of his neck in deep, smoothing circles. Ohara made small sounds of pleasure. Moving down, her fingers slid over the knife scar on his upper right arm. It was a souvenir of the dangers that were part of his life. He'd been lucky so far, but she lived with the haunting fear of the next time. Though her fingers paused briefly, she said nothing. Now, as always, she kept her dark thoughts to herself.

He knew, and loved her for it. Police marriages were notoriously vulnerable, but love and mutual respect plus Peggy's rare understanding had kept theirs alive.

As she worked, she admired his strong, muscular body, which was trim and fit. He kept it that way by regular practice in the aikido dojo and his preference for light, plain food.

By the time she had finished the massage he was almost asleep. She sat beside him, looking at his face, which she thought handsome with its high forehead, long straight nose, and full, well-shaped lips. Glad to see him rest, she did not disturb him, but let herself daydream about how nice it would be if they could go away together for a few days. He was due some time off, so . . .

Her pleasant daydream was shattered by the ringing of the phone. She rose and answered softly, but Ohara had woken up at the first ring. "It's the station," she said, trying to keep the disappointment out of her voice.

As he came over to take the phone, he kissed her on the cheek. "Probably just routine," he assured her.

Ohara listened, frowning, then began to write something down on the pad they kept handy by the phone. Peggy sighed. It wasn't routine. They wouldn't be going away together as she'd hoped.

When he had hung up, she went to him and locked her arms around his body. "Couldn't someone else take it, Isamu? You've just come in."

"I know," he said gently, "but this time I'm really needed. I promise that after this one, I'll take my time off. We'll go away somewhere, just the two of us. Would you like that?"

"I'd like that very much, Isamu," she said, wondering if this time it would really happen.

After Ohara had showered and dressed, he phoned his partner, Ted Washington, who was still enjoying the last of his day off. Ohara felt a little guilty at breaking in on it, but he valued Ted and wanted him along.

21

The phone rang a long time before Ted answered. When he heard what was wanted, he groaned, "But I'm working on Ethel!"

Ohara could imagine the annoyance on Ted's broad, black face. Ethel, his pride and joy, was a 1925 Ford he'd recently inherited from his grandfather. She'd turned him into an antique-car buff. On his free time he was either replacing her temperamental innards, polishing her antique exterior, or driving her to rallies with his dog, Irish, in the front seat. Even his usually exuberant love life was temporarily in abeyance.

"Technically you're still off, Ted," Ohara admitted, "so if . . ."

"What's an hour or two more? My back's aching anyway. I'll come."

Glad that his own back didn't ache anymore, Ohara was cheerful. "Good! I'll pick you up in fifteen minutes."

Ohara parked behind the police cars lining the curb, and both he and Washington clipped on ID badges. The cops at the scene greeted them, not surprised that "Irish" Ohara was on this job. He'd acquired the name "Irish" from Desk Sergeant Reagan, an old-fashioned Irish cop to whom the idea of an "O'Hara" named Isamu was just too much. Only his partner and close friends called him Sam.

Together Washington and Ohara pushed through the crowd of curious bystanders and went into the cordoned-off area, where a small cluster of men stood around a body.

The lab specialists and ambulance people were waiting for the M.E. to finish his examination. Ohara was sorry to see that the M.E. was not his old friend, Bob Abrams, whose mournful beagle face and wacky sense of humor he'd grown used to and liked. Instead, it was a new man named

Fellows, who was reputed to have a computer for a soul and no sense of humor whatever.

Fellows acknowledged Ohara's greeting with a perfunctory nod. Dispensing with further amenities, he reported his preliminary findings. "The victim was struck between the eyes with a narrow-edged, blunt instrument. He was also severely beaten on the right side of his face and his jaw broken, probably with the same instrument. No sign of it around. He's got neck injuries, too."

"You're saying it was a hammer job?" Washington tried to pin him down.

As Fellows considered, Brewster, one of the lab specialists, spoke. "I'd say a wrench made the mess. It's a handy piece of mugging equipment. Your knuckles don't get bruised."

Fellows's mouth tightened into a thin line. "It could have been a wrench," he conceded, "but wringing the victim's neck is certainly a new twist for muggers." He glanced at Ohara to see if he'd caught the small attempt at humor.

Ohara's faint smile told him he had. The others stared at Fellows, dumbfounded that he'd actually made a joke. The little M.E. smiled himself, enjoying his minor triumph. "Anything else?" he asked.

"When do you think he was killed?" Washington recovered enough to ask.

Fellows frowned. "Not long ago. Something under an hour."

"I'd like to examine the body," Ohara said.

"Be my guest." Grudgingly, Fellows stood back. The body was his and, unlike some other coroners, he was jealous of it. To him, inspection of the body by the detectives was unnecessary. It was his facts and figures that would count in the end. But protocol was protocol.

"That's the contents of his pockets." He indicated a plastic bag beside the victim, hoping to hurry things along. Fellows was never comfortable for long away from his stainless-steel lab and precision instruments. He walked impatiently toward where the ambulance men waited.

Ohara was not intimidated by Fellows's testy manner. He looked at Brewster. "What have you got so far?"

"Pictures of the body; some shots of the scene. I sort of held back. Fellows doesn't like us buzzing around while he's working."

"Well, you can go ahead now. Scour the place for the weapon. I can't see anyone walking down the street carrying a bloody wrench. Take some shots of all the approaches to the alley, too. We might get lucky."

"Will do," Brewster said. "We've already checked the immediate area. I suppose the rubbish bin is next."

The patrol officer who had taken the call was waiting to report. He read the brief facts from his notebook. A Mrs. Walker had called in at 8:15 to report the body. Their car had responded by 8:25. Mr. Walker was waiting by the body, but could not identify it. He thought the victim lived in the apartment complex. The apartment manager was summoned, and he identified the victim as Tak Shimizu, a tenant in apartment 2B who was unmarried and lived there alone.

His report finished, the officer pointed to the garage just behind them. "That's the garage for 2B. You'd better have a look. That's the victim's car, and it's a mess."

They all walked over to the garage and stared, appalled at the vicious way the car had been vandalized. A few drops of oil still dripped like blood from the ravaged engine. It had literally been hacked to death.

"I've never seen anything like it," Washington murmured.

"Nor have I." Ohara had seen cars stripped for their parts, but this was something else. "There's hate in this," he said quietly, and turned to look back at the body. "The same kind of hate that beat him to death. This rules out a run-of-the-mill mugger.''

Aware that the coroner's men were still waiting to remove the body, Ohara went back over to where Shimizu lay sprawled under the police floodlights. Following him, Washington saw that his partner's face had the same closed, meditative look he had seen before when they'd stood over a victim. He'd often wondered what Ohara thought at such times, but had never asked.

If he had, Ohara probably wouldn't have put it into words. He was always touched by the pathetic muteness of a body newly dead. He seemed to sense its voiceless protest against dying, against the impersonal, uncaring hands that would touch it, the silent plea that this terrible rending of body and spirit would not go unnoticed.

After a moment, Ohara bent down for a closer look at Shimizu's face. He wondered if the plump little Japanese had put up a fight. There were no indications that he had. Why not?

"Here's his wallet." Washington took out his handkerchief and picked it up off the ground. "Nothing in it but a driver's license and credit cards. But look at this, Sam." He showed Ohara the fresh-looking smears both inside and outside of the expensive wallet, then took it over to Brewster.

Ohara went back to studying the body. When Washington returned to stand beside him, Ohara indicated the victim's left hand.

Washington squatted down for a closer look. "Yes. I noticed that before. The little finger's gone, down to the last joint. Maybe he had an accident."

"No." Fellows spoke from behind them. "It was chopped off."

"Thought so," Ohara said. "How much do you know about the Yakuza, Ted?"

25

"I've heard the name. Sort of Japanese mafia, aren't they?"

"That and more. In Japan most people don't even say the name out loud. The Yakuza are everywhere. They control money, businesses, gambling, prostitution, and human beings. When a Yakuza soldier makes a mistake, he can atone by cutting off one joint of his little finger and sending it to his overlord. A second mistake takes the next joint."

"What happens when he runs out of fingers?" Washington's tone was light, but his eyes were grim.

"Then he's dead," Ohara said.

"You think he might be a Yakuza?"

"Possibly. It's something to check out with the Organized Crime Unit." Ohara sat back on his heels. "Might turn up something useful."

Then he went through the things that had been in the dead man's pockets: a matchbook from Flynn's Pub, some small change, a gold pen, and an expensive gold-plated case containing business cards indicating that Shimizu had been an agent for Guardian Insurance Company.

"No keys," Washington commented.

For a moment more Ohara studied Shimizu's crushed temple. Then he looked at Fellows. "Wouldn't you say some time elapsed after the blow between the eyes and those on the side of the head?"

Fellows shrugged. "It's possible."

"I find that unusual," Ohara said as he stood up. "You can have him now."

"It is unusual," Washington said as he watched the coroner's men zip the body into a black bag for transport, then lift it onto a gurney. "But only a nut case would wait around before taking a second whack. Still, the way that car's been savaged, a psycho may be what we're looking for."

"Could be," Ohara agreed, "but I've got another idea."

26

"So? Come on, Sam, don't go the inscrutable Japanese on me. I'm too tired."

Ohara grinned. "And I'm too tired to be inscrutable. I think two people, possibly three, did this."

Washington stared at him in disgust. "You won't buy a nice simple mugging; it has to be complicated. Well, which one got lucky: one, two, or three?"

"That remains to be seen, Ted, but I think three different people wanted him dead."

Chapter Four

As the coroner's men loaded the victim's body into an ambulance, the small crowd of spectators jostled one another for a closer look. There was no sympathy in the curious faces, only a morbid fascination with violent death safely removed from themselves. It was the same every time, Ohara thought.

"Three killers!" Washington's expression was gloomy. "It could be worse, though. I saw a movie where a whole committee of killers stabbed a guy on a train. The detective damn near went crazy."

Ohara laughed. "I saw that movie, too, but with our killers I have the feeling it was every man for himself."

"Hey, Irish." They were interrupted by Bill Talbot, one of the brighter wizards of the crime lab, who was walking toward them holding out a plastic bag.

"Got this out of the trash bin," he said. The bag contained a torn and bloody handkerchief. "Course, somebody may have had a nosebleed. We'll check it out."

"Thanks, Bill. No sign of a weapon?" Ohara asked.

"Nope. But we'll keep looking."

They were interrupted by a shout from Brewster, who had been photographing the alley. He was squatted down, pointing his flashlight into a garage several spaces down.

"I'd bet money that's what bashed your guy's head in." Brewster's light picked out a heavy mechanic's wrench lying half-hidden behind the wheel of a station wagon.

Talbot carefully fished the wrench out from behind the wheel. "Could be we'll find some joy in this. It's been wiped, but they never do a complete job of it."

"Doesn't look like the usual wrench," Ohara commented.

"It's an auto mechanic's wrench, and an old one," Washington put in. "I could sure use one like that for Ethel, but that make is almost impossible to find these days."

Ohara turned to Brewster. "That was good spotting."

"Thanks, Sam." Brewster looked pleased.

"I'll swing by that automotive plant near here tomorrow," Washington said, "and check it out."

Ohara nodded absently. "It bothers me that Shimizu's keys are missing. Maybe it wasn't just his car they wrecked. It's time I checked his apartment. The manager should have a key."

"I'll come with you," Washington offered.

"I can handle it, Ted. Why don't you interview the Walkers before they start forgetting the details."

Washington smiled. "On my way, Sam."

Ohara watched Ted walk away with his fast, swinging stride. He had a controlled energy in that big body that made itself felt, yet he was a surprisingly gentle and compassionate man.

Walking over to the manager's apartment, Ohara was remembering how he and his partner had come together. Washington hadn't wanted a Japanese senior partner any more than Ohara had wanted a chip-on-the-shoulder trainee. Ohara had had to remind himself that he hadn't been much different a few years before, when he'd been the minority pebble on the beach. They'd rubbed each other the wrong way for a time, until they discovered that they were the same kind of cop. Now they were friends as well as partners.

It didn't take Ohara long to locate the building manager. "Look," he said, wheezing and snuffling with a cold. "The

29

officer already dragged me out to look at the dead guy. I'll give you a key, but I'm not going out again." He shuffled over to his desk, got the key, and thrust it into Ohara's hand. "Bring it back when you're through."

But Ohara was not finished. "I'd appreciate your opinion of the dead man. What was he like?"

"Like? He wasn't a bad guy. Smiled a lot. Guess that was 'cause he sold insurance. I was afraid he'd start pestering me, but he never did." The manager sneezed again and closed the door.

When Duke Walker had finished with the patrol officers, he had been sent back to his apartment to await questioning from the detectives. When he reached it, he couldn't bring himself to go inside. He stood staring at the little Japanese good-luck figure Midori had hung on the door, a small wooden *kappa*. Its supposed good luck, like Midori, had turned out to be a fraud. Reluctantly he took out his keys, let himself in, and closed the door behind him. There was no need now to playact for the police. He let his body sag as he stared at Midori, who stood facing him across the room. He clenched his big rawboned hands as his inner conflict of anger and bewilderment shook him.

Midori's eyes searched his face a moment, then a sob caught in her throat. She didn't move, only stared at him, like a small animal expecting to be kicked.

He didn't care. His own hurt was too great. He pulled the picture out of his pocket and held it so she could see it. "I thought you were stealing his wallet, but this was what you were after, wasn't it?"

She wet her lips nervously, unable to speak.

"Was he going to spoil your game? Show this to the poor stupid guy who got you into America and fell crazy in love with you?"

"No, Duke, no, I tell you true I . . ."

30

He cut her off. "You wouldn't know how to tell the truth. You've lied to me from the beginning."

"No," she said, fighting back tears. "No!"

"What about your letter in the magazine? 'I from small farm village. My father teacher village school. Speak only little English,'" he mocked. "A pack of lies! You're a city slut and always have been."

She jerked as if he'd struck her. "Don't say such thing. You don't know . . ."

He walked toward her, his anger flaring.

"I believed your stories about your simple home, your cooking and cleaning and learning how to be a good wife, and all the time *this* was the truth!" He held the picture before her eyes a moment, then dropped it like filth. His arm drew back to strike her, but he couldn't. Instead he stumbled over to the couch and sat down with his head in his hands.

"I ate it all up, the pretty words, the cute little ways. I never had anyone to love before, but when you walked toward me off the airplane, I knew it could be you. And it was. Just the thought of you waiting for me at home made the whole day good." He began to laugh, a harsh, grating sound that chilled her. "What a joke! How much more time was I going to get for my money before you walked out?"

"Duke, don't." The words were like a cry of pain as Midori ran over and knelt beside him. She reached to touch him, but drew her hands back, afraid. "Yes, I lie, but only little bit. I must get away from Japan, and letter only way. But you I respect from first, my husband. I swear myself I be best wife to you, and I try. Then I find strange thing. I not respect only. I come feel so big love. Never such thing happen me before."

31

Duke raised his head and looked at her, his eyes bitter with disbelief. "What a con!" he said.

"I not know what is con, but you must listen, please!"

He brushed her fingers away. "I'm listenin'. Tell me some more lies!"

"No lie, Duke. You my life. I only want live with you always, have little ones, grow old together, happy, peaceful. So lovely dream!" She choked back a sob, but the tears slid down her cheeks. "Now you think I bad, not want. You will send away."

She paused, then looked up at him. "But first, my husband, you must listen what I say."

Duke grunted and threw himself back on the couch.

"Is true I grow up in small village in Japan. My mother die when my sister born."

"You didn't say you had a sister," Duke interrupted, but she went on as if he had not spoken.

"My father good teacher, but bad farmer. He try grow just our food, but weather kill. We not have enough eat. So he sell me to geisha house."

Duke jerked upright. "A geisha house? He sold you?"

"Cannot help. He think good for me, and money help at home."

"You're lying again. No father would sell his kid to be a hooker.'

She straightened. "I know what is hooker. Not like that. My father good man. I hear in America how some fathers and mothers sell little ones for bad picture and other thing. That not like me."

He knew she was right. "But a geisha house!"

"Many peoples not know how is geisha. Real geisha not like you say. She sing, dance, talk nice, fun at party. Man who buy geisha for dinner friends pay big money, gain great face. Other thing pillow girl do, not geisha."

"That's all you did? Dance, sing? That sort of stuff?"

"Yes. When first go geisha house I be maid, cook, but master see I grow pretty face, so he teach me be geisha. I learn dance, play *shamisen*, *koto*, how talk guests. When I am full geisha he buy me many beautiful kimono. Important men ask for me."

"In this day and age! I can't believe it. Couldn't you get away when you had worked off what your father got for you?"

She gave a sad little smile. "My debt never go. I owe master for kimonos; they sometime thousand dollar each one. Then is hairdresser, other clothes, many thing. I always owing him."

"And you never slept with anyone?"

"Never," she said, lifting her head with a pride he found unexpectedly touching.

Then he remembered the picture. His face hardened. "Don't stop now. How did you get from being an untouchable geisha to prancing around naked in a bar?"

Midori lowered her head and looked at her hands twisting nervously in her lap. "I tell." Her voice was so low he could barely hear her.

When she didn't go on, he said, "Well?"

She raised her head, and her face became a mask, showing nothing. "My master die. His son live Tokyo, not want old geisha house in small place. He say he own all geisha now. We must come work Tokyo. Maybe not so bad, I think. But we not work geisha. He sell to man who have club. We must work pillow girl, serve drink, wear no clothes like picture. One girl say she not do; they beat so bad she die. They tell us, we not do what they say, or try run away, they kill." Her head dropped and tears ran down her cheeks.

"They couldn't get away with that." Duke was angry, for her sake this time.

"They powerful men. All things they do. No one can stop."

Duke knew what she said was true of organized crime all over the world. "You met Shimizu there? Was he one of them?"

"Yes. He one. Very bad man."

"You poor kid." Duke looked at the small figure at his feet as he struggled with his own changing emotions. He marveled that she had lived through so much. Who was he to judge what she had done?

"I must tell all, my husband. I afraid, so I obey, be bargirl, must no wear clothes like in picture, but always I think how I can run away. One time man give me big tip; I hide, not give to boss. Is for buy ticket home. When I get chance I run away. Hope they not find and kill."

"Was that when you wrote the letter and sent the picture to the magazine?"

"No, before I come home our father die. Sister all alone, so she write letter in magazine, send picture. Tell me nice man want she come America. But when hear what happen me, she say I must go, marry nice man so I be safe. I not want, but she say must do or I be kill. Give me ticket you send, and passport. No one guess I not Midori."

Duke stared at her. "She wrote the letters. It was her I promised to marry. All the things she wrote were true."

"Yes, all true. My sister good girl, not like me. When she think I not know, she cry very hard for not marry her Mr. Walker. I try make her go, but she not listen."

"She's one hell of a woman to do that." Duke's voice was gentle.

"Yes. I promise I bring her America some day. Now too late."

Duke tried to speak, but she hurried on, pressing her fingers against his lips. "You want me go away, Duke. I understand."

34

"Like hell I want you to go away." Suddenly Duke was on the floor beside her, gathering her into his arms. "Don't ever say that again! Your sister's wonderful, but you're everything I've ever wanted. Nothing matters except that you're mine, and you're safe. No one is ever going to hurt you again."

He held her so tightly she could hardly breathe. They clung to each other for a long time; there was no need for words. At last Duke pulled her over to lean against the couch, his arm still around her. "Midori must be your sister's name, since it was on the passport. What's yours?"

"My name Miyuki."

"Does it mean something?"

"Mean 'beautiful snow'."

"Miyuki." He tried it and smiled. "I like it!"

She snuggled against him, glad to blot out for a moment the ugliness and fear. But all too soon he said, "Tell me about Shimizu. How did he find you?"

She looked at him and sat up, not sure how he would feel about what she must tell him now. He smiled. "It's all right, honey. I must know because of what happened tonight. That's all."

"Shimizu knew me from club. One day he see me come out our apartment. I hope he not know me, but he do. He come to apartment, say I must pay or he tell about me. Show bad men where find me."

"Blackmailing son of a bitch!"

"He say I buy insurance his company. He come get money for company and extra money for him. I must pay cash."

"Why didn't you come to me?" Duke's face was red with anger.

"I afraid. Wait, I show you paper." She went into the bedroom and came back with an insurance policy.

Duke laughed bitterly when he read it. "Life insurance with himself as beneficiary. Even if you died he'd make out."

Miyuki looked shamed. "I know bad thing, but don't be angry, Duke, I not spend house money. I get job."

"What job?"

"I learn geisha house how make beautiful flower arranging, so ask flower man in shopping center if he want. He give me job in afternoon."

Duke shook his head in amazement. "You know, you're one gutsy little kid." His face grew sober. "What happened today?"

"Today he come show me picture. Not know he have. Say he want fifty more dollar each time for self."

Duke's hand involuntarily tightened on her shoulder, hurting her. "The slimy little bastard. Go on, honey."

"Then when he leave your dinner all burn, so I must do again. After, I go outside and wait for you come home. Pretty soon I hear sound in alley. I look, think I see something on ground and go close. Then I see is Shimizu. I think maybe dead, but not sure. I try find picture so no one see. Then you come."

He was silent, looking at her. He was sure she hadn't told him everything. It didn't matter; he could guess. Almost fiercely, he pulled her close. "It's all right. I understand and I don't blame you." He kissed her gently, then said, "Now don't worry anymore about it. I've taken care of everything."

"What you take care, Duke?"

"Never mind. He's dead; it's over."

"Tell me, Duke!" Fear gripped her.

"It's all right, I tell you! I wiped the wrench on my handkerchief and got rid of it. I buried the handkerchief in the trash. They'll never find it; the trash is picked up tomorrow."

36

Miyuki stared at him, horrified at the implications of what he'd said. "But Duke . . ."

The doorbell rang, making her jump.

"That's the police," Duke said. They stared at each other. Miyuki was trembling. "I must tell true . . ."

He took her by the shoulders, forcing her to look at him. "Now listen. I'll do all the talking. I'll tell them I found the body when I came home from work. I told you to call the police. That's all you know about it. Understand?"

She nodded. "But if police . . ."

The bell rang again. "It'll be all right. Trust me!"

Chapter Five

Ohara let himself into Shimizu's apartment, turned on the light, then stood for a moment trying to sense the man who had lived there. The room was expensively furnished with a white leather divan and chairs, black lacquer tables, crystal lamps, a large-screen TV, and a bar. The carpets were so thick and white Ohara was tempted to take off his shoes, Japanese-style. For an insurance salesman on commission, Shimizu had done himself well.

The first room on the left was a den. Here Ohara found a businesslike desk with all the drawers pulled out. A large filing cabinet had been opened; most of the folders had been spilled onto the floor. Examining them, being careful not to destroy any latent fingerprints, he found they were individual insurance policies. Folders containing photographic negatives had been left untouched. They were labeled by what appeared to be a number and letter code. Double doors ran across an alcove at the far end of the room. When he opened them he found a small but efficient darkroom.

A bedroom and bath adjoined the den. Here Shimizu's sybaritic tastes had been given full rein. There was more thick, white carpet, dark red satin drapes, and in the middle of the room a huge, circular bed with a custom fur spread. Three photo floods on standards stood near one wall. It wasn't hard to guess what kind of photography Shimizu did here.

The sliding mirror doors of a large walk-in closet were open. Several expensive suits on the clothes rack had been pushed back to reveal a hinged panel in the wall. It hung open; the small space it had concealed was empty.

Next he examined the kitchen. There were dirty dishes in the sink and a bag of doughnuts on the breakfast bar. The doors and windows were securely fastened. There was little doubt that the intruder had used keys on the door, files, and cupboard. Had he killed Shimizu to get them?

When Ohara came back through the living room to explore the other rooms on the left, he stepped on something hard. It was a bunch of keys almost embedded in the thick pile of the carpet. He knelt, pushing his pen through the key ring, and lifted. One of the keys matched the one the manager had given him.

He was about to call to Brewster when a sound from one of the rooms on the left made him pause, listening. It was not repeated. Laying the pen with the keys on a lamp table, he pulled his gun from its shoulder holster and went to investigate. Opening the first door, he found the heating plant. The next concealed a linen closet. The door at the back of the small hallway had a spring lock on the outside. Below it was another lock. Wondering if he would need a key, he tried the knob on the spring lock. It turned easily, and he was able to open the door. The room beyond was dark. Remembering to push up the button that kept the latch from locking, he stepped just inside the door and felt for the light switch. It eluded him, so he stepped farther into the room, running his hand along the wall. He had time only to hear a sharply indrawn breath before the back of his head exploded with pain and he fell to his knees, his gun spinning out of his hand into the darkness.

Stunned as he was, Ohara felt his assailant trying to get past him. Reaching out into the darkness, he managed to grab a foot, and held on despite the violent kicks that pounded him. Then, using an old judo trick, he rolled his body to one side and jerked hard. When his assailant fell, he grabbed the body in a bear hug, surprised at its light weight. Fingernails scraped at his face.

Thrusting his arm up, he pushed hard at his assailant's throat while he gripped the thrashing legs with his own. The struggle ceased at once.

"Don't hurt me, please, don't hurt me!" The voice was female, and frantic with fear.

Ohara got to his feet, pulling his captive up with him. He found the light switch and flicked it on.

He was holding a girl, no more than a teenager, he would guess. She was a pretty little thing with a heart-shaped face and large pansy-blue eyes. Blond curly hair fell to her shoulders and across her forehead. She winced and looked down at his hand gripping her arm. He let go at once and she rubbed the spot, staring up at him resentfully. He was sorry he'd been so rough; she was as defenseless as a kitten. The girl couldn't have been much older than his daughter Susie, a pathetically vulnerable age.

Like Susie, she wore the inevitable jeans and T-shirt, but unlike Susie, her jeans looked pasted to her body, outlining her slender thighs and buttocks. The T-shirt was blue and stretched tightly across her rounded young breasts.

"I'm sorry if I hurt you," Ohara apologized as he retrieved his gun and returned it to the holster. "But you didn't give me much choice."

"You came to kill me," she burst out.

"No, that was your idea." Ohara touched the back of his head, probing a sticky wetness. "Was this what you used?" He picked up a heavy onyx ashtray from the floor.

She ignored it. "You're one of them. Tak said you'd come."

"Whoever they are," Ohara said, "I'm not one of them. I'm a police officer." He pointed to the badge on his jacket.

She studied it, looked suspiciously at his face, then threw her arms around his neck and clung to him. "Oh, I'm so glad!" She nuzzled her face closer to his neck, like a child seeking comfort.

Ohara gently patted her shoulder. "Don't worry, no one's going to hurt you now." After a moment he loosened her arms from around his neck, but she clung to his hands.

"Don't leave me!" she begged.

"I won't," he promised. "Now, what's your name?" he asked, trying to sound as casual as possible.

"Jody," she said with a little smile, her lips parting slightly, their softness accented by pale pink lipstick. Young as she was, there was a sexual awareness in the look she gave him that his daughter Susie had not yet learned.

"Just Jody?" he asked.

"No, it's Baxter," she said slowly. "Jody Baxter. And I'm sorry I scratched your face." Raising her hand, she touched the red welts gently.

"It's all right, Jody." Ohara heard someone coming up the steps to the apartment. "Now, you sit down in that chair. I'll be back in a minute."

He went into the other room and found Brewster and the others at the door. He told them to come in and began to outline what had to be done. Suddenly he realized he'd lost their attention. He looked behind him to find Jody standing there, smiling. There was no trace of her previous terror.

"Jody, I told you to wait . . ."

She ran her fingers up his arm. "I don't want to be alone. Besides, I'm hungry. Awfully hungry!"

"We'll find you something soon," he promised, and turned back to the amused faces of the lab crew.

"Where'd the baby doll come from?" Brewster asked, grinning at Jody over Ohara's shoulder.

"Her name is Jody Baxter. Shimizu had her locked in a bedroom." If Ohara hoped the explanation would shut them up, he was mistaken.

"I'd lock her in the bedroom, too," someone murmured as they trooped into the den with their equipment.

Embarrassed, Ohara turned to Jody, but apparently she hadn't heard. She was admiring herself in a wall mirror, fluffing her hair with her fingers. "I'll be back in a few minutes, Jody," he said. "Wait here."

He went into the den to tell Brewster what photographs he wanted, then came back with Bill Talbot to have him check the keys.

Jody was sitting on the white leather divan, humming to herself as she picked at the nail polish on her fingers. Ohara went to the lamp table for the keys, but they were gone. "I just put them there," he said. "I know it was on that table." He began searching the floor around the table, in case they had rolled off.

"Are these what you're looking for?" Jody asked, holding up the bunch of keys. "These are Tak's. He must have left them home this morning." Then she frowned at Ohara. "Hey, how did you get in?"

The two men looked at each other. "The manager gave me a key," Ohara said.

"Now, why would he do that?" she asked.

"Jody," Ohara said, "Mr. Shimizu was killed this evening."

She stared at him, then said in a small voice, "Killed?"

"Yes. I'm sorry." Ohara reached over and took the keys, then handed them to Bill Talbot.

Jody stared in front of her, her face pinched and afraid. "Tak said somebody might try to kill him."

"Why?"

"I don't know. Tak told me somebody had broken in, so he'd had new locks put on. He didn't want to give the manager a key, but he had to."

"Did he call the police?"

She shook her head. "He said police couldn't help him." Her lips began to tremble. "Now they'll come and kill me."

Ohara sat down beside her, put his arm around her shoulders, and held her secure, as he might have done for his own daughter. "No one's going to kill you, Jody. We'll see to that." He held her gaze with his own. "You don't need to be afraid. Understand?"

She nodded and put her head on his shoulder.

Bill Talbot cleared his throat. "I'd better get started on these keys, Sam. I'll have to have her prints, too."

Still clinging to Ohara, Jody turned her head and looked at Bill with interest. "You mean you'll take my fingerprints, like in the movies?"

"That's right."

She sat upright and looked at her two hands. "I've never had that done before. Can we do it now?"

Startled by her sudden mood shift, Bill looked at Ohara. "Sam?"

"Later," Ohara said. "I want to talk to Jody now." He hadn't expected her fears to be so easily lulled, but he was grateful. The important thing was to find out what she knew.

Jody's mouth held the suspicion of a pout, but when Talbot went into the den she turned back to Ohara and put her hand trustingly in his.

He smiled, then said, "It would help me a great deal if you would tell me how you came to be locked up here."

"Can I call you Sam?" Jody asked.

"If you want to," Ohara said, a little off balance from the unexpected interruption.

"Sam . . . Sam." She tried it out, her mind off on a new tangent. "I like Sam." She looked up at him, her eyes teasing. "Do you like me?"

Calmly, Ohara gazed back at her. "Suppose you tell me how you happen to be here."

She sighed and leaned back against the divan. "I don't know where to start."

"Well, where's your home?"

"I was born in Chicago," she said, "in a beautiful house. My mother and father loved me very much."

"I believe you told me your family name was Baxter," Ohara said.

"Yes. My father was Peter Baxter. He was a painter. My mother's name was Alys. She was very beautiful. Daddy said I'd be beautiful, too, when I grew up." She looked at Ohara for a reaction, but was disappointed.

"We must call your parents, Jody. They must be very worried."

She stared straight ahead, then shook her head. "My parents were killed a year ago in a car crash. It was my birthday." Her voice broke and she looked down at her hands.

"I'm sorry," Ohara said, and waited for her to go on.

She looked up at him with a pathetic little smile. "It was terrible, but worse than that, I had to go live with my aunt, and everything changed."

"How did it change?"

"It was awful. She hated me, but she had to take me in because of the will. But that still wasn't the worst." Jody paused and shut her eyes as if to blot out the memory.

Ohara watched her, fascinated. Her story so far had all the drama of a soap opera. How much was true, and how much Jody's imagination had colored the facts, was yet to be seen. As she took breath to tell him the worst, he asked,

44

"What was your aunt's name, Jody? Where did she live?"

She didn't like being interrupted with minor details. "Matthews." Ungraciously, she threw the name at him, reproving him with a frown. "Paula Matthews. She lived in Evanston. Do you want to know what happened, or not?"

"Please, go on," Ohara leaned back and gave her his full attention.

"The worst part," she continued, "was her live-in boyfriend. He was always hanging around me." Reaching up one hand, she began to play with her hair, twisting a long strand around her fingers. "Then one night he came into my room and started kissing me and pulling my pajamas off. My aunt came in and caught . . . saw us. Of course, she blamed me. She hit me and said she was going to put me in a tough boarding school where they had ways to make kids like me behave. She'd threatened to do it before, but I knew she meant it this time." Jody's hand clenched. "She locked me in my room, but I got out the window. I had some money of my own, so I hitched a ride to the bus station and took a bus to Los Angeles."

"Why Los Angeles? Do you know someone here?" Ohara asked.

"No, I wanted to get to Hollywood so I could be a movie star. Everyone knows the talent scouts pick you up off the street, or sitting in a drugstore. I've been practicing, too." She jumped up and struck a pose: back arched, one leg thrust forward, her eyes beaming sultry heat. After a moment she flopped back on the couch. "I'll be good, won't I? Do you know any talent scouts?"

Someone started clapping, then a deep voice said, "I'll bet you get a lot of offers." Much to Ohara's relief, it was Ted Washington. Jody looked at him, not sure his words were the compliment they sounded.

"Sit down, Ted," Ohara said.

45

As Washington settled into one of the white leather armchairs, Ohara told him what had happened so far, then turned to Jody. "This is my partner, Ted Washington. It's important that he hear your story, too."

She apparently had taken a dislike to Washington. The movie siren had turned into a sulky teenager. "I don't want to talk to him."

"Come on, kid." Ted was smiling. "You're doing great, from what I've heard so far."

Jody turned her back on Washington and turned to face Ohara beside her on the divan. "I'll tell you, Sam. I'll do anything you ask me."

"Where did you meet Shimizu?" he asked, hoping to get her back on the track.

"He picked me up on Hollywood Boulevard. I was running out of money, so I let him buy my dinner. He was real nice at first and said he could get me a singing contract for a club in Japan. I thought that was neat, so I went home with him."

Ohara knew that racket. Jody was luckier than she knew. "What happened then?" he asked.

"At first it was OK. He took some publicity pictures to show around. Then he said he'd gotten me a screen test. He took me to a place where there were a lot of men. At first it was fun, getting my picture taken, but then Tak said I had to take my clothes off so they could take some more. He said if I didn't do it, and wasn't real nice to them, I'd blow my chance to be a star."

The thought of a kid like that in the hands of a bunch of perverts made Ohara sick.

"It wasn't the way I'd thought it would be at all." Jody was hunched back on the couch. Whatever stories she'd spun before, her face told them this was the truth.

"Bastard!" Washington's voice was hard, but his eyes were full of pity.

"After that," Jody went on, "I tried to split, but Tak caught me. He said he'd signed a contract for me and gave me fifty dollars advance. I was supposed to go to Japan in a week to make movies. I told him I didn't want to make any more movies, but he said I had to because those were real tough guys and they'd kill me if I didn't, and him, too. Then he locked me in the room."

When she had finished, Jody's self-assurance seemed gone. She was a frightened child, haunted by what she'd been through.

"Sam." Bill Talbot had come into the room. "I'm ready to take her prints now, if you're finished."

"Yes," Ohara said, grateful for the distraction; it was just what Jody needed. She was already on her feet, smiling at Bill, holding out her hands.

When they had gone, Washington reported on his interview with the Walkers. "Guess what I found out about him?"

"What?"

"He's an auto mechanic and works in a garage near here."

"Maybe we should ask him about wrenches."

"Now?"

"No. I want to talk to Jody again. Maybe she saw something tonight. Her room's just off the alley."

Jody had come unnoticed into the room. "I did," she said, "but I don't think I'll tell you till I get something to eat."

"Hey, Jody." Washington played the bad guy. "This isn't a game. What did you see or hear, if anything?"

She flushed and turned to Ohara. "I'll tell *you*, Sam. I did hear something. I heard a gun go off."

Chapter Six

"When did you hear the gun go off?" Ohara's dark eyes gazing steadily into Jody's compelled her attention and stilled the restless movements of her hands. Washington had seen him do the same thing with violent suspects, calming them with the force of his own inner serenity.

"I don't know." She shrugged. "But it was dark. I almost didn't see the man running away." She smiled a little cat-with-cream smile, pleased with the effect of her words.

Ohara held on to his patience. "Tell me about the man, Jody."

"Sure." She jumped up, took Ohara's hand, and pulled him toward the bedroom.

Washington had been skeptical of Jody's story from the beginning, but now, intrigued, he followed. In a quick glance, he took in the room: a rumpled bed littered with magazines, a small portable TV, a chair, and a table on which sat a tray of half-eaten food. He could see a small bathroom through a half-open door.

Jody stood close to Ohara and pointed to a set of louvered windows whose opaque glass hid an unappealing view of the alley. A lever at the side opened and closed the glass slats. They were open a few inches.

"I looked out there and saw him."

As Ohara went to the window opening, Washington joined him. They could see a small stretch of alley, the wall of the left-hand garages, the edge of the refuse bin, and the first garage on the right-hand side. Even though it was dark outside, the light at the end of the garage lit the area enough for her to have seen someone, as she claimed.

Jody had lost interest and was sitting on the bed eating a cookie. "Like one, Sam?" She held out a crumpled plastic bag of cookies.

Ohara smiled. "Not now, Jody. I want you to start at the beginning and tell us everything you saw or heard."

"Well, I was reading a magazine and waiting for Tak to come home. Then I heard this shot outside, so I ran to the window and looked out."

"Why did you think it was a shot?" Washington asked. "It could have been a car backfiring."

"It was a shot!" she shouted back at Washington. Then she turned to Ohara. "Make him stop, Sam. He gets me all confused."

"Detective Washington's just trying to get things clear," Ohara soothed. "Go on, please."

Jody looked back at Washington, as if daring him to say something. "Well, at first, after the shot, I didn't see anything. Then I saw this man run out of the alley. Pretty soon I heard a car start up. Nothing more happened, so I went back to my magazine."

"What did the man look like?"

"He was a big guy, like him," she looked over at Washington, "but he was a white man." She stressed the word *white*.

"Did you see anything else?" Ohara asked.

She thought a moment. "Not then. Later on, I got up to turn on the TV and looked out again. A woman was walking down the alley." Jody fished for another cookie and bit into it.

"What did she look like?"

"I didn't really see her, only the back of her dress. I think she had dark hair."

Ohara looked at Washington. "What was Mrs. Walker wearing when you saw her, Ted?"

"White slacks and a green top."

"Go on, Jody."

Jody licked her fingers and considered. "I stayed at the window, watching for Tak. He was awfully late bringing dinner, and I was hungry. I heard a car stop and pretty soon a man got out and walked up the driveway. He sort of stopped and looked, then he went down the alley. I heard him yell something, but I didn't catch any words."

Jody was enjoying herself, playing with them, making them dig for what she knew.

"Describe this man, Jody." Ohara continued the questioning, since she seemed so antagonistic to Washington.

She examined the polish on her fingernails, then said, "He was tall and thin. Oh, yes, he was carrying something."

"What?" Washington asked. "A bag, a lunchbox, a toolbox?"

"It could have been a lunchbox."

"Did you see or hear anything else?"

"No. I got bored and watched TV for a while. Then I heard car doors slam and people talking. When I looked out, I saw some cops go down the alley."

"Then why didn't you yell for help?" Washington asked. "Weren't you trying to get away from Shimizu?" From her expression he could see the question disconcerted her.

"No way! I didn't think those cops would believe me. Besides, yesterday Tak said he'd be nice to me again if I didn't make any more trouble. So I promised. Then he brought me food, magazines, even the TV, though he still kept me locked up.

"After a while I got to thinking it might not be so bad to go to Japan. Besides, he told me if I ran away the bad guys would find me and I'd be in for a world of pain."

Ohara felt his throat tighten at the thought of what would really have happened to this eager, pretty kid. "We understand, Jody," he said. "Now, get your things together, then we'll get you some supper and a place to stay."

He went to see how the lab crew was getting on. They had just finished after packing the negatives and files for checking at the office.

Jody came up to him ready to go, a denim bag slung over one shoulder. All her possessions, Ohara thought, in that one bag. He had a vision of his daughter's room filled with books, posters, and mementos, not to mention her menagerie of stuffed animals.

On impulse he put his arm around Jody's thin shoulders as they left the apartment and walked to the car.

At a nearby coffee shop, Jody wolfed down a hamburger, fries, and a malt. The two men settled for coffee. After Ohara had made a phone call, and they were again in the car, Washington, who was driving, asked, "Where to? Juvenile Hall?"

Jody heard him from the back seat. "Don't take me there!" she pleaded. "I won't go!"

"No Juvenile Hall, I promise," Ohara assured her.

"You're not really going to take her home?" Washington's expression told Ohara he had read his mind.

Jody clutched Ohara's shoulder. "Please, Sam! That would be great."

Ohara wished he could give her a taste of a normal life. He knew Peggy's heart was big enough to do a little extra mothering, but professionally he couldn't consider it. "No, Jody, I can't take you home, but I'm going to take you to a friend of mind. Her name is Harriet Takai. I called her from the restaurant. She's a wonderful person; I know you'll be happy with her until we get things sorted out for you. It's a real home with some other girls your age. You won't be lonely."

Washington thought Ohara had found a good solution, since he was too softhearted to take Jody to Juvenile Hall. Harriet, a former probation officer, ran a halfway house for teenage girls in trouble. Even the toughest cases seemed to respond to her intelligent understanding and down-to-earth common sense.

Jody continued to plead and cry, but Ohara's only response was, "Trust me, Jody. It'll be all right."

Harriet greeted Jody warmly and tried to make her feel at ease, but the girl did not respond by as much as a nod. Ohara went over to her. "I have to go now, Jody, but I'll see you again tomorrow."

She stared at him, her eyes accusing. "Tomorrow, Sam? Promise?"

"I promise," he said, putting his arm around her shoulders as he might have done with Susie.

Ohara was silent as they drove away, his face troubled. "What's wrong?" Washington asked.

"It's that poor kid back there. She's so vulnerable and defenseless. Someone's got to give a damn about lost children like her."

"Not you or me, Sam. She's streetwise enough to get what she wants out of people. Kids like her really know what survival of the fittest means."

"Cynical bastard, aren't you?" Ohara said.

Ted looked at him, surprised at the coldness in his voice.

"Depends on how you look at it," he said. They didn't speak again except for a brief "Good night" as Ted got out of the car. For the first time since they'd been partners, they weren't completely sure about each other.

Feeling more secure now that he'd made it home, Bill Stack limped to the bathroom, stripped off his shirt, and sat swabbing with a towel at his arm. He'd vomited into the bowl and was still feeling queasy. Ginny should be there to help him.

The apartment door opened, making him freeze with fear. Then he heard Ginny's complaining voice and went limp with relief even to hear her bitching because he'd not picked her up.

"Get in here, Ginny," he shouted. "In the bathroom."

"I work all day and you can't even remember to give me a ride—" She broke off, shocked at the sight of him.

"Don't just stand there," he grated through clenched teeth. "Tie up my arm."

Gently, she lifted the bloody towel. "You've got to see a doctor."

"No doctor!" Bill grabbed at her arm, wincing in pain from the effort. "That's a bullet hole. He'd call the police."

"So what? You need a doctor for that."

"Shut up and listen! I just killed a guy. Got it? No doctors, no police."

Ginny stood as if frozen, unable to react.

"Come on!" Bill shouted. "I'm gonna bleed to death."

She pulled herself together and fixed up the arm as best she could, then helped him onto the bed. "Get me a drink," he mumbled.

When she had brought the whiskey and helped him to get it down, he shut his eyes and lay still. "What happened?" Ginny tried to sound calm, but failed. "Tell me!"

"Leave me alone," he moaned, and rolled his head away from her.

Usually when he'd been drinking and got in a fight, he'd boast to her about what he'd done to the other guy. This time he'd gone too far; she could see he was afraid.

53

When he still said nothing and she could see he wasn't going to die, she stared at him with a grim satisfaction. It seemed as though drinking and fighting was all he did lately. When he couldn't pick a fight outside, he'd beat up on her. Sometimes he'd hurt her so much she could only crawl into bed and lie there, not caring whether she lived or died. The next day, seeing the ugly bruises on her face and body, he'd be sorry and promise it wouldn't happen again.

She should have left him long ago, because it kept happening. But he was so pitiful, begging her to give him another chance, threatening to kill himself if she left. What could she do?

Involuntarily her hand reached out to push back the thinning gray hair from his eyes. He reached up and caught her fingers, holding on. It was reassurance he wanted. There'd been no real feeling between them for a long time. They'd stayed together through mutual need, and a habit hard to break.

Wearily Ginny sat down on the edge of the bed, letting him hold her hand. She didn't press him to talk. What could she do about it, anyway? She slipped off her shoes and let her body slump.

She was always tired these days. Too tired to care even about this, just as she'd been too tired to leave him and start over, to play the old man-woman game with someone else. Once she'd been a good-looking woman, with a nice shape and red hair that made the men come running. Now she hated to look in a mirror at what she'd become. To keep her job she piled on the makeup and tinted her fading hair, but she wasn't kidding anybody, least of all herself. She smiled a lot, so people wouldn't notice the lines in her face or the dullness of her eyes.

"Ginny?"

"Yes, I'm here. Want another drink?"

"No. Just . . . thanks."

A tear rolled down his cheek; he was beginning to feel sorry for himself again. Ginny felt a stir of pity and laid her fingers against his forehead. It was hot. "Feels like you got a fever," she said.

"I didn't mean it to happen like it did," he mumbled.

It was the same old story, Ginny thought. He never meant it to happen the way it did.

"It was the Jap started it. He pulled a gun on me, so I threw a wrench at him and knocked him down. His gun went off and the bullet nicked my arm. He could of killed me!"

Ginny showed no reaction, so he went on. "I might of helped him, honest, but I'd nailed him. He looked dead to me." There was a hint of macho pride in his voice, but only for a moment. He paused while his mind took in the meaning of what he'd said, then a look of new fear grew in his eyes. "They're gonna come after me, aren't they?"

"But it was self-defense! Just tell the police the truth."

"You think so?" His fingers clutched tighter on her hand.

Ginny guessed she hadn't heard it all. "Tell me the rest, Bill."

He started with what had happened at Flynn's. As he talked, he relived it all: the rage, the destruction of the car, his pain, his fear. When he finished, he was pitiful again. "You gotta help me, Ginny."

He was hanging on to her like a scared kid. "I promise, if you help me out of this, things'll be different for us. We'll go away; I'll get another job. Please, Ginny, help me!"

"It'll be all right," she said. Whether it would or not, it was what he wanted to hear. Besides, that was about all the help she knew how to give.

Joe Flynn didn't get back to the bar until closing time. He explained that Mary hadn't been feeling well and he'd had to take care of her. Barry didn't question that; it had happened before. Joe seemed a bit keyed-up, but that was understandable. He had a big load to carry.

Benny Polser let himself into the frame house where he lived with his mother. She was snoring in front of the TV and didn't know when he came in. He went into his room and threw himself on the bed. Time enough to take care of her later, get her settled for the night. Now he wanted to be by himself. He needed to think.

Lying on the bed, he looked at the posters and photographs hanging on the dingy brown wall: Clint Eastwood, John Wayne, the musclemen, the athletes. They were Benny's idols, full of the macho bravado he dreamed of in himself. They wouldn't have let Bill Stack run them out of the bar! His face grew hot at the memory. They wouldn't have let any Japs rob them of their father's store!

He sat up suddenly, his thin arms hugging his body. Well, things would be different now! Excitement surged through him. What had happened tonight had changed everything. Bill was going to learn to treat Benny Polser with respect from now on. He pictured the moment when he would tell off Bill, savored the words: "I know what you did to the Jap's car, and I know you clobbered him with the wrench."

The thought of the power he held was dizzying. He'd get the Japs, too; Bill had shown him the way.

He remembered what else he had seen in the alley, but the very idea of using it scared him.

Carefully, he drew the Jap's small black gun from his pocket. He'd never seen a gun up close before. Straightening his arm, he aimed it at the wall and made a clicking sound with his tongue. "Tchok! Tchok!"

Nobody would push him around anymore.

Chapter Seven

The following morning before going to the office, Washington stopped at the automotive plant near the murder scene, hoping to get some expert information on the oddball mechanic's wrench.

After being passed from receptionist to secretary to manager, he was finally directed to Billy Hamilton, the plant foreman. Hamilton was a sinewy little Irishman with shrewd gray eyes, who carefully sized up Washington as he listened to his request.

"In the first place, hardly anybody uses that make of wrench nowadays, especially not here. Come take a look." He led Washington into a section of the plant where robots were servicing the assembly line. "Don't need guys with wrenches here. Machines make the machines."

Looking at the long metallic arms that plugged, twisted, fitted, and tapped in silent monotony, Washington felt depressed. "I see what you mean."

"Put a lot of guys out of work, they did." Billy nodded at the robots. "Everybody blamed the Jap imports, but it was these things. Bosses figured they'd work cheaper in the long run with no union squawks. Course, the Japs invented them, so maybe the boys were right after all."

Next Billy led his visitor to a smaller section, where some handwork was still being done. He pointed to the racks of tools neatly hung above each workspace. "Every plant's different. Here the company supplies the tools, and they're kept here. Don't use an older wrench like you asked about."

"Well, who does?" Washington asked as he followed Hamilton back to his small office.

"A few old duffers like me." He picked up a well-worn toolbox and opened it. "I got one of them wrenches. Better than the new ones." Lovingly he picked up a wrench just like the murder weapon, but this one gleamed with polish and care.

"I'd sure like to get a hold of one for Ethel."

"Ethel? She a mechanic?"

Washington grinned and explained about his antique Ford. It turned out that Billy's pride and joy was an antique Buick. They talked old cars for a while until Washington reluctantly came back to why he was there.

"Anybody else around here have his own tools?"

"Used to be a guy named Bill Stack. Worked here until the big layoff. Might have stayed on then, except he was a troublemaker."

"Know where I could find him?"

"Nope. Him and me weren't close. Office might know."

Washington thanked Billy, who promised to come have a look at Ethel. Then he went to the office. He had to apply a little official pressure and considerable charm, but he got Stack's address, which had to be dug out of the back files. Feeling good, he headed for the office.

As he waited for Ted, Ohara sat at his desk trying to get his thoughts together. It still bothered him that he'd been so edgy with his family that morning. After a restless night thinking about the Shimizu case, he'd been looking forward to a peaceful breakfast with the family. It was a time he always enjoyed; instead he found nothing but arguments.

Peggy, who was usually perceptive of his moods, pressured him about coming to some community center meeting. When he said he expected to be too busy, Susie and young Jim started on him.

"You've got to come, Dad," Jim stared at him accusingly. "It's about what's happening to Asians right here."

"Good," Ohara said. "You go, and tell me about it."

"Don't you remember how you and Grampa and Grandma were sent to Manzanar? Don't you care if it happens again?" Susie looked outraged.

"We were at war then; it's different now," he snapped. "You're getting worked up over nothing."

Jim looked at him, his young face tight. "Nothing? Get with it, Dad. Haven't you read about what they did to Victor Chin? And that's only one incident. We've got real problems."

Ohara disliked Jim's tone, but made allowance for his adolescent passions. "All of you had better understand that I've got a particularly vicious murder case on my hands. As you ought to know by now, it doesn't leave much time for meetings, so stop pushing."

"The late news said a Japanese was murdered yesterday," Peggy said quietly. "Is that your case?"

"Yes." He stood up to leave.

"That's what the meeting's about: violence against Asians. Somebody has to care." With that, she began clearing the table. He walked out without saying good-bye.

In a calmer mood later, he wondered if anti-Asian violence had triggered the Shimizu killing, especially considering the savaging of the car. He was sorry that he'd allowed his annoyance to drive a wedge between himself and those he loved most. He picked up the phone and called home, but no one answered.

Realizing he'd accomplish nothing in his present frame of mind, Ohara resorted to his usual technique to restore mental balance. Sitting very straight, he closed his eyes and began breathing slowly and deeply, in and out, concentrating only on the movement of his own breath until his mind was empty of all thought and he felt the great breath of the universe in his own body.

When he opened his eyes again, minutes later, his mind was peaceful and clear, his energy renewed. It was time to get the wheels rolling. He picked up Shimizu's business card, dialed the Guardian Insurance Company, and arranged an appointment with the head man, a Mr. Takematsu, for three o'clock.

As he hung up the phone, Ted arrived, looking pleased with himself. While he drank a cup of what passed for coffee, he briefed Ohara on what he'd learned at the auto plant. "I stopped to see Bill Stack, but no one was home. We'll have to try again."

Ohara told him about their appointment at Guardian Insurance.

"Afternoon's OK. I've got to testify in the Arlen case this morning. Oh, yes, I've started some inquiries on Jody. See you later." Washington took a last swallow of coffee and left for his court date.

Ohara decided to interview Jody again. He phoned Sergeant Reagan for a policewoman to accompany him and take a formal statement.

When he went downstairs, he heard an angry, white-haired Japanese complaining to Reagan that the tires on his car had been slashed. Ohara went over and introduced himself to the man, who gave his name as Sego Hirata.

"I've parked my car on the street for years without trouble. We don't have garages in the neighborhood. Now somebody's gone berserk and slashed tires all down the block."

"Every single car?" Ohara asked.

"No, that's the point. My neighbor's Chevy wasn't touched, or a Ford van. The ones they did were Japanese makes. But that's not the worst. They painted 'Get out Japs' or 'Fuck the Japs' on the cars." Hirata was almost incoherent with rage. "What's that for? I'm an American, born and raised here. I served with the 442nd in Italy."

Ohara knew the famous brigade that had fought so valiantly in World War II. It had been made up of American-born Japanese who wanted to serve their country. Their families were in internment camps, but even in the face of that, they were Americans, and America was at war.

Promising Hirata that he would look into the matter, Ohara hurried out to the parking lot, where Officer Amy Byers was waiting. She was a pretty girl with red hair, brown eyes, and fine creamy skin. Also, she was young enough for Jody to relate to easily. Ohara nodded approvingly. "Glad you can come along. You'll be a real help."

Amy was delighted to be on an assignment with Irish Ohara. She liked trim, good-looking men, and his Japanese heritage seemed to add a special touch of glamour. She'd seen most of Toshiro Mifune's samurai movies and could easily imagine Ohara in such a role. It was exciting to be working with him, however small her part. She listened carefully as he outlined the case for her and filled her in on Jody's background.

"I'm going to make a stop on the way, Amy. Some cars have been vandalized on a street not far from Shimizu's apartment. Might be a connection."

When they arrived at Maple Street, three cars were still at the curb, their tires slashed and the ugly slogans painted in red across the sides.

It was a block of old-fashioned wood-sided houses. From what Amy could see, the population was largely Oriental.

Ohara studied the damage and talked to the owners, who were standing around looking at their cars. Some were angry and others were frightened. Growing more and more agitated, one old man clung to Ohara's arm. Ohara spoke to him in Japanese; the man became calmer. Finally Ohara bowed with great respect to the old man, who bowed in return. The scene, Amy thought, was right out of old Japan. As they drove away, she remarked to Ohara how frightened some of the people had seemed.

"The older people remember what happened once before in World War Two," he said. "Something as ugly as this makes them wonder if it is all starting again, or if something worse will happen."

"But that's not possible," Amy protested. "That was wartime; people were edgy."

"You'd be surprised what can happen when people start hating like that. You saw what was painted on the cars." Though his voice was quiet, there was a tight set to his mouth.

He pulled up before a small white house about a block from Maple Street. "My parents and I lived there until we were sent to Manzanar. I was only four at the time, and I couldn't understand why we left our nice house to live so far away with soldiers and people we didn't know. We never came back here."

They drove on in silence until Amy asked, "Do you think the person who wrecked Shimizu's car vandalized the ones on Maple Street?"

"No," he answered. "The cuts are different and there was no painted slogan on Shimizu's. It could be an imitation."

"But no pictures of Shimizu's car have been released. How would anyone imitate something they hadn't seen?"

Ohara looked at her and almost smiled. "Because someone did see it."

When they arrived at the hostel for girls, Harriet Takai showed them into her private sitting room and sent for Jody. The young girl came in carrying her denim bag, a big smile on her face. Dropping the bag at the door, she ran to him, arms outstretched, only to stop short when she saw Amy. "Who's she?"

"A police officer." Ohara introduced Amy, whose pleasant greeting to Jody was ignored.

"Let's sit down." Ohara led Jody over to the couch. "Are you feeling better?" he asked.

She shrugged. "Now that you've come to take me away, I am. I brought my bag down."

"Actually, I came to get a formal statement of everything you told me yesterday, and anything you might have remembered since then. Amy will take it down for the record."

Jody frowned. "Oh, all right, but then let's go."

Ohara took her through her story again, but it remained substantially the same. "Can you describe the second man you saw any better, Jody? It would help."

"Well," she said slowly, "I think he had a scar on his cheek."

"Which cheek?"

She hesitated. "His right cheek."

Ohara realized she was probably making up details to please him; she couldn't have seen the man's right cheek from the window. But he let it go. "Anything else?"

"He had on a red jacket with something written on it. I couldn't read it."

That was more reasonable. She said she would recognize either of the men if she saw them again.

Ohara thanked her and rose to go, adding, "We're trying to work something out for you and . . ."

She jumped up and flung her arms around him. "Sam, don't leave me here, please! Take me with you!"

Ohara tried to be gentle. "It just isn't possible, Jody. I told you that yesterday."

She looked up at him, her eyes filling with tears. "Please! I hate it here." She buried her face on his shoulder, her arms tightening around his neck. "You said you liked me, Sam. If you did, you'd take me with you."

He loosened her arms from around his neck and stood holding her hands in his. "Right now this is the best place for you. Give it a chance."

Jody wrenched her hands away from him. "Well, I don't like it. You can't make me stay here!"

Amy came to Ohara's rescue. "Stop it, Jody. You're in no position to play games. If you don't like it here, we can take you to Juvenile Hall right now. You decide."

Jody jerked her head around to stare angrily at Amy's pleasant but determined face. Then she looked back at Ohara. "You pigs are all alike. Who needs you." She stalked over to the door, picked up her bag, and left. They could hear her angrily stamping up the stairs.

When Ohara and Amy left the hostel, he said, "I want to visit the crime scene again. I want to check out a hunch." As they drove, Ohara explained that a gun fired during the crime was missing, then said, "But unless the bullet is lodged in somebody's body, it's got to be there."

"Didn't the lab guys already check the scene thoroughly?" Though she wouldn't say so, Amy didn't see the point.

"They did, but I want another look."

Shimizu's vandalized car had been towed away, so it was easier to survey the garage. Ohara pointed out the faint traces of blood on the floor that led out to the alley. "Judging from this and the position of the body, the victim must have fired before or as he fell. So the bullet, if it's here, must be somewhere on that wall."

"That simple," Amy said.

"Yes, that simple, but not that easy," Ohara answered.

The garage space was ample, allowing for tenant storage. In Shimizu's space, the back wall was stacked with cartons. They were tightly packed, with the barest space between rows, and none showed signs of any damage. Ohara and Amy began moving them. They continued silently until long past the time when Amy would have given up, when Ohara suddenly said, "Got it!"

Amy spotted the bullet hole in the wall about three feet from the ground. Carefully Ohara dug out the bullet and held it in his hand. It hadn't stopped Shimizu's murderer, but it might yet convict him.

Chapter Eight

Ohara returned to the office to find Ted already there. "How did it go in court?" he asked.

"Case dismissed. Fellows sent us a preliminary autopsy report." Washington indicated the papers on his desk. "I've just finished reading it."

"Has he pinned anything down?"

"Only that the victim was overweight, drank too much, and would probably have died of liver cancer in a couple of years. Right hand showed he might have fired a gun."

Ohara smiled. "I got lucky. I went back to Shimizu's garage after I'd finished talking to Jody, and found the bullet. It's at ballistics now."

"Brewster and the others scoured that place. How come they missed it?"

"It was a fluke." Ohara explained how the bullet had slipped through the space between two rows of cartons. "We had to have the car out and start unpiling the cartons to find it."

"Nice work!" Washington brightened.

"It's something," Ohara admitted, "but not enough. First, whoever has the gun will have to shoot somebody so we'll have a bullet for comparison."

"That can happen. I don't imagine it was taken for a keepsake."

Ohara picked up Fellows's report and scanned it. "Not much help here, either. According to this, the blow with the wrench came first, and might have killed the victim if he'd lived long enough to die of it."

Washington sighed. "More bullshit for the defense to jump on. Looks like the blows to the face and head were lethal enough."

"I wonder if whoever wrung his neck knew that," Ohara said.

Washington considered the point. "Makes you wonder what kind of person would do that."

"It would take a strong pair of hands, some knowledge, maybe even experience," Ohara said. "Professional assassins sometimes use that technique. It's quick and silent."

"Do you think it was a professional?"

"It's possible."

"If not a professional, who else?" Washington probed.

"A masseur, maybe a chiropractor or osteopath," Ohara answered.

"How about a wrestler?"

Ohara looked thoughtful. The question poked at his mind, but brought out nothing useful.

"You think it could be a woman?" Ted asked, looking thoughtful himself.

"It could be."

"There are too many possibilities in this case," Washington grumbled. "Did you turn up anything else?"

Ohara told him about the vandalized cars.

"Nasty." Washington could guess how Ohara felt. "Could be a connection with Shimizu's murder, considering what was done to his car. There are still people around who kill blacks just for the hell of it. From what you've told me, somebody doesn't like Japanese, either."

"So it appears." Ohara let it go at that and went on to report on the interview with Jody. "Only new thing really was her description of the second man, his jacket and the scar on his cheek. I got the feeling she was trying too hard to please. That kind of jacket is common, and she couldn't see the scar from where she was."

"Agreed, Sam, but she's not lying about Walker's scar. He does have one."

Ohara looked at his watch. "Walker . . ." Ohara said, almost to himself. "Maybe we should give him a little more thought, but not now. I'd like to leave a little early so we can stop at the lab on our way to Guardian Insurance."

On the way, Washington told him about his inquiries on Jody. "She told us her aunt, Paula Matthews, lives in Evanston. I've checked Motor Vehicles, Voter Registration, the telephone company, and Credit Bureau, but drew a blank. Apparently there is no such person in Evanston."

"How about Chicago where she grew up?"

"The Chicago police were cooperative, but her parents, Peter and Alys Baxter, don't appear in any of the usual records. Missing Persons has no girl matching Jody's description reported missing. There's no birth record of a child born to an Alys and Peter Baxter. The police checked back fifteen years, but couldn't find a trace of either Jody or her parents."

Ohara looked depressed at the news. "Maybe we can get something from her prints."

"Maybe," Washington agreed, "but I've also made up an Identikit picture for distribution throughout the state."

"Hope it works," Ohara said. "Poor kid. What a life she must have had if she needs to make up a better one."

At the lab, Brewster didn't look exactly delighted to see them, but he gave them what he had. "The wrench has three faint prints left even after being wiped. Two different thumbprints, both large, and a smaller print. One large thumbprint is superimposed over a small one."

"Anything on the handkerchief?" Washington asked.

"It's good-quality linen. The initials on it are DW. Blood and dirt on it. The blood's the same as the victim's, which is type O."

"I know we're pushing," Ohara said, "but is there anything on the blood scrapings from the driveway?"

"They're type A."

"We need to send the girl's prints in to records," Ohara said. "How soon can we have them?"

"Soon." Baxter was almost out the door. "Along with the negatives, files, scene sweepings, the lot." He was out the door before he finished his sentence.

Ohara glanced at his watch. They just had time to make their three-o'clock appointment. With Washington he went back to the car, drove out of the low-rent neighborhood where the lab was located, and headed for the high-rent community of Beverly Hills.

"Hope we don't step on any sensitive toes here," Washington commented, remembering that Beverly Hills had its own elite police force.

"Don't worry about the local police, Ted. I've a friend on the force. He's Japanese-American, and one of the best cops I know. Name's Masuto."

Going slowly, they drove past gracious mansions with smooth green lawns, their driveways parked with Porsches and Mercedes. Once this had been "movie star row," and though many of the stars had departed for Malibu or places farther afield, the glamour still remained. Washington was enjoying himself. "This is the kind of life I'd like to get used to," he sighed.

"Cops don't bowl in that league," Ohara said.

"No. Only the guys who play cops in the movies. Maybe I should take a screen test. What do you think?"

"Sidney Poitier got there first." Ohara grinned. "Stay in police work!"

They turned onto a boulevard of expensive shops, banks, and landscaped office buildings. Guardian Insurance was in a new high rise that had been designed for the space age, a soaring tower with black mirrored sides. After parking in the underground garage, they took the elevator to the twenty-fourth floor.

The Guardian office, judging from its decor, lived up to its address. A blond receptionist who looked like a Hollywood starlet took their names, checked the appointment sheet, then directed them through the busy working office to Roger Takematsu's sanctum. His secretary, a pretty Japanese girl, admitted them.

The office was expensively furnished and impressive, more so than the anxious little man who stood up from his oversized mahogany desk to greet them. The courtesies completed and his offer of refreshments declined, he invited them to sit down. Then he seated himself behind his desk and asked, "What did you want to see me about?"

"Your employee, Tak Shimizu," Ohara answered. "He's been murdered."

Takematsu seemed to shrink back into his chair. "Murdered?" He almost whispered the words; his face was ashen.

"Yes, last night. I'm sorry to give you such a shock. It was in the news."

"I seldom read the papers."

Washington studied him with interest. The man was shocked, all right, but not with grief. He was badly frightened. Washington wondered why.

Ohara, who had made the same observation, continued. "Do you know of any enemies Mr. Shimizu might have had?"

Takematsu had been staring straight ahead of him, absorbed in thoughts of his own. Ohara repeated the question.

71

"I'm sorry. It's just such a shock. No, I don't know that Tak had any enemies. Why should he?"

"He had enemies, all right," Washington said. "Do you know anything about his private life?"

"No, nothing. You must understand. We had a strictly employer-employee relationship." Apparently, this sounded a little callous even to Takematsu. "Tak was an excellent agent. He brought in more clients than anyone else on our staff. We're going to miss him."

"Who recommended him? We might like to talk to them."

Takematsu looked uncomfortable. "My backers in Japan, actually. He had worked for them before. Er . . . have you any idea yet who might have killed him?"

"There have been some developments," Ohara answered.

Takematsu waited for more information, but he didn't get it. He cleared his throat nervously. "Tak Shimizu had some files that are the property of Guardian Insurance. I'll send someone over to get them."

"They're being held as evidence at the moment. We'll return them eventually."

The little man leaned back in his chair as if the air had been let out of him. "Evidence of what?" He was having trouble with his voice.

"We don't know . . . yet." Washington leaned forward. "Do you know of any reason why Shimizu's desk and files should be ransacked?"

"No."

"Your property will be returned to you in due course, Mr. Takematsu." Ohara did not look up from the small notebook in which he was writing.

"I've no idea what could be in them," Taketmatsu looked earnestly at his visitors, "but probably it's confidential information about our clients. It shouldn't fall into the wrong hands.''

"It may already have." Ohara closed the notebook and laid it and the pen on Takematsu's desk, then reached into his pocket for a tissue and began wiping his fingers. "Pen leaks sometimes," he explained.

After saying they might need to come again, Ohara and Washington got up and left. Outside Takematsu's closed door, Ohara paused a moment, searching his pockets, then said, "I left my notebook and pen on the desk."

The Japanese secretary rose to get it for him, but Ohara forestalled her by opening the door to Takematsu's office and walking in, followed by Washington.

Roger Takematsu didn't even hear them. He was on the telephone. "Yes, they were here. You've got to find out what happened—" He broke off as Ohara reached the desk to stare up at him, his expression suddenly fearful.

"Sorry. Don't let me interrupt." Ohara smiled pleasantly. "I just came back for my notebook and pen."

When they were alone in the elevator going down to the garage, Washington grinned in appreciation. "You're a sneaky devil.''

"Have to be sometimes." Ohara grinned back. "He's terrified, and I want to know why. Let's check with Organized Crime, and see if we can get a line on his Japanese backers."

"Yakuza?"

"That's likely. If we can prove Shimizu's connection and tie Roger in with him, we've got another murder suspect."

Washington looked surprised. "Takematsu? He wouldn't have the guts to beat a man to death."

"I agree," Ohara said as they got into their car. "But he could hire it done."

"Back to the professional." Washington seemed to like the idea.

Ohara nodded, then, reaching into his pocket, took out the green shamrock matchbook advertising Flynn's Pub. "This was in Shimizu's pocket. Let's go see what they can tell us about him."

"Never heard of the place."

"Flynn's Pub is in the same neighborhood where somebody painted 'Fuck the Japs' on a lot of cars."

Chapter Nine

Ohara pulled up in front of a compact brick building sandwiched between a dry cleaner's and a fast-food stand. Its front had once been shingled in dark wood, which had mellowed with the years to a soft brownish-gray. A green neon sign proclaimed FLYNN'S PUB.

"Homey sort of place, isn't it?" Washington said as they got out of the car and with a look down the rather dreary street headed for the bar.

As Ohara reached to pull open the sturdy wooden door, it was swung outward, knocking him to one side. The man who emerged stood blocking the entrance. "Dumb yellow bastard," he said, "look where you're goin'!" Then, shoving past, he went down the street without a backward glance.

Ohara started after the man, but Washington gripped his shoulder. "Take it easy, Sam. The guy's an asshole, but you'd better let it go."

Angry as he was, Ohara knew Ted was right, if for no other reason than that the retreating figure had one arm in a sling. He let his breath out in a long sigh, pulled the door open, and entered the pub.

It was empty except for the bartender, a well-set-up man with thick, graying hair and a ruddy face. He stared at the two men who had entered, then, as if remembering what he was there for, said, "Hi, what'll it be?"

"Nothing," Ohara snapped as he walked up to the bar. "Are you Flynn?"

"No, he's out," the bartender said, then added, "Sorry you had to run into one of the neighborhood bigots."

"How many are there?" There was bitterness beneath the calculated calm in Ohara's voice.

"We get a few," the bartender said mildly.

Ohara showed his ID. "My name's Ohara. This is my partner, Ted Washington. We'd like to talk to Flynn. When will he be back?"

Smiling, the bartender extended his hand. "Glad to meet some members of the lodge. I worked patrol in West Valley Division before I retired. Name's Barry Sawyer. Take a Code Seven and I'll buy you a beer."

"I'd like that." Washington grinned. "How about you, Sam?"

"Why not? I could use a break," Ohara said, though it was the last thing he wanted at the moment.

For a few minutes they sat at the bar talking shop. Finally Barry brought the conversation back to Joe Flynn. "Joe's not in trouble, is he?"

"Not that we know," Ohara reassured him. "We want to ask him some questions. That's all."

Barry nodded. "He's an all right guy. I've known him from before he took over the pub. Used to watch him wrestle."

"He was a wrestler?" Washington asked with more than usual interest.

"That's his picture on the wall over there."

Washington and Ohara went over to look at the pictures lining the wall while Barry gave them a fan's-eye view of the wrestling greats.

"Who's that?" Washington pointed to a bald-headed giant of a man posed with the Mighty Flynn.

"Oh, that's Joe's brother-in-law. Billed as 'Dirty Mike Muldoon'; always played the heavy. Nicest guy you'd want to meet. Got hurt in the ring and couldn't work afterward. Joe was real good to him. Saw him through the bad times, then bought him a little motel to run."

"Not many guys would do that," Washington said, "especially for a brother-in law." He looked at his watch. "What do you want to do, Sam, wait?"

"Joe probably won't be back until tonight," Barry said. "His wife's an invalid, so he goes home to get her dinner and spends a little time with her. Anything I can do?"

Ohara took the green shamrock matchbook out of his pocket. "This was found on the body of a murder victim. He's a Japanese named Tak Shimizu. Was he a customer here?"

"He was Joe's insurance agent. Came in once a month to collect. He was here yesterday about six-thirty when I came in to relieve Joe."

"Tell us about it."

"Well, when I came in, Shimizu and Bill Stack, the guy you bumped into, and a pal were having some kind of rhubarb with him. Bill was on his feet spoiling for a fight, yelling how he didn't drink with no Japs. His buddy, Erne Smith, told him to cool it and held him back, but Bill keeps goin' on about how he's going to get the Jap. Shimizu was pretty hot, too. I saw him reach inside his jacket, and was sure he was going for a gun."

"What happened then?"

"Bill's yelling gave him a coughing fit. Finally his buddy was able to get him shoved out the door."

"Was Stack's arm in a sling then?" Ohara asked.

"No, it wasn't. When he was in for a beer just now he said he fell down some stairs last night and dislocated his shoulder."

"My heart bleeds for him," Washington grunted.

"When did Shimizu leave the bar?" Ohara asked.

"He stuck around awhile. Told Joe to get him a drink. Said he wanted to talk some business. They sat down in the front booth and Shimizu began talking, keeping his voice down. I took the hint and busied myself further down the bar."

"Go on," Ohara encouraged.

"You understand, I wasn't trying to overhear them. Joe's personal business is his own, but cop to cop I'll tell you. Joe starts getting excited and pretty soon he says real loud, 'I can't pay that! I can hardly make it now.'"

"What happened then?"

"Shimizu hands him an envelope. I saw Joe open it and take something out; but I couldn't see what it was. Then Shimizu talked some more. Pretty soon he gets up and leaves."

"Did Joe say anything to you about what had happened?"

"No. He just said he was going home and he wouldn't be back so I should close. He seemed pretty upset."

"Will he be in tonight?" Ohara asked.

"Should be. Didn't say he wouldn't."

"Do you know where this Stack character lives?" Washington asked.

Barry smiled. "Happens I do. He went on a drunk one night, so I piled him into his old blue Chevy and drove him home. He lives in the first of those old-fashioned apartments on Chestnut Street, just past Maple."

When Ohara and Washington left the pub they headed for Chestnut Street, which looked much like its relative Maple Street, except that the substantial frame houses had given way to small stucco bungalows. On the corner stood the two-story apartment building in which Stack lived. A pair of stone steps led to the hallway, which was lined with slotted mailboxes.

"I'll take him on, if you want," Washington offered.

"Thanks," Ohara said, "but don't deprive me of the pleasure." When they rang the bell under Stack's name, there was no response.

As they walked back down the stairs, Ohara noticed a beat-up blue Chevy among the cars that crowded the curb. It was too dark to see inside, but they took the license number.

There was nothing more to be done for the moment, so they got back into their car to return to the station. On the way they discussed the next step, which was talking to Duke Walker. "Even money says that handkerchief with the DW monogram was his," Washington concluded. "Maybe he can explain how it got so bloody."

"The blood doesn't necessarily mean he killed Shimizu," Ohara reminded. "People do weird things when they stumble on a crime scene: pick up the weapon, drop it in horror, move the body to see if it's alive. Then they panic and try to cover it up."

"He's covering something up. Let's shake him up and see what falls out."

Bill Stack had almost panicked when the bell had rung. He'd been watching for Ginny and had seen the two men coming. There was no mistaking that they were cops. Watching from behind the window drapes, he'd scarcely breathed until he'd seen them go back down the apartment steps. When they'd stopped to check his car, he'd been thrown back into torment. The Jap was the guy he'd bumped into coming out of Flynn's.

That was why they'd come after him. Barry must have blabbed, even given them his address. He watched them drive away, but he knew they'd be back. Wiping the sweat from his forehead, he tried to think what to do. Why had they looked at the car? Had somebody seen it at Shimizu's?

He wasn't sure Ginny's scrubbing had gotten all the blood out of the front seat, so maybe he'd better get rid of it.

What else? His head ached as he tried to think. An alibi . . . he'd get Erne to say he'd come home with him that night and stayed around. Good old Erne would do it, too. He hated cops.

After Washington left him, Ohara drove to Tashimura's, his favorite small restaurant, for a bowl of noodles. It wasn't too far from Flynn's, so afterward he could check out Joe Flynn and maybe try for Stack again.

Ohara ate leisurely, enjoying his conversation with Tashimura-san, who'd been a longtime friend of his parents.

When he'd finished eating, Tashimura laid a yellow flyer in front of him. It was about the Asian Concerns meeting at the center that night. "Isamu," he said, "you think bad times come again for us?"

Ohara sighed. He'd stayed away from home to duck this. "There have been some scattered incidents of anti-Asian violence, Tashimura-san, but don't worry. It's just the unrest in the country, not like during the war."

"Not sure, Isamu. They not think so." He pointed to the yellow flyer.

"It could be they're overreacting," Ohara said. "Remember, there is violence against other ethnic groups as well."

Tashimura nodded, but he didn't look too convinced. "I go listen what they say, anyway."

When Ohara reached Flynn's, the parking spaces at the curb were taken, so he swung his car around back and into the weed-studded parking lot behind the pub. The place was fairly full, but Barry saw him come in and waved him over to the bar.

"Is Joe in?" Ohara asked.

"No. Didn't call, either," Barry said, "but Erne Smith is here." He nodded toward a booth where a tall black man wearing a baseball cap sat nursing a beer. "The little guy with him is another of Stack's pals, Benny Polser."

Ohara was aware of the growing silence around them. The relaxed, friendly atmosphere he'd sensed when he came in seemed almost hostile. "They don't like strangers here," Barry said under his breath.

Ohara looked at him. "Or Japanese?"

Barry shrugged.

"Paper says they found a dead Jap," a voice spoke from nowhere in particular. "Good riddance, I say."

Ohara stiffened, but did not rise to the bait.

"Better look out," another voice said. "They got Japs in the police now. They'll see a white guy gets pegged for the killing."

Ohara leaned back against the bar so that he faced the room. Instantly, heads turned away. No one appeared to look at him, but when he walked to the booth where Erne Smith sat, he could feel every eye on him.

Producing his ID, he said, "I'm told you were in the bar with Bill Stack when Tak Shimizu came in. What happened?"

"He's the Jap guy got killed, isn't he?" the little guy interjected before Erne could answer.

Ohara's expression didn't change. "What do you know about it?"

"Me?" Benny's voice skidded into high. "Nothin', only what I hear. I left before he came in."

"And you?" Ohara turned to Erne, who finished his beer before answering.

"We were here when the Jap came in, but we left, me and Bill."

"Barry says there was an argument."

"That's his opinion. I didn't hear no argument. Like I said, we left."

"I saw you guys come outside." Benny was filled with importance. "Ol' Bill was so pissed he kept slammin' his fists on the Jap's car."

"Shit, Benny." Erne glared at Polser. "What you know about anythin'. Bill was just lookin' at it. I done the same."

"I seen him, Erne," Benny insisted. "Then he . . ." Benny suddenly wilted under Erne's glare.

"Do you know where Stack would be now?" Ohara looked from one to the other.

Erne didn't bother to answer. Benny looked at him defiantly. "He's home, I guess." Then Benny's eyes glittered with malice. "But I betcha he won't like talkin' to no Jap cop. He's a mean ol' boy."

Ohara ignored the taunt. "Do either of you recall anything else?"

"No, we don't." Erne stood up. "Don't like the smell here, neither. I'm goin' home. Any objections, Mr. Police Officer?"

"None." Ohara stood back as Erne pushed past him.

Benny got up, too. "Yeah, it's too crowded in here." He followed close behind Erne out the door.

Ohara went back to the bar, got a beer from Barry, and settled down to wait for Joe. As he waited, people came and went. There were no more pointed remarks, but the silent hostility made itself felt.

Finally Ohara gave it up, paid for his beer, and left.

His car was the only one in the dark back lot. He could barely see to unlock the door. As he bent to fit the key into the lock, something cracked against his temple, knocking him sideways, then bounced against his car and fell at his feet. Dazed, he turned and stared into the shadows near the pub. He could see no one, but he could hear the sound of running feet escaping into the darkness.

Leaning against the car, Ohara took out a handkerchief and wiped away the trickle of blood from his temple. Then, bending down, he picked up the object that had struck him. It was a large, ragged piece of paving. He tossed it aside, unlocked his car, and got in. As he started up there was only one question turning in his mind. "Did it happen because I'm a cop, or because I'm Japanese?"

He headed for home, then changed his mind and drove to the meeting at the Community Center.

Chapter Ten

Ohara arrived at the Community Center complex of low brick buildings to find the parking lot was full. More people than he would have guessed seemed to be interested in the Asian Concerns meeting. He parked on the street and made his way to the entrance in the brick wall that enclosed the patio, classrooms, kitchen, gymnasium, and judo hall. When he'd first brought his kids to the Center for judo, Scouts, and other activities, it had consisted of only two buildings. He was impressed by what the money and volunteer labor of a lot of good people had accomplished over the years. Wings had been added to the original buildings, and the patio had been landscaped.

At one end a simple, serene Japanese garden commemorated the achievements of the first Japanese immigrants, the Issei. At the other end another small garden set off the bronze plaque that had been placed in honor of the Nisei veterans who had fought for America in World War II. It seemed to him that the two small gardens symbolized the blend of heritage and birth that was Japanese-American. It had made him the kind of man he was.

Light streamed out of the open rear door of the gymnasium so Ohara went in and stood at the back, along with a few others. He looked over the capacity crowd trying to spot his family, but he couldn't locate them.

The speaker on the small stage at the other end of the gym was Roy Moneta, a man whom Ohara knew and respected. He was outlining the causes of the growing anti-Asian feeling in the country, among them the Oriental stereotypes so frequently used in books and movies: comic buck-toothed Japanese, sinister Chinese villains, and vicious karate killers.

To Ohara these had always been fantasies of entertainment, nothing more, and hardly typifying Orientals in general. Yet, thinking about it, he could see how they would tend to create a subconscious image in people's minds. Ordinary Asians were little publicized even in TV commercials, the popular norm of the American way of life, or what it was supposed to be.

He and his family were American by birth, by outlook, and everything else that counted. Apparently that didn't matter to someone who believed you couldn't be a real American if you had an Oriental face. He'd often heard the saying, "a gook is a gook," but like all such racial labels, gook, spade, honkey, or whatever, they destroyed the common human bond, and bred distrust and resentment.

Still he could understand the attitude of people for whom the sudden influx of Asian and other refugees had become a job threat and an unwelcome burden on the welfare rolls. It made them afraid, and, as so often happened, fear could change to hate, expressing itself in violence. Shimizu might have been killed because he was "one of those yellow bastards" and for no other reason.

Ohara's hand went to the cut on his temple. He'd had worse injuries, but never just because somebody hated him impersonally for the color of his skin. With a new awareness he listened to the accounts of recent anti-Asian violence across the country.

The facts were shocking and brutal. In one Los Angeles community the construction of a Buddhist temple had been blocked. Residents didn't want any more Asians coming into the neighborhood. They "looked funny," "ate dogs," and had "weird diseases."

The litany of senseless violence went on. Anti-Asian slogans had been painted on walls and sidewalks of a California schoolyard where a Vietnamese student had been killed by a "whites only" gang. Ohara wondered if this was how it had begun in Hitler's Germany, when it was a crime to be a Jew. Here and there public officials had spoken out and committees had been formed to study human relations. So far they hadn't accomplished much.

When open discussion was invited, the man whose car had been vandalized on Maple Street told what had happened, describing the "Fuck the Japs" slogans painted on the cars.

"What are the police doing?" somebody shouted.

"They said they'd look into it," the man answered with a shrug. A quick burst of sarcastic laughter rose from the crowd.

There were more stories, but Ohara barely listened, as once more he tried to find his family in the crowd. Then he felt a small hand on his arm, and turned to find his wife smiling up at him. "Peggy!" He put his arm around her and drew her close to his side, his expression a mixture of relief and pleasure. "I'm sorry about this morning. I tried to call you." They had eyes only for each other, intent on mending the rare breach that had come between them.

"Jim went too far," she began, then broke off as she saw the cut on his temple. "What happened, Isamu?" She touched it gently.

"It's nothing serious. Where are the children?"

She pointed over to the left about ten rows from the back, and he saw them. Suddenly Ohara heard his name being spoken.

"Detective Ohara," the speaker asked, "was the murder of the Japanese yesterday a racial incident? I've been told you're handling the case."

"I can only say that he was beaten and robbed. There's no real evidence of a racial incident."

"What about his car being vandalized?" someone asked. "That sure sounds racist to me."

"True," Ohara admitted. "His car had been vandalized, but unlike the cars on Maple Street, there was no slogan painted on it."

From one side of the hall a voice shouted, "It's time we took things into our own hands if we want any protection." A young man stood up. Ohara recognized Kaz Shimoda, who was the son of old friends. He was in college now, majoring in political science, and had gained a reputation as an activist. Young as he was, he had the kind of charisma that makes leaders or demagogues.

"Don't kid yourselves that what you've seen and heard tonight can't happen right here," he told the audience. "It's already started . . . the vandalism, the slogans, the killing. Yesterday an innocent Japanese was brutally murdered, yet Detective Ohara tells us he doesn't see any racial overtones. Maybe he doesn't want to, or maybe he has orders not to see."

Here and there Ohara saw people turn to look at him. His son Jim was one of them, disappointment and condemnation in his face. It shocked Ohara that the boy so misunderstood him.

"Ask your kids what's happening in school," Kaz was saying. "They can tell you about racial overtones." He paused dramatically, gathering full attention, then went on, "The damn *hakujin*, or should I say 'Whitey,' pushed you around before, sent you to camp, and took your homes. Ever since then we've had to buck prejudice in jobs, housing, and society, same as the blacks. Forget the speeches and committees! What we need is action!" He sat down amid a buzz of excitement.

87

Few people saw old Fred Hata walk heavily up to the microphone before his voice boomed out. "I want to say something!"

About everyone there knew him. His ruddy, weatherbeaten face and black hair disguised the fact that he was close to eighty. With a simple dignity that was arresting, he stood there, solidly planted, his big hands, in which every crack was permanently indented with the soil he loved, hanging at his sides.

Too old for the arduous work of gardening, he now spent his time on his beloved bonsei, and in working with young people. He firmly believed that a kid who learned to plant and grow something could never go bad. He owned a small piece of land, where he helped senior citizens, and others with little income, to grow their own vegetables. Respectfully the audience quieted to hear him speak.

"That kind of talk won't make things any better," he began, "but it could get a lot of us hurt. We lived through a worse time than this when they interned us: men, women, and little kids behind barbed wire. Not for doing anything wrong, but because we were Japanese. You think we weren't mad as hell then? And sick at heart because we'd been betrayed by our country. But we tried to understand because America was at war, and we were American citizens. That's why our boys joined the army." Fred paused for a moment. His eldest son had died in combat in Italy.

Ohara could almost feel memories of that time come alive in the room as Fred's husky voice continued. "That's why, when the war was over and they let us out of the camps, we didn't complain. Maybe, like our boys, we felt we had to help ourselves, the American way. And we did it, starting from nothing, working hard, gaining people's respect. That's somethin' no law can give you. You gotta earn respect. Sure, Asians got new problems now, but they got to solve

88

them like we did. If a plant gets sick you work with it, you don't tear it out by the roots! That's all I got to say."

There was a moment's silence, followed by enthusiastic applause, as Fred walked back to his seat.

But before it died down Kaz was at the microphone. "Listen, people, that sounds great, but that kind of thinking won't work today. I'm not talking against the system, but what can it do? Pay for studies on why people are beating up on Asians? Send the police to find out who killed your kid, or your wife, or you?

"What we need is a vigilante patrol to walk the streets of our community. We need one at each school, too. Anybody wants trouble, we'll give it to them!"

He paused, looked round him, sensing every eye on him, then said, "Those who agree, follow me outside. We'll find ways to protect ourselves." Assured and purposeful, Kaz walked out of the meeting.

With mixed feelings Ohara watched most of the young people follow him. He knew the local white, black, and Chicano gangs would take their vigilante patrol as a fighting challenge to their turf.

That broke up the meeting. To Ohara's relief, his daughter Susie came to stand beside them. "Hello, Dad," she said. Smiling he put his arm around her and hugged her close. "Jim went with Kaz," she said, "but I couldn't. He sort of frightens me."

"He frightens me, too," Ohara said.

"Our son mustn't go," Peggy said. "You must stop him, Isamu!" Her voice was strained with worry.

Ohara wished he could. Like Peggy, he wanted to protect Jim, spare him some of the hard lessons that lay ahead, but he knew his son was in no mood to listen. "Don't worry, Peggy." He tried to sound confident, "Jim will stop himself when he finds the answers he needs. We have to give him that chance." He put his free arm around Peggy's shoulders. "Now let's go home. It's been a very long day."

Chapter Eleven

The next morning was bright and sunny, one of California's best, but it did nothing to cheer up Ohara. He'd hoped to talk to Jim at breakfast, but his son had already left. As was his custom, he went quickly through the morning paper. The story of the meeting was in the local news under the headline "Asians Strike Back." Most of the article dealt with Kaz Shimoda's dramatic action in organizing a vigilante patrol. It concluded by saying, "Shimoda says the visible presence of patrols should prevent violence, but that if his people are attacked they will fight back."

Gloomily Ohara thought that if they were a visible presence on the hotly disputed gang turf of the neighborhood, they'd be attacked, all right. Kaz Shimoda, fresh from the ivory tower of his college campus, probably hadn't reckoned on that.

Peggy broke in on his thoughts. "Isamu, you must talk to Jim tonight. Those patrols could be dangerous. I keep thinking about that young boy who was stabbed on the school grounds, and I'm afraid for our son."

Ohara reached over and took her hand. "You can be sure we'll have an eye on things."

He had lost his appetite, so he got up from the table. Peggy walked him to the door as usual and clung to him for a long moment. "I've never felt this afraid before," she said. "How can this be happening?"

"I don't know," he answered. "I never thought it would."

As he drove to the station he realized that, even more than the vandalism, the Shimizu killing brought home to people the fact that they too might become victims. He needed to solve it quickly and prove, if he could, that the motive was not racial, but something else. That would go a long way to dispel the growing suspicion and fear that would soon reach out far beyond Maple Street. It had already reached into his own home.

When he arrived at the station, Sergeant Reagan stopped him. "Hey, Irish, what the hell is goin' on in that Maple Street neighborhood? We just had another call from there, somebody named Tom Fujiwara. He was crying like a baby because his bushes are ruined; somebody poured acid on them."

"When?"

"Last night. Seems he had some bushes round his place that he kept trimmed like animals: a deer, an elephant, a rabbit, like that. Said he'd been growing them for twenty years."

Ohara remembered seeing Fujiwara's green menagerie when he'd driven over to look at the vandalized cars.

"Then, as if that wasn't enough," Reagan continued, "they painted 'Fucking Jap' . . . oh, no offense, Irish . . . on the sidewalk." He let his voice trail off and looked away, embarrassed for a man he liked and respected.

"Is somebody working the call?" Ohara's voice showed nothing of his feelings.

"Yes."

"Let me know what they come up with, will you?"

"Sure, Irish."

More depressed than he liked to admit, Ohara went up to the detectives' office. His corner desk and Washington's next to it were piled with material from forensics. He greeted Reyes and Liebman, the only other detectives around at the moment, and sat down at his desk, glad to have something concrete to work on. He was deeply absorbed when Washington arrived.

"Up early catching worms?" Ted asked.

"Some choice ones," Ohara answered. "There were traces of cocaine on a scale and some plastic envelopes in the cupboard of Shimizu's closet."

"Doesn't surprise me," Washington said.

"Also some prints, similar to those on the wrench, appear on Shimizu's wallet. One might be a woman's."

"Now we're getting somewhere."

"Wait, more to come. Remember the smears on the wallet? The lab report says they're mostly sugar and chocolate."

"Don't remember Fellows mentioning anything like that in Shimizu's stomach contents, do you?"

"No," Ohara admitted. "That's a good point, Ted."

"But what does it get us? A killer with a sweet tooth?"

"Well, leave that and take a look at these pictures from Shimizu's negatives." Ohara handed over a folder of eight-by-tens. "Some of them are ordinary enough—Shimizu and friends, for example—but there are others that look like blackmail."

"Maybe that's why Roger Takematsu was worried that the files might fall into the wrong hands." Washington opened the folder. "Could be they were in on it together."

"Takematsu's scared of something," Ohara mused, "but I don't think it's the police. Barring a lucky break, there's no way for us to prove why these photographs were taken. The only notes Shimizu kept are dates and numbers."

"Why those?"

"I don't know." Ohara got up and walked over to the small window that looked out on the parking lot. The more he uncovered, the more he felt he was climbing through deep, sliding sand. "Take a look at those, Ted, and see what you make of them."

Washington examined the pictures carefully. There were some porno shots of pretty girls, but most were of individuals who obviously didn't know they were being photographed: a man leaving Los Angeles airport; a car full of Mexicans; a man running down the street; a young man lying in an alley next to garbage cans.

Ohara had come up behind Washington and was looking over his shoulder. He pointed to the picture of the boy lying in the alley. "I've a feeling I've seen his face before, but I can't think where."

Washington looked at the picture again. "Me, too. It'll probably come to me." He dropped the picture and continued through the pile. Suddenly he stopped and said, "Bingo!"

He handed Ohara a picture of a half-naked girl standing between Shimizu and an unknown Japanese. "Know who that is?"

Ohara looked at it. "Shimizu and friends."

"The girl is Duke Walker's wife, Sam."

"And they claimed they didn't know Shimizu." Ohara felt as if he'd just come out of the sand onto solid rock. "OK, Ted, let's pick Walker up and see if he has anything to add to his story."

"Hey, Duke, a couple of cops want to see you." Fred Monk, the owner of the repair garage where Duke worked, seemed to enjoy the sensation he was creating. Duke slid out from underneath the Porsche he was working on and stood up.

"Knew they'd get you sooner or later, Duke," his buddy joked. But Duke, watching Ohara and Washington walk toward him, knew it was no joke. The usual noises of the garage grew suddenly quiet as everyone stopped work to hear what was said.

When it appeared that the cops wanted to take Duke into the station, a small group of men left their work to stand beside him. "He ain't done nothin'," one of them said. "What you want him for?"

"Just to make a formal statement. He's a witness," Ohara said pleasantly.

"I shouldn't be long," Duke said to the boss, and hurriedly put on his jacket. "And keep your cotton-pickin' hands off that Porsche, Frank!" He looked at Ohara and Washington. "Let's go and get this over."

As they walked toward the car, Ohara could feel the hard stares following them. He turned back to look at the ring of faces filled with suspicion and distrust. One of them was Erne Smith, the man he'd talked to in the bar, Bill Stack's buddy. He guessed it wouldn't take long for this news to circulate.

When they arrived at the station, a reporter was quizzing Sergeant Reagan on the latest vandalism incidents. It was Ed Burns, whom Ohara had met before. That he had come was significant. The police-blotter detail was usually handled by a rookie. "Something new on the Shimizu case, Irish?"

Ohara signaled to Washington to take Duke on ahead and turned to answer. "Not yet, Ed."

"That guy a suspect?"

Ohara passed that off. "A witness, that's all."

"Come on, Irish, give me something. If this is a racial murder, it's news, especially when a white guy is brought in for questioning."

"Ed, do me a favor. Play down the racial angle. It's not confirmed and could cause a lot of trouble."

The reporter's eyes narrowed. "OK, Irish, if you say so, but I want first crack at the story. Deal?"

"Deal," Ohara said, feeling like he was holding his finger in a dike that would overflow anyway.

Ohara stopped at his desk to pick up the handkerchief and the photograph. Then he went to the interrogation room, where Washington and Walker waited. A police stenographer was seated unobtrusively in the corner. Ohara sat down at the table opposite Duke. "You've been advised of your rights."

"Yeah," Duke answered, "but I don't know what for. I just found the body."

"It's a necessary formality," Ohara answered. "Do you want a lawyer present?"

Duke looked shaken, but said, "Don't need one. Just let me tell the damn story and get back to work."

"All right," Ohara said. "Let's hear it."

With a nervous glance at the stenographer, Duke told the same story as he had before. When he had finished, Washington said, "You sure you didn't know the dead man?"

"No! How many times do I have to tell you?"

Washington looked at Ohara. "Maybe we should ask Mrs. Walker if she knew him?"

Duke jerked his body forward. "My wife never saw him in her life. Leave her alone. She's not well." Duke took a handkerchief out of his pocket and wiped his palms.

"Nice handkerchief," Ohara said mildly. He reached over and lifted one corner. "Embroidered initials. Don't see many of those anymore."

"My wife gave it to me. She embroidered it." He ran his thumb over the initials as though they gave him some kind of comfort.

"Then this must be yours, too. It was in the refuse bin near where you found the body." Ohara laid the bloodstained handkerchief on the table.

Duke stared at it, his throat working. "It . . . it might be. I cut myself and tied up the cut with my handkerchief, I remember. Then I threw it away."

Washington opened the folder he held. "According to the lab reports, the blood is the same as that of the victim. Now, how did it get on your handkerchief?"

"I told you, I cut myself."

"Yes, you did," Washington said. "What is your blood type, Mr. Walker?"

Duke's eyes flashed with panic, then he seemed to pull himself together. "I want a lawyer," he said.

Washington and Ohara stood up. "Call any lawyer you want."

"I don't know any lawyers. Besides, I can't afford one."

"We'll get one for you, then."

"Do it." Duke flung himself back in his chair and looked at his hands.

Washington called the public defender's office, and before long Bess Summers was at the station. They knew her, and felt Duke was in luck.

Bess was a bit eccentric, often dressing in whatever came to hand first in the morning. Her wiry red hair did nothing to flatter her rather plain face, but somehow she managed to inspire a confidence in her clients that was well deserved. Shrewd and impatient, Bess fought for them with everything she had.

After a brief conference with Duke, she was ready for them. "My client is willing to cooperate. He has a perfectly reasonable explanation for that handkerchief. Tell them, Mr. Walker."

Duke admitted that in his excitement at finding the body he had inadvertently picked up the wrench. Then, realizing that if his fingerprints were found on it he might be accused, he had wiped the wrench, tossed it away, and put the handkerchief in the refuse bin.

"That's tampering with evidence," Washington countered.

"Maybe." Bess was not disconcerted. "But not proof of murder."

Ohara nodded. "We'll take your prints for the record," he told Duke. "There were some prints on the victim's wallet also. Did you pick that up in your excitement?"

"Don't answer that!" Bess cut in.

"It's no use," Duke said. "When they take my prints, they'll find them on the wallet, too. Yes, I did pick it up. I wouldn't have done it, but I wanted to see if the man had been robbed."

"Why?" Washington asked.

"Because I . . ." Duke caught himself. "I don't know why."

"Is that all you've got against my client?" Bess began.

"Not quite," Ohara said, and laid down the picture.

Duke stared at it, his face losing all color, his body shrinking in on itself.

"That's Mrs. Walker," Washington said. "Mrs. Walker and the victim. I'd say she knew him rather well."

"Damn you!" Duke slammed his hands on top of the picture, covering his wife's naked body. "That was a long time ago in Japan. She's got nothing to do with this!"

"Was Shimizu blackmailing you?" Ohara asked.

Walker, sensing the sympathy in Ohara's voice, looked up at him. "Yes. My wife knows nothing about it." Duke looked down at his hands, which were gripped together on top of the picture. "But I didn't kill him."

"Mr. Walker, don't say anything more now," Bess cautioned. "Are you going to hold him? If so, on what grounds?"

"Obstruction of justice will do for now," Ohara said, "unless he wants to change his story."

"We'll let you know." Bess smiled politely, but her blue eyes showed worry.

When the formalities concerning Walker were concluded, Ohara said he was going to send Amy Byers to pick up Jody. "I want her to ID him."

As they waited for Amy to bring Jody in, they began going over the photographs from Shimizu's file. Washington stared longest at the one of the kid lying in the alley. "You know, Sam, I just realized who that kid looks like. Remember those pictures of the Mighty Flynn we saw at the pub? This kid would be the image of him if he wasn't a washed-up hype."

"It might explain a lot of things. If Shimizu was blackmailing Duke Walker, why not Joe Flynn?"

"It does add up," Ohara conceded.

Washington developed his point. "There's something else, Sam. Joe Flynn's an ex-wrestler. He'd be pretty good at snapping necks."

"We're just guessing that this is Joe's boy."

"Give me five minutes to run this past Bob Reilly in Narcotics. If it is Flynn's kid, he's a local and they'll have something on him." Washington took the picture and went across the hall to Narcotics.

In a few minutes he was back. "Bob says they've picked the kid up more than once. It's Joe Flynn's son, all right."

"Then we'd . . ." The phone rang and Ohara picked it up. As he listened, Washington knew by the look on his face that something had gone wrong. "Stay there, Amy. We're coming over." He put down the phone. "Jody's gone," he said. "She attacked another girl and escaped through a window."

99

Chapter Twelve

Beyond putting out an all-points bulletin on Jody, there was little more they could do. Still, Ohara wasn't satisfied. "Let's go talk to Harriet," he said.

Washington nodded. "Want to see Joe Flynn afterward? We've got something solid to hit him with now."

"Good idea." Ohara put the picture of Mike Flynn into a folder and tucked it under his arm.

When they reached the halfway house there was little more that Harriet or Amy Byers could tell them about what had happened. "You'd better talk to the girl Jody attacked," Amy said. "She tried to tell me what had happened, but she was too incoherent. Her injuries are painful, but not serious."

Since Amy was no longer needed, she returned to the station. Before the two men went upstairs to see the girl, Harriet told them about the long talk she'd had with Jody just that morning. "She really opened up to me, told me about losing her parents, how unhappy she was living with her aunt, and that dreadful experience of being molested by the aunt's boyfriend. Poor little thing. She acts so grown up, but she's just a child."

"I'd say it was just the other way around," muttered Washington. Then he patted Harriet's shoulder. "Don't feel so bad. Jody took us in, too. Her story doesn't check out. She has no parents named Baxter, and no aunt, either."

Ohara blamed himself. He'd been aware of Jody's sudden mood changes, her exaggerations, the inconsistencies in her story. But his sensitivity to kids like Jody had made him see what he wanted to see: an abused teenager, a frightened, helpless young girl the same age as his daughter Susie.

Lisa, the girl Jody had attacked, looked up from her bed as Harriet and the two detectives entered the room. She stared at them nervously, drawing the sheet up to her chin.

"Visitors, Lisa," Harriet said cheerfully as she went over to the bed and smoothed the girl's lank hair back from the bandage on her forehead. "How are you now?"

Lisa just shook her head, but her badly scratched and bruised face was mute testimony to the violence of Jody's attack.

"These police officers would like to hear your story," Harriet said, smiling encouragingly.

"I already told it to the woman cop," Lisa said fretfully. "I hurt. Why don't you leave me alone."

Ohara came and stood beside the bed. "I know you've told your story once." He smiled in sympathy. "But you were in shock. Maybe you'll remember it better now." He held out his hand. "I'm Detective Ohara."

Lisa looked surprised at the gesture, so Ohara guessed her contacts with police up to now had not been social or friendly. Still, she reached up and took his hand, giving a small smile that must have hurt her bruised mouth.

Then Lisa told her story for the second time. She admitted that she'd been going through Jody's bag while Jody was out of the room. "I wasn't going to take anything," she said. "I was just curious, 'cause she kept it with her all the time." Lisa looked anxiously at Ohara.

"I understand," he said. "What happened then?"

"Jody caught me at it and just went crazy. She kicked me and beat me with her fists. I was fighting back, but she was too strong. Then she hit me on the head and I fell down. Jody just picked up her bag and starting climbing out the window. That's all I remember until Mrs. Takai was bending over me."

"Thank you," Ohara said, and patted her thin hand, which was clutching the sheet.

"Wait." Lisa caught Ohara's hand and held it. "There's something I didn't tell the woman cop. Underneath some clothes Jody had a plastic package filled with white power. Had to be some kind of drugs. Then in the very bottom of the bag she had a knife. Looked like a penknife, but bigger."

Lisa hadn't much more to tell, so they left. Washington and Ohara sat in the privacy of their car a few minutes, discussing the latest development.

"Lisa's lucky Jody didn't use the knife on her," Washington said. "I suppose the load of drugs came from Shimizu's place."

"Most likely," Ohara agreed. "Forensics found traces of cocaine in the closest cupboard."

"But how would Jody get into a locked cupboard hidden in Shimizu's bedroom?"

"I can't answer that."

"You know, I think Jody's in a lot deeper than we gave her credit for." Washington glanced at his partner. "She's probably hitting the streets right now to peddle her little stash, if it is cocaine."

Ohara looked grim. "I think we can assume that. I wonder where she'd go to sell it."

"No matter where you're from," Washington said, "you've probably heard of Hollywood Boulevard. I'm betting that's where she'll head."

He picked up the radio mike. "I'm going to notify Bob Reilly at Narcotics. His undercover guys may find her before we do."

102

Ohara nodded. "I'm thinking we should check out the boulevard ourselves."

"It's a little early yet. Why don't we go see Joe Flynn first?" Washington tapped the manila folder lying on the seat. "This could be our motive, and so far Joe Flynn has no alibi."

Bill Stack was feeling pretty good. Things were working out all right, now that he'd shut Ginny up with all her talk about giving himself up. A good beating was all most women understood.

Early that morning Bill had taken his blue Chevy and parked it on a little-used back street, where it looked as run-down as the rest of the cars at the curb. Then he'd removed the plates and left it. Afterward, when it was safe, he'd get it back.

Ginny had been gone when he'd returned, which wasn't unusual. She frequently had an early shift. He got himself something to eat and watched TV for a while. It was lonely stuck in the apartment, so he was damn glad to see Erne Smith when he came at noon. Over a beer Erne told him how the guys at Flynn's had treated the Jap cop. "Made it plain he wasn't wanted," Erne said with relish. "Then he comes over to Benny and me and wants to know about the argument with Shimizu."

Bill tensed. "That's the Jap cop come here yesterday with his spade partner. I didn't answer the doorbell, so they went away. What'd you tell him?"

Erne grinned. "You know me, Bill. I said I wouldn't call it no argument, and besides, you and me were just leavin'." He frowned. "Too bad that idiot Polser had to get in the act and talk about how you pounded on the Jap's car."

"Shit! Now they'll be back. Damn Polser!"

"Maybe not." Erne took a swallow of beer. "They picked up Duke Walker at the garage this mornin'."

"Who the hell is he?"

"A guy who works at Fred's with me. It seems he lives in the same apartment block as Shimizu. He found the body."

"If that's all, why'd they take him in?" Bill wondered.

"I don't think that's all. He's got a Jap wife, you know. Maybe she and Shimizu had something going and ol' Duke killed him."

"Yeah!" Bill, considerably heartened, opened two more beers.

By late afternoon Bill was feeling a lot more confident, so he decided to go to Flynn's for a drink. However, his good mood was soured when he saw a couple of young Japs, wearing white headbands with Oriental writing on them, heading in his direction. He'd seen two others on the street outside his apartment earlier. What the hell were they up to? Ganging up on the whites, he'd bet. Well, let them just try something on him! He'd show the little punks! Planting himself on the sidewalk, fists clenched, he waited, but the boys walked around him and on down the street.

Bill stared after them, then continued on his way toward Flynn's. He was almost there when he saw the two cops going in the door.

Suddenly his good feeling of safety evaporated. He didn't want to meet any cops. So he turned back toward home, worried about what Joe might tell them.

A familiar voice shouted his name, and he looked up to see Benny Polser crossing the street toward him. Benny was smiling, sucking up, as usual. "Hey Bill, how's yer arm? Erne says you fell down."

"Never mind my arm, Polser." Bill caught Benny's shirt and pulled him close. "Whatcha mean talking to the cops about me? You trying to get me in trouble?"

"No, Bill, honest! I didn't think . . ."

Bill gave him a shake and pushed him aside. "You can't think. You ain't got the brains of a moron. If I hear you been doin' any more talking about me, I'm gonna beat you to a pulp. You got that?"

Benny was trembling. "I got it." He wet his lips and timidly touched Bill's arm. "I wouldn't do nothing' to hurt a good buddy like you, Bill."

Bill jerked his arm loose. "Knock off the 'good buddy' stuff, Polser. You ain't no buddy of mine. Now, piss off!"

Benny watched Bill go, then angrily scrubbed away the weak tears on his cheek. "No, you piss off, big man," he said under his breath. "You ain't gonna kick me around no more." He looked down the street toward Flynn's, then made up his mind. He was going to tell those two cops what he knew.

When he reached the pub, the cops were talking to Joe at the far end of the bar. Joe looked up and recognized him. "Sorry, Benny, but we're not open yet. Come back in twenty minutes."

"But I gotta—"

"Twenty minutes!"

Benny went out and stood in the doorway. Well, he wouldn't tell them what he knew. Let them screw themselves! He went home, got his ma her supper, washed up afterward, then turned on the TV and settled her in front of it.

"You're a good boy, Benny," the old lady said, peering at him affectionately. Moved by her tenderness, he went over and kissed her cheek. His ma was the only person who ever said anything nice to him. She reached up and stroked his hair. "You should go out more, Benny. Get yourself a nice girl, maybe get married."

"Ma, you know I don't make enough delivering for the drugstore to get married."

"We could maybe sell the house. It would bring a lot now. It's yours, anyway."

"And where would you go?"

The old lady's face fell; she'd not thought that far.

"Besides, I'm happy just as I am," he lied. "I'm going to turn in now, maybe read a little and go to sleep. Will Molly be coming in?"

"Yes, our show is on in half an hour. Don't worry about me. She'll help me get to bed."

"OK, Ma. Good night." Benny went to his room and shut the door. Now his time was his own. He threw himself on the bed and thought about what he could do. When he finally decided, he was both excited and scared. This time Bill would listen to him and find out what a good buddy Benny Polser was.

Benny lingered over the ending of his wonderful daydream. He imagined Bill saying he was sorry, wanting to be pals. From then on he'd show some respect, do anything so Benny wouldn't tell what he knew. Oh, that would be good!

But there was another ending to the dream that tempted him, satisfying his long-suppressed craving to strike back. This time he saw Bill plead and beg for mercy, promising him anything he wanted, but the new Benny Polser would stand tall, his face a mask, and say, "Bill, you go to hell!"

Benny lay on the bed a long time, his eyes half-closed, a smile on his lips. Then he got up, went to his dresser, and pulled out the bottom drawer. Reaching under a pile of socks and shorts, he pulled out the small black gun. It made him feel safe just to hold it. If Bill got rough, all he'd have to do would be pull out the gun, let him see it.

He laid the gun down while he put on his baseball jacket. Then he picked up the gun and thrust it into the side pocket. He took a last look at his heroes' pictures on the wall and climbed out the window and down the drainpipe to the ground.

Bill was glad to get home. He poured himself a beer and settled in front of the TV. The local news had shots of the white-headband gang, some kind of Asian violence patrol. Next came pictures of the vandalized cars on Maple Street and some Jap's yard sprayed with acid.

Bill was puzzled. Who the hell was doing that? He'd like to give him a hand. A news bulletin said that a Caucasian was being questioned in the recent killing of a Japanese insurance agent. Bill smiled. There was nothing more of interest.

Bill switched to a talk show and fell asleep halfway through it. He didn't know what woke him, but finally heard the faint knocking at the back door. Ginny must have forgotten her key again, the stupid bitch. Yawning, he stumbled to the back door and opened it. When he saw who it was, he started to slam the door shut. But Benny was too quick for him and pushed inside. He faced Bill defiantly, his hand bunched in his pocket. "I got somethin' to tell you, Bill, and you gotta listen."

"Like hell I do!"

"I know what you did to the Jap!" Benny rushed out with it. "How you beat his face in, and got shot. You're gonna do what I say, now, Bill, or I go to the cops."

Bill moved so fast Benny didn't see it coming until his throat was gripped in an iron vice and he was shoved against the wall. "You ain't gonna tell nothin' to nobody." Bill's angry face was so close, Benny could smell the beer on his breath.

The vice on Benny's throat tightened as his head was banged against the wall. He could hardly see Bill's face for the growing red haze in his eyes. Desperately he gripped the gun and struggled to pull it from his pocket. No longer able to see or hear, he didn't know he'd fired it until the hands on his throat let go and Bill fell at his feet.

Chapter Thirteen

Joe Flynn was behind the bar polishing glasses when the two detectives entered. Ohara, observing the powerful shoulders and arms, and the solid stance of the man's body, knew that even now he would be a formidable opponent. But beyond that there was little trace of the cocky young wrestler in the pictures. His rugged, handsome face with its unusual dimpled chin looked old and defeated. There was a taut set to the generous mouth.

Without interrupting his polishing, Joe said, "You'll be the police, I expect. Barry said you were looking for me."

"Yes." Ohara produced his ID and introduced Washington. "You've been away from the pub the last two nights."

"The wife's been sick."

"I'm sorry," Ohara said, then asked Joe for his version of what had happened between Shimizu and Bill Stack in the bar.

Some of his obvious tension easing, Joe told them what had happened. "Bill's a hothead. He blames the autoworker layoffs that cost him his job on Japanese imports. Most of my customers are from the automotive plant. A lot of them are out of work, so they feel the same as Bill."

"What started the trouble with Shimizu? Was it just because he was Japanese, or did something else happen?"

"Well, a little of both. The guys had been watching the news about the Victor Chin case, and were pretty worked up about the two autoworkers being found guilty. Then

Shimizu comes in and starts going on about his new hotshot Nissan. He'd heard Bill sounding off about Japanese imports, like just about everybody around here, so he couldn't resist rubbing the guy's nose in it. Then he says, 'Don't take it so hard, Bill. I'll buy you a drink.'

"That lit Bill's fuse. He started yelling at Shimizu so bad he got a coughing fit. Then his buddy, Erne Smith, took him out."

"What did he shout?" Washington asked.

Joe looked uncomfortable. "He said he didn't drink with Japs. Then Bill shoved a half-filled beer glass down the bar so it spilled on Shimizu's sleeve."

"Was that all?" Washington persisted.

Joe hesitated, but went on. "Bill shouted something like 'I'm gonna get that dirty Jap,' and got up like he was going for Shimizu. He was drunk, that's all."

Ohara changed the subject. "I understand Shimizu came in regularly to collect insurance premiums. Isn't that a little unusual? Most companies mail the bill."

"He did it as a favor." Unconsciously Joe was crumpling the polishing cloth into a tight ball.

"What kind of insurance was it?"

"Life insurance."

"Barry told us you had a conversation with Shimizu after the others had gone. What did you talk about?"

"It was private." Joe's voice grew cold.

"Since you were about the last person to see him alive, anything he said to you might be important," Ohara said smoothly. "Barry says you were shouting at him about something. What was that about?"

Joe looked down at the polishing cloth and began smoothing it out on the bar. "He told me my premium was being raised. I guess I shouted about how I couldn't pay it."

110

The door to the bar opened and a skinny little guy started to come in. Ohara saw he was the one who'd been sitting with Bill Stack's pal Erne. He'd talked about Stack beating on Shimizu's car.

Joe told him the bar wasn't open yet. When he started to protest, Joe abruptly cut him off, and then turned to Washington and Ohara. "If you've finished, I've still got work to do."

"Not quite finished," Ohara said, and laid a manila folder on the bar. "We found this in Shimizu's file." He opened the folder and laid Mike Flynn's picture in front of Joe.

Joe looked down at it, his breathing stilled, his big body motionless. After a long moment, he raised his eyes. "So?" He seemed to pull the word from the depths of his being.

"So Shimizu was a blackmailer," Washington said. "Your son's picture was in Shimizu's file with that of a blackmail victim we've already identified. There's only one reason it could be there."

"It has nothing to do with me."

"We think it has," Washington went on. "When a blackmailer is killed, it's usually by one of his victims."

Ohara was watching Joe's face as his partner played the heavy. He saw the flash of fear, quickly suppressed, followed by well-simulated anger.

"Are you saying I killed him?" Joe's tough Irish chin jutted forward and his fists clenched.

"Are you saying you didn't?" Washington countered.

Joe took a deep breath, pulling himself under control. "Listen to me, and get this straight. Shimizu couldn't blackmail me over Mike. I knew what my son was, and when he took up that kind of life I told him to get out and never come home again. I just stopped caring about him. Most people knew that."

Ohara saw that the shock treatment had failed and tried another tack. "Where were you the night Shimizu was killed?"

"I was home taking care of my wife. She's an invalid."

"Well, that's something we can verify when we talk to her." Ohara put the picture back in the folder and looked at Washington. "If you'll give us your address we can see her now and clear this up."

"No!" Joe flung the crumpled cloth onto the bar.

"What do you mean, 'no'?"

"All right!" Flynn spoke more quietly. "Leave my wife out of this and I'll tell you the truth."

"We're waiting." Washington kept up the pressure.

Joe sighed, then came out with it. "Mary, that's my wife, thinks I came back to the bar like always. But I didn't. I was worried about where I was going to get the extra money Shimizu had demanded and I didn't want her to guess anything was wrong. So I got in the car and just drove, trying to think of what I could do."

Washington pinned him down. "Where did you drive? Did you stop anywhere? Talk to anyone?"

"I drove out to Venice to look at the ocean. It always makes me feel better. I bought coffee from a stand where Venice Boulevard hits the beach." Joe fell silent, but his face betrayed the turbulent emotions he tried to hide.

Ohara recognized a temporary stalemate when he saw it. "We'll do some checking, then get back to you."

"You won't disturb my wife?" Joe's eyes were anxious again. "She's not well."

"No, Mr. Flynn." A touch of gentleness softened the cold, official tone of Ohara's words. "Not unless you make it necessary."

As they were leaving the bar, the TV news was talking about Kaz Shimoda's vigilante patrol. Ohara knew some

112

elements of the community would consider it a threat. The repercussions would be far-reaching, turning neighbor against neighbor and friends into foes. He hoped young Jim would not be hurt.

"What now, Sam?" Washington broke in on Ohara's thoughts.

"We've got to talk to Stack," Ohara said. "Maybe this time he'll be home."

They drove to Bill Stack's apartment building and got out of the car. "Records says that blue Chevy we looked at is his, but I don't see it. Could be he's away again."

As before, no one answered the bell. As a long shot, they tried some of Stack's neighbors to see if they knew when he'd come in that night. But it didn't pan out. No one knew anything about Stack except that he fought with his wife.

Once more back in the car, Washington said he'd like to check out Joe Flynn's alibi. "If he did buy coffee where he says he did, somebody might remember."

"OK," Ohara said. "I've got to do some thinking about Walker. I don't think he killed Shimizu, but he's doing nothing to help himself. I think I'll go see his wife. Also, I want to do some homework on the material Forensics gave me."

"All right," Washington said. "I'll get on Flynn first thing tomorrow. Do you buy his story about kicking his son out and not caring who knew it?"

"No, not a man like that," Ohara replied. "Besides, there's another way Shimizu might get to him. He's very protective about his sick wife. If she doesn't know about Mike, and if Shimizu threatened to tell her . . ."

"I see what you're getting at, but you know where that leaves us." For all his tough exterior, Washington was a compassionate man. "I'd hate to be the one to tell her."

"I know." Ohara sighed. "If we *can* find any other way
. . ."

Washington turned to him. "Remember what Barry told
us about Joe's brother-in-law? An ex-wrestler running a motel
shouldn't be too hard to find. Maybe we can get what we
need from him."

"I like it," Ohara said. "Let's give it a try."

Benny was sweating and trembling by the time he reached
home. Bill's heavy body had fallen against the door, and it
had been a nightmare trying to move it so he could get
out. He'd run down the steps and out onto the street, panic
keeping him running till he gasped for breath. Then he
spotted a man walking his dog and somehow made himself
slow to a walk. When he reached his street, he clung to
the shadows and with his last ounce of strength climbed
the drainpipe, tumbling through the open window into the
safety of his room.

He lay in a heap on the floor for a long time, till the
pounding of his heart quieted and he could think. He'd
have to have an alibi, and the sound of his old lady's TV
gave him an idea. He hid the gun in the drawer and wiped
his hands as best he could on a Kleenex. Then he put on
pajamas and robe, stuffing the Kleenex into the pocket,
mussed his hair, and went into the other room.

He was pleased to see Molly, his mother's friend, was
with her. "Hi." He yawned. "I've been trying to get to
sleep for over an hour, but the TV's real loud. Would it
be OK if I turned it down a little?"

The two old ladies assured him that it would, and offered
him some coffee and cake, which he refused. The very
thought of food nauseated him. All he could think about
was Bill's crumpled body and the ooze of red that had
stained his hands as he'd tried to move him.

114

He stopped at the bathroom, washed his hands and flushed the Kleenex down the toilet, then went back to his room.

He sat down on his bed, overcome by a fit of shivering, and stared at the pictures on the wall. But the strong, confident faces of his heroes gave him no comfort. He was alone with what he had done, and he was afraid.

Rudy Balzac gulped down a handful of popcorn, eyes glued to the TV as he watched the gory conclusion of a martial-arts movie. "You see that, Steve?" he enthused to his friend and fellow fan. "Man, that Lee guy was great!"

"Yeah, he was pretty good," Steve agreed. Having taken some judo and karate lessons once, Steve spoke with authority. He knew all the karate and kung fu stars in the business, and had seen all the movies. He'd even collected various pieces of equipment, or made replicas.

But Steve's mind wasn't really on the movie at the moment. He was thinking about the news broadcast they'd watched earlier showing Kaz Shimoda's vigilante patrol. It had given him an idea, one of the best he'd had in a long time.

When the movie was over, he ran his idea past Rudy, who stared at him wide-eyed. "Hey, man, I don't know; it might not work."

"Trust me, it will! I know where we can get what we need. We'll pick up some easy money and have a blast. You in?"

Rudy could not resist the adventure Steve proposed. "I'm in."

Steve grinned. "The real thing, man. The real thing!"

Chapter Fourteen

Sergeant Reagan looked up from his desk and saw the girl standing timidly in the doorway. He noted that she was Japanese and very pretty. Probably she'd come to report some new vandalism. "Can I help you?" he asked.

Her face lit with relief and she hurried over to the desk. "Yes, thank you." She inclined her head in a small bow. "I need see Officer Washington. This one." She handed Reagan a calling card.

Reagan looked at her over the tops of his glasses. "Washington is out of the station at the moment," he said. "What did you want to see him about?"

The girl looked crushed. "No, thank you. Must see him; tell him big mistake put my husband in jail. Is me should take!" Her lips were trembling as she fought back tears.

"There, there, now!" Reagan's big, rumbling voice softened in sympathy. Women tended to get emotional when their men landed in jail; he wanted to help her. "What's your name, miss, er, ma'am?"

"Walker," she said. "Mrs. Duke Walker."

Reagan's gaze sharpened. This was a surprise. "I'm sorry, Mrs. Walker. Officer Washington won't be back for quite a while."

"I wait," she said, and started to turn toward a bench by the front door.

"I tell you what." Reagan smiled. "Why don't you talk to Washington's partner? He's familiar with the case."

116

"Oh, thank you. You so kind man!" The brightness of her smile warmed Reagan's heart.

"Sure, and it's nothin' at all. Now you just go up those stairs to a room marked 'Detectives' and ask for Sam Ohara."

"Thank you," she said again, and this time bowed low. Reagan found himself bowing back, an awkward proceeding behind his big desk, and something he hadn't done since he'd been an altar boy.

When Miyuki reached the room to which Reagan had directed her, she stood staring in bewilderment. It seemed full of people too busy to take any notice of her presence. She was wondering how she would ever find Sam Ohara when she saw a tall Japanese walking toward her. It was like the sun coming out from behind a cloud. "Mrs. Walker?" he asked in a low, pleasant voice.

"*Hai.* I mean, yes. Mrs. Walker am." She was so nervous, her English was deserting her completely. She couldn't think what to say next.

He smiled at her, then switched to flawless Japanese. "The sergeant phoned that you were coming up. I'm Isamu Ohara, Mr. Washington's partner. Let's sit down over here."

Miyuki was glad of the reassuring touch of his hand at her elbow as he guided her across the busy room, but most wonderful of all, he had spoken to her in her own language. He set a chair beside his desk for her, then sat down himself.

"You speak Japanese." She made it a statement.

"Yes." Ohara smiled, "I was born here after my parents had emigrated to America from Japan. So I have the best of two worlds."

He was surprised by Duke Walker's wife. She was a lovely woman. Her face was a classic oval with delicate features framed by long, ebony-black hair. He noticed her hands, as he always did in a woman, lying quietly in her lap, the soft, slender fingers gently clasped. Her quiet manner,

117

the way she carried herself, her voice, all spoke of training and culture. This was no bargirl, as he'd assumed from Shimizu's picture.

"I am so relieved to speak in Japanese," she said. "I must tell you many things so you will understand, and though I am studying hard, my English is not good."

"In Japanese, then," he said, and leaned back in his chair.

Taking courage from the kindness she saw in his dark eyes, she hurried on. "My husband, Duke, did not kill this Shimizu. He is trying only to protect me, because he thinks I killed him." She looked down at her hands.

"Did you?"

"No!" Her head lifted and her eyes looked straight at Ohara. Then she seemed to droop. "I found Shimizu lying like a dead man in the alley."

"It was *you* who found him, not your husband?"

"Yes. He lied to the police to protect me."

"Why would he do that?"

Her hands tightened in her lap. "I will try to explain. Shimizu was a bad man. He had," she hesitated a moment, then went on, "he had something that belonged to me in his pocket. When I thought he was dead, I tried to get it back. I was reaching into his pocket when Duke came up behind me and saw what I was doing." She looked up at him, her face agonized. "He thought I had robbed an injured man."

"What were you trying to get back from Shimizu?"

"A picture." She spoke so softly he could barely hear her.

Ohara's hand lay on the manila folder that contained Shimizu's copy of the photograph. He did not take it out, but merely said, "I've seen the picture. We took a copy that Shimizu had in his files."

She closed her eyes as a red flush stained her throat and crept up into her cheeks. "I am so ashamed, but I must explain. One day many months ago when we moved into our apartment, Shimizu recognized me from Tokyo and came to see me when I was alone. He said if I did not buy what he called 'insurance' from him, and pay cash, he would tell my husband what I did in Japan. I knew my Duke would never understand. I could not risk that he might find out."

She paused, finding it difficult to go on. Ohara waited quietly until she was ready. "Then, early on the night Shimizu was killed, he came to me with a picture." Miyuki avoided Ohara's eyes. "He said next month I would have to pay him more money or he would show Duke that picture. I told him there was no way I could get more money, but he just laughed and put the picture back in his jacket pocket. He said men paid money for me in Tokyo, so why not here." Her lips trembled and she pressed her fingers against them, fighting for control. "Later, when I found him dead, I thought that by some miracle I had been saved. I could get the picture back and no one would ever see it."

"Then he was not blackmailing your husband?"

"No. Me only. Now, you let Duke go free!"

"It's not that easy, Mrs. Walker. Your husband's fingerprints are on the murder weapon. His bloody handkerchief was thrown in the trash bin."

"That was only to save me because I had picked up the wrench."

"Why did you pick it up?"

She could see in his eyes what he was thinking, and felt suddenly cold. "When I knelt beside Shimizu's body, I felt something hard under my knee. I pulled it out and saw it was a tool, all bloody. I was so horrified, I dropped it and wiped my hands on my skirt."

"You were wearing a dress, not slacks?" Ohara leaned forward.

"Yes. When Duke saw the blood on my dress, he told me to change my clothes before I called the police. I knew then he thought I had killed the man. I tried to explain, but he just sent me away."

"What color was your dress? Describe it, please."

Miyuki looked surprised. "Pink, with buttons down the front. It had a belt with a white buckle."

Ohara nodded and made a note. "Did you touch anything else?"

"I picked up Shimizu's wallet when I looked for the picture."

"How much money was in it?" Ohara studied her face without appearing to do so.

"There was no money." She flushed at the implication of the question.

"Mrs. Walker." Ohara straightened. "Before you tell me anything more, let me read you your rights."

"No, please! That is not important, only that you let Duke go free. You do not understand, because I haven't told you everything. Please, let me explain what happened from the beginning."

Ohara could not refuse, because she might not open up again. He would see that she had a lawyer when the time was right. She was still more a witness than a suspect. Right now it was important to let her talk comfortably in Japanese. "All right, tell me from the beginning."

He listened without interrupting as Miyuki talked in her soft, surprisingly sensual voice. What a story it was: from trained geisha, to bargirl, to fugitive, to mail-order bride for a man she had never seen. Then, just as she'd found happiness, fate, in the person of Shimizu, had tripped her up.

120

As she told him how Duke had found the picture and confronted her with it, the tears flowed unheeded down her cheeks. "Never did I want to hurt my Duke. No one in all my life was so good and kind to me as he has been. At first I had dreaded the thought of marrying a stranger, but then I did not know what a wonderful man Duke was. When we were married, I grew to respect him and to love him more than I had ever thought possible."

She paused, her face gentle with her thoughts. Then the pain was back again. It had shamed her, telling her story to this policeman, but she was grateful that he was Japanese. She could never have told it in English to an outsider.

"While I was calling the police, Duke found the picture. When he came back to the apartment he was filled with anger. He showed me the picture and said I had lied and made a fool of him. I thought he would beat me, but he did not even touch me. I would not have blamed him for beating me, after what I had done to him."

She looked directly at Ohara, her eyes brilliant. "Do you think such a man would kill anyone? Kill a man he did not even know?" There was a proud defiance to her as she confronted him with the truth of her argument.

"You've made a very strong case," Ohara conceded. "Did you tell Duke the story you've just told me?"

"Yes. I told him everything. But even then he did not despise me. He forgave me the lies I told and destroyed the terrible picture. He said he understood what I had done, and that I would never have to be afraid of anyone again. He still loves me!"

Watching her, Ohara marveled at the complex emotions of human beings. All she could think of was saving her Duke, while he, despite the shock of the ugly photograph, had instinctively tried to protect the woman he loved.

Suddenly Miyuki leaned forward and grasped Ohara's hand. "Ohara-san, my Duke is innocent. I have told you the truth."

"I believe you have," Ohara said, and gently withdrew his hand to pick up the manila folder. "There will be some legal complications, but I think we can have Duke released this afternoon. Of course, later you must make a formal statement."

Miyuki looked radiant. Ohara wished he could let her keep her happiness, but he could not. "There are some things you must do to help me."

"Please, Ohara-san, I will do anything."

He began by taking her back over Shimizu's last visit to her apartment. "Did you see or hear anything after he left you?"

She thought a moment. "I heard something like a car exploding."

Ohara realized what she meant. "You mean you heard the noise a car makes sometimes, like a gun?"

"Yes, it was like that."

"What did you do after Shimizu left you?"

She looked embarrassed. "I had burned some vegetables while he was there, so I had to take them off. Then I heard a car out front and went to the door to see if it was Duke. But it wasn't."

"Did you see anything, or anyone?"

"Only an old blue car driving away."

Ohara asked what kind of a car it had been, but she didn't know. "What did you do then?" he continued.

"I made more vegetables and finished icing a cake for Duke. After that, I went outside to wait for him. I thought I heard a noise in the alley. When I looked, I saw something in front of one of the garages."

"Was it light enough to see?"

"There was some. The garage night-lights were on. When I went to see what it was, I found Shimizu."

"What time was this?" Ohara asked.

"I'm not sure. I think it was around eight o'clock."

Ohara made a note, then remembered the smears on the wallet. She said she'd picked it up when looking for the photograph, so he asked, "What kind of icing did you put on your cake?"

She looked surprised, then smiled. "Chocolate. That's Duke's favorite."

Ohara smiled briefly, then asked a more disturbing question. "Where did the blood stain your dress?"

"On the skirt at the bottom, where I wiped my hands."

Though Ohara felt she was telling the truth, he wanted to see the dress. Shimizu had been bludgeoned with such savage force that his blood would have spattered the clothes of whoever had done it.

"Do you still have the dress?" he asked.

"Yes," she said. "I washed it, but the stains didn't come out very well."

Inwardly Ohara groaned. Still, the lab should be able to find traces of blood. People usually didn't get them all out. "I'd like to see the dress, perhaps send it to the lab. Will you permit this?"

"Of course, Ohara-san." She looked back at him, showing no concern. He suspected she had followed his thinking perfectly.

"Thank you," he said. "Now, forgive me, but I must ask you to identify the other man in the picture with you." He laid the picture in front of her and pointed to a tall Japanese posing with her and Shimizu.

"That is Shigero Kano," Miyuki said without hesitation. "He is a very evil man, a Yakuza. They said he killed a

123

girl who ran away from the club. That is his job: killing people."

"Were he and Shimizu friends?"

She shook her head. "Nobody was Kano's friend, but everybody pretended to be. They were afraid not to."

Ohara studied Kano's handsome, arrogant face and his powerful body. He was probably a martial-arts expert. Miyuki's identification had opened up new possibilities. If Guardian Insurance was backed by Yakuza money, and they had discovered that Shimizu was skimming their take, they'd use someone like Kano to get rid of him.

It was a long shot, Ohara realized, and depended on whether or not Kano had been in the country at the time of Shimizu's murder. Still, it was worth checking out with Joe Spielberg of the Organized Crime Unit. He recalled how worried Shimizu's boss, Takematsu, had been about the dead man's files. He'd been very upset when he'd heard the police had them. Carrying the scenario a step further, if Takematsu had been involved in Shimizu's scheme, he could be next on the hit list.

Ohara had been so engrossed in his thoughts that he'd almost forgotten the girl beside him. He looked up to find her smiling a little as she studied his face.

"I'm sorry," he said. "I was thinking. I'd like you to come with me and talk to a police officer who specializes in gangs like the Yakuza. We need to find out about Kano."

Her eyes widened as the meaning behind his words struck her. "You think Kano may be in this country?" She was suddenly afraid. "He will find me, and punish me like the other girl. There is no escape."

"You'll be protected, I promise you. Besides, he may not be here at all. I'd just like to find out. Will you help?"

"I will help," Miyuki said quietly. "I cannot run away anymore."

Ohara saw how badly shaken she was and said the one thing that might make her feel a little better. "I will make some calls to arrange for Duke's release from County Jail . . ."

"When will he be here?" Miyuki interrupted eagerly, her face bright.

"It will take a little time," Ohara said, "so first we will go to see the officer I spoke of about Kano. Then we can pick up Duke. Is that all right with you?"

"Oh, yes," Miyuki said.

Ohara made his calls, including one to Joe Spielberg, who was in, and would see them as soon as they could get there.

On the drive to Parker Center, where Spielberg's office was located, Ohara did his best to divert Miyuki by general conversation, easing her tension about the coming interview.

Soon she relaxed and, true to her old geisha training, followed his conversational lead back to her early life in Japan. She told him about her family, and the mix-up in names caused by having to use her sister's passport. "Duke must learn to call me Miyuki now, not Midori. It is very funny sometimes."

Ohara thought the name, which meant 'beautiful snow,' suited her quiet, serene personality. "Miyuki has a beautiful sound," he said. "May I call you by that name?"

"Oh, please, I would like that very much."

When they arrived at the Organized Crime office, they were shown in by Spielberg's assistant, a young Japanese, who eyed them curiously from behind his thick-lensed glasses.

Spielberg was a spare, graying man who had worked Organized Crime for years. He was soft-spoken and relaxed, which seemed to put Miyuki at ease. As she told her story, this time in halting English, he listened carefully, smoothing his empty pipe bowl between his fingers. He had long ago

125

given up smoking, but he still enjoyed holding the old pipe between his fingers.

When Miyuki had finished speaking, he nodded thoughtfully. "I don't know offhand if Kano's in the country, but I can check."

Then he asked her to look at some pictures for him. Reaching for a file of photographs, he laid them before her. As she studied them there was a brisk knock at the door and the young Japanese entered. "Need me, boss?"

Spielberg shook his head. "No translation needed, Eddie. Mrs. Walker speaks English." He smiled at Miyuki. "Detective Ohara can interpret, should it be necessary. Thanks anyway."

The young man smiled at the visitors and glanced casually at the collection of photos in front of Miyuki. "Just trying to help," he said, and went out.

"Eddie interprets for me in several Oriental languages," Spielberg explained. "He's been with me for quite a while."

Miyuki wasn't listening; she was staring at a photograph in her hand. It showed an unusually corpulent Japanese with heavy brows and a fat, mean face getting into a limousine. "This man is big Yakuza boss," she said. "I not hear name, but he come many times to club."

Spielberg whistled. "That's Seiko Wakari. We don't have much on him. We just know he owns a large import-export business and travels between here and Japan on a treaty trader visa. We've never been able to connect him with anything out of line. Are you sure he's a Yakuza boss, Mrs. Walker?"

"Yes, I very sure," Miyuki answered. "Shimizu, he tell me."

Spielberg looked at Ohara. "We do know the Yakuza are importing drugs and exporting guns, but we haven't been able to find their connection. Wakari has the perfect

126

setup to do it. With Mrs. Walker's identification, we may be able to get a warrant to check his warehouse."

Miyuki was going through the rest of the pictures. Suddenly she held one out to Spielberg. "Here is Kano," she said.

He took it and studied the notes on the back. "Your hunch was right, Sam. Kano arrived in this country two weeks ago on a tourist visa."

Miyuki tensed and turned terrified eyes on Ohara.

Chapter Fifteen

"I think Kano come look for me," Miyuki said. "He always kill girl who run away."

Seeing the desperation in Miyuki's eyes, Ohara countered quickly. "No," he said. "He's here for something else; Shimizu may be part of it. You used your sister's passport to leave Japan. Now you're a Mrs. Walker. It's not likely Kano will know where you are." He did not tell her that Shimizu's files had been broken into before his murder. If the Yakuza had seen the files, they would have seen her picture, but he knew she was too close to the edge to handle that.

As she listened, Miyuki felt a small flicker of hope, but she was afraid to trust it. "They always have ways to know," she said.

Joe Spielberg tried to be reassuring. "I think Ohara's right," he said. "Whatever Kano's after, we'll find him and keep an eye on him. If he steps out of line just once, we'll take him in."

Miyuki smiled at him gratefully.

"We can get both Wakari and Kano deported as undesirable aliens," Spielberg went on, "if you are willing to testify that you know them, and that they are Yakuza."

"What is testify?" Miyuki looked at Ohara, who explained in Japanese that she would have to state in court how she knew they were Yakuza, which would mean telling her story and perhaps showing the picture. She looked at him, stricken.

Spielberg was afraid she was going to back down. "If luck is with us, we may be able to do more than just deport them. We may be able to hit them with something big. Will you testify, Mrs. Walker?"

She looked at him for a long moment. "That is only way? Duke be shamed, people find out about me."

Spielberg sighed and leaned back in his chair.

"From what you've told me, Miyuki," Ohara said in Japanese, "Duke isn't the kind of man to be ashamed of you. Maybe the Yakuza won't find out where you are. You have a right to refuse; we won't force you. Only you can decide what to do."

Spielberg wished he knew what Ohara was saying to the girl. It was maddening to be this close to a big bust, only to lose it.

When Ohara had finished speaking, Miyuki seemed to come to a decision, then spoke in English. "I not think Shimizu find me, but he do." She looked at Spielberg, and her voice was unsteady with emotion. "These men do so bad things. Many people they kill, give pain. Someone must stop. I will say what I know."

"Wonderful! You're a courageous lady, Mrs. Walker. Now, don't worry about a thing. They won't even know about you until we get to court. Even if the most we can do is deport them, the Tokyo police will be waiting for them. It's a brave thing you're doing, and we're very grateful." He looked at Ohara. "Tell her, Sam. I want to be sure she understands."

While Ohara translated, Spielberg rang for Eddie and asked for another file. "I'd like you to look at a few more pictures for me, Mrs. Walker."

Eddie brought the file, laid it in front of Miyuki, then left. She pored over the pictures and found several other

Japanese she recognized as Yakuza who had been at the club.

Well pleased, Spielberg thanked her and asked her to wait in the outer office while he spoke with Ohara. When she had left them he said, "I've a feeling this is going to be a lot bigger than a deportation hearing. We've been sniffing around this Wakari she identified as Yakuza for a long time. We've even put an undercover man in his warehouse, but so far he's found nothing that shouldn't be there. If we can get him as a dangerous criminal, we may be able to check the house he keeps in Beverly Hills."

Ohara brought Spielberg down to earth. "If they find out about Mrs. Walker, she won't get a chance to testify."

"I know," Spielberg replied, "but if we try to hide her away, it might draw more attention to her than leaving her at home. I'll keep a man on watch. Nobody will get close to her."

"How much are you prepared to level with her husband?"

"No more than absolutely necessary. The husband might rock the boat." Spielberg was inclined to think in terms of results rather than human beings.

Ohara did not protest the plan, because only by nailing Kano and his boss could Miyuki's safety be assured. It might be necessary to move her to a safehouse, but for now they could take it one step at a time.

"How long have you had Eddie with you, Joe?" Ohara asked.

The question surprised Spielberg. "Two or three years. He's good. He's got a clearance, if that's what's worrying you."

"It was worrying me," Ohara admitted. "But if you say he's been cleared, I have to accept that. He seemed very interested in what we were doing."

"That's only natural. He helps me with everything."

"On a need-to-know basis, keep him out of this. I'd feel better." Ohara's expression was pleasant, but his words made Spielberg uncomfortable.

Though he didn't look pleased, Spielberg nodded. "Have it your way, Sam. I'll be in touch."

A short time later, Ohara drove away from Parker Center and headed for County Jail. Miyuki had little to say, but Ohara sensed how afraid she was of what she had promised to do. She said nothing of her fears, only asked, "When will we see Duke?"

"We're on our way to pick him up now," Ohara said, glad to see her smile again. Then, while they could still talk alone in Japanese, Ohara explained that Spielberg felt she should not tell her husband too much about what her testifying would mean, since it might worry him.

"No," she said at once. "I have told my husband too many lies. This time I must speak the truth. Though he will be afraid for me, I will make him see that I cannot be safe by keeping silent." She paused a moment, then went on. "There is something else, Ohara-san. That girl Kano killed, she was my friend. I cannot forget how she died. They told us, so we would be afraid, how they tortured her before they killed her. Other girls were beaten and tortured, too. Shimizu told me Wakari liked to watch. I want to stop them, so they never hurt anyone again. Duke will not forbid me."

Looking at her pale, determined face, Ohara knew that, poor English or not, Miyuki would make her husband understand. Ohara's job now would be to reassure both of them that they would be protected.

Arriving at the massive gray monolith that was County Jail, Ohara had Miyuki wait while he went to get her husband. When he and Duke came in sight of the car, Miyuki jumped out and ran toward them. "Duke! Duke!"

she said. Then his arms were around her and they clung together with no need of words. Ohara went back to the car, giving them their moment of privacy. When at last they came over to him, the joy on their faces gave him real pleasure.

He offered to drive them home. On the way, Miyuki told Duke about her interview with Spielberg and that she had decided to testify against the men she had identified.

"No!" he protested, "it would be too dangerous. You said those men will stop at nothing . . ."

"My husband, you must listen . . ." Then in her quiet, gentle way she made him understand. By the time they reached home, he had reluctantly agreed. As Miyuki got out of the car, she said, "I will go get the dress you want to see, Ohara-san, if you will wait a moment."

Duke looked after her as she ran to the apartment, then turned to Ohara. "You guys better look out for her. You hear?"

"That's a promise," Ohara assured him.

Duke nodded and followed Miyuki inside. In a few moments she was back, the dress in a paper bag. "I don't know how to thank you," she began, "you give me back my Duke."

Ohara smiled. "No, Miyuki, you did that yourself. Don't worry, now, we'll be looking after you."

"I know," she said. "So will Duke."

Driving back to the station, Ohara tried to fit his idea about Kano into the Shimizu killing. It had blossomed as a possibility, but that was all it was. The whole case depressed him. What leads he and Washington had found so far were dead ends. He wondered if Washington had turned up anything more on Joe Flynn. Their other prospect was whoever had taken Shimizu's gun, but unless it was used, it would be hard to find.

132

If he could see into Jody's kaleidoscopic mind, he might discover a connection with Kano among the Japanese men she'd met. He also needed to talk to her about the burglary in Shimizu's apartment. First they'd have to find her.

He tried to freshen his mind by thinking about something else, but it was no good. He was worried about his son Jim and the kids who'd been maneuvered into those well-intended but potentially dangerous patrols. With a sense of relief, he pulled into the station parking lot and went to his office.

The only message was a note from Washington saying that the Identikit picture and description of Jody that they'd sent statewide had brought results. People who thought she might be their daughter were coming to talk to him. Ohara didn't relish the prospect of telling them the girl was still missing.

He took out the forensic reports and began going over them, thinking as he did so that tomorrow they would have to get tough with Bill Stack. The only hard evidence they had was the wrench—an odd make known to be used by him—some blood scrapings, and his argument with Shimizu witnessed by Joe Flynn and Barry.

Flynn himself was a prime suspect. He seemed to have a motive, and no established alibi. Maybe Jody had seen him, too, and in her haphazard account had failed to mention it.

Forensic vacuuming of the murder scene had turned up some bits of thin silvered metal. What was it? Unexplained elements bothered him. They'd also found some threads of red cloth on the windowsill. A cleaner's rag? That didn't worry him too much, because Shimizu had been killed in the alley, not inside his apartment.

A voice broke in on his concentration. "Hey, Irish, I've got something you may be interested in." It was Bert Macklin, a veteran homicide detective.

133

Ohara looked up with a smile. He liked Macklin, who had broken him in on homicide. He also respected the brain behind Bert's easy manner. "What is it?"

"I took a homicide call a while ago from an apartment on Chestnut Street. Guy named Stack, shot in the chest."

Ohara drew in a sharp breath. "Bill Stack?"

"That's him. He one of yours?"

Ohara nodded. "He's involved in the Shimizu case. When was he killed?"

"They're doing the autopsy now, but the doc says roughly early last evening. His wife and a friend found him around noon today. When I saw her I figured we had an open-and-shut case. Seems Stack beat the hell out of her the previous night. One eye was swollen shut and she had other cuts and bruises you wouldn't believe. But she's got a solid alibi. She was at work all day yesterday, and with her friend from then on. She'd decided to leave her husband after the beating, and just came home for her things."

"How did you connect him with me?"

"When we questioned the neighbors, one of them said that a Japanese cop had talked to him yesterday about Stack. Mind filling me in?"

"Bill Stack had an argument in Flynn's bar with a Japanese named Shimizu shortly before Shimizu was found beaten to death. Washington and I have been handling it. We've been trying to get hold of Stack for two days."

"That's what Stack's wife was going on about, then. She claims that the Japs—her word, not mind—had killed her husband. Sounds like she knows something."

"I'd like to talk to her, Bert."

"Sure. She's down in interrogation waiting to sign her statement. I want to hear what she says to you."

Ohara, following Bert's bulky figure into the interrogation room, was not at first visible to the woman waiting there.

When she saw him, she stiffened. "Who are you?" she asked, her bruised lips barely moving.

Bert answered. "No cause for alarm, Mrs. Stack. This is Detective Sam Ohara, who's investigating the beating death of a Japanese named Shimizu. He'd like to talk to you."

Seeing Ginny Stack's battered face, Ohara was moved by pity. He went over and sat down beside her. "I'm sorry to trouble you just now, Mrs. Stack. I can guess how you must be feeling, but I'm hoping you can answer some questions. I tried to see your husband, but wasn't able to do so."

"Nobody knows how I'm feeling right now. If you mean this," she gestured to her face, "I've had this kind of pain before. About Bill, I don't have any feelings left. I just want to see justice done."

"Justice?"

"Yes. You should know the truth. It was self-defense, how he killed that Jap."

Ohara's expression didn't change. "Tell me about it."

"Bill wasn't a bad guy, you know " Ginny looked at the two men as if she expected them to deny it. "It was just that he lost his job and couldn't get work. Then everything went sour for him. He blamed the Japs and got to hating everything and everybody. Sometimes he'd boil over, do crazy things like smashing up that Jap's car. He didn't really mean to hurt anybody."

She saw them looking at her face and knew what they were thinking. "OK, so he'd beat me up sometimes when he'd had too much to drink, but he was always sorry afterward, and I always believed him." Pausing, she dug in her bag for a tissue and wiped her eyes. "We had some good times at first. I don't forget that."

Ohara said nothing, so after a moment she went on. "It wasn't all his fault. That Jap pulled a gun on him and he threw the wrench in self-defense." Then she told them how

135

she had come home to find Bill bleeding from a bullet wound, and his account of what had happened. "He was sure the cops wouldn't believe his story, because of what he'd done to the car and because everybody knew how he felt about Japs."

Ginny's fingers pulled absently at the rumpled tissue. "I was going to leave him after he beat me this time. He was a louse in some ways, but now that he's dead, I remember him like he used to be, and I want to see him done right by."

"We understand," Bert Macklin said.

"You do," she said, "but I'm not so sure about him." Her eyes challenged Ohara. "You're a Jap, so maybe you don't want to believe what I'm saying. But he never set out to kill that man, even if he was a Jap. I don't want nobody calling Bill a murderer. He was always a decent man before things went sour for him."

Ohara gazed back at her. There was no anger in his eyes, only compassion and understanding. "Thank you for telling me what happened," he said. "We'll do our best to see that he gets justice."

When Ginny Stack had left, Macklin turned to Ohara. "She could be charged as an accessory, Irish."

"Not by me," Ohara said quietly.

"You're probably right," Macklin said. "I'm only interested in who killed Stack. What do you know about him?"

Ohara filled him in, then went back upstairs to his office. It had been a long day, and it was already almost seven o'clock. As he was about to leave for home, the phone rang. "Detective Ohara?" the crisp voice on the other end of the line inquired.

"Yes, this is Ohara."

"This is St. Mary's Hospital. Your son has been injured and is in emergency."

136

Chapter Sixteen

"How is my son?" Ohara asked the emergency-room doctor, trying to keep the fear out of his voice.

The young doctor was brusque; he was tired of having to talk to distressed parents. "About the way you'd expect after a gang fight," he said. "A stab wound in the side is the worst of it, but he'll make it this time. You can see him now; ask the nurse." He pushed his way back through the swinging doors to the emergency room.

"Wait . . ." Ohara began, then turned at a touch on his arm.

It was a young patrolman who said, "I'm sorry about your son, Lieutenant. I was with him when he was brought in. He didn't want us to call his home and frighten his mother, so I gave the nurse the station number. I was sure they would reach you."

"Thank you," Ohara said. "That was the right thing to do. Tell me what happened."

"We rolled on a gang disturbance," the officer said. "When we got there the local gangs were beating up on the vigilante patrol your son was in, as well as on each other. It seems the patrol went into disputed turf claimed by both the Swords and the Contras."

"Many hurt?" Ohara asked out of habit.

"Quite a few. One dead. Your son was trying to pull an injured boy away when he was stabbed. He's a real gutsy kid. How is he?"

"I don't know," Ohara replied. "I'm going in to see him now." He went over to the nurses' desk to ask where his son was. The nurse in charge delayed him long enough to sign some papers, then directed him to the proper ward.

It jolted him to find young Jim lying on the bed so still and pale, with his eyes closed. Ohara took his hand and held it. The doctor had said he would make it, that was all that mattered. He clung to the words as he would a talisman.

Ohara knew he must call Peggy, but he couldn't make himself leave just yet. He was painfully aware that he'd spent very little time with Jim lately. It was true that under the pressures of police work the family often had to take second place, but he knew, too, that he and Jim had been growing apart. They hadn't really tried to be together. They seemed to have different viewpoints on almost everything of late, and had become immersed in separate worlds.

There'd been a time in his own youth when he'd experienced the same thing with his father, who, being a wise and loving man, had finally found a bridge of understanding and respect for their differences. Because he had, their bond of filial love had become strengthened and dignified by friendship. Now that he'd been given a second chance, he vowed that he would make it happen for Jim and himself.

Filled with emotion, Ohara had unconsciously tightened his hand on his son's. Suddenly Jim's eyes opened and tried to focus on his face. "Dad?"

"Take it easy, son." Ohara's heart lifted just to hear Jim's voice.

Jim tried to move, then winced in pain. "What's wrong with me?"

"You were stabbed and beaten up, but the doctor says you'll be all right."

"I remember now. The Swords . . . Eddie Ho . . . how is he?"

"I suppose he's the one you pulled out of the fight. He's being cared for, too."

Jim seemed to relax at the news.

"I'm very proud of you," Ohara said.

Jim's hand tightened in his father's. "Does Mom know?"

"I'm going to call her now. I waited until I could give her some good news. Now, why don't you rest while I go get her." Ohara laid Jim's hand down, smoothed his son's hair back from his bandaged forehead, then left to telephone Peggy.

Murray Feinbaum sighed as he closed his account books and tried to ease his aching shoulders. He knew he and Miriam were getting too old to keep on a busy dry-cleaning store. But he liked being active, talking to the people who came in. Besides, the store did a good business. With what things cost today, everybody needed a little extra income.

He called out to his wife, who was putting up orders in the back. "Close the back window. It's time to go home."

She didn't answer. Murray muttered to himself that the woman was getting deaf as a post, then picked up his cash box and receipts to take them to the safe. As he pushed through the curtain that led to the back of the store, something hard and cold snaked around his ankles, jerking him to the floor. His books scattered as he threw out his arms to save himself. His head struck the floor and pain shot through him. When he could focus his eyes, he saw Miriam kneeling on the floor, her hands tied behind her.

Two figures stood over her, dressed all in black with black cloth wrapped around their heads so that only eyes showed. One was tall and thin, the other medium height and on the heavy side.

139

"You know who we are?" the tall one asked.

Lifting himself on his hands, Murray shook his head, unable to speak.

"We're Ninja!"

The voice was young-sounding, which made Murray bolder. "What's Ninja?"

"Ninja are the greatest of the Japanese martial-arts fighters, the secret assassins. We've come to right a wrong!"

"Wrong? What wrong?"

"You know, all right! The crimes people like you are committing against Asians. Now you're going to pay."

Miriam moaned.

"We don't hurt no one, you bastard!" Despite his fear, Murray was angry.

Suddenly the accuser drew a stick from behind his back that had a chain and an iron ball attached. As he swung it around his head, it cut the air viciously. "Give us your money, or we'll use this on her."

Miriam screamed. "Murray, for God's sake give the money, or these Japs will kill us!"

Murray shoved over the cash box he'd dropped. "So take the money. Just don't hurt my wife!"

The tall Ninja stopped whirling the ball and chain. "Pick it up," he said to his companion, who got the box and tucked it under his arm.

"Let's go!" he urged.

"Not yet," the tall one said. With his foot he pushed Miriam facedown on the floor, then, spinning around, kicked backward and knocked down the shelf holding Murray's tailoring tools. Next he smashed his hand down on the little drum table where they ate their lunch. It crashed to the floor in pieces.

The Ninja with the cash box edged toward the door. "Come on!"

"Wait!" Then the tall one reached inside his jacket, drew something out, and threw it at Murray's head. "Remember the Ninja!" he shouted.

What followed was terrifying. The black-clad figure raised his hand. Suddenly there was an explosion, and a cloud of smoke hid him from sight. Murray, sure his end had come, cowered on the floor. By the time he could see again, and found himself unharmed, both the black-clad figures had disappeared.

Lying in front of him where the Ninja had thrown it was a sharp pointed silver star. Murray picked it up and stared at it, gripped by an old fear. Then he heard Miriam moaning and crying. He untangled the chain from around his ankles and staggered over to her.

By the time the police arrived, she was in hysterics. An hour later the whole neighborhood was in turmoil, repeating and embroidering on the atrocities the Jap Ninjas had perpetrated on the Feinbaums.

Then word got out that a pharmacist several blocks away had also been visited by the Ninjas. He'd been tied up and left with a silver star at his feet. His store had been wrecked and his register robbed.

As the news spread, the phone at the police station was kept busy. Several unlucky Asians were roughed up. Angry citizens armed themselves to walk the streets searching for the Ninjas. They had to be dispersed by police patrols. One man, dressed in black pants and black turtleneck sweater, was shot in the shoulder by his neighbor as he went out late at night to empty the garbage. Japanese-Americans and other Asians locked themselves inside their homes.

The Ninja panic had put quiet little Maple Street and the area around it in a state of siege.

141

Chapter Seventeen

Their black Ninja outfits hidden in the back of the closet, Steve and Rudy sprawled on the floor of Steve's room over the family garage. As far as their respective families were concerned, they'd been there all evening studying for exams.

Elated by the success of their evening's exploits, they gorged on pizza and beer as they relived each exciting moment. "Man, Steve, you were great," Rudy said admiringly. "Just like Bruce Lee!"

Steve smiled complacently and stretched his arms over his head. He knew he looked like a drip, with his pimply, nondescript face and mousy blond hair. Nobody but Rudy appreciated the real Steve, or was awed by his hidden power. "You weren't so bad, either," he conceded, then spoiled it by adding, "after you got over being chicken."

Rudy covered his embarrassment by draining his can of beer, then said, "We scared 'em shitless, didn't we?" He caught up a long string of cheese falling from the pizza and ate it off his finger.

"Yeah, I never had so much fun as this. My smoke bomb worked real well, too." Steve folded his legs into the lotus position, as befitted a great Ninja, then reached to turn on the TV. "Maybe we made the news."

They had. Both boys watched the screen, hearts pounding. The announcer was already well into the story. "There were two intruders dressed in black, who told the victims they were Ninja, Japanese assassins. In each case, after robbing the victims and wrecking the premises with kicks and karate chops, they left behind a pointed silver star, then disappeared in an explosion of smoke.''

Beer dribbled from the can unnoticed as Rudy punched his buddy on the shoulder. ''All right! They think we were the real thing!''

There were follow-up shots of the wreckage at the dry cleaners and the shambles at the drugstore. ''Just like the movies!'' Rudy shivered with excitement.

Then Murray Feinbaum was briefly interviewed. He described the black-clad robbers, the iron ball and chain they'd used to threaten his wife, and the silver star they'd left behind.

''Did they say anything?'' he was asked.

''They said people like us would have to pay for the crimes against Asians. What crimes?'' Murray was indignant. ''Miriam and me don't hurt nobody.''

Next came a shot of a gurney being loaded into an ambulance as the newscaster said, ''The other victim had to be hospitalized for a broken hand and shock.''

''You shouldn't have kicked him, Steve.'' Rudy looked worried. ''You said nobody would get hurt.''

''I wouldn't have kicked him if he hadn't pulled a gun on us,'' Steve blustered. ''I saved your neck! Now shut up and listen.''

''We'll be bringing you more information on the Ninja attacks during our 'Night Talk' show.'' The news segment ended, replaced by a commercial.

Steve snapped off the TV and turned to face his friend. ''OK. Let's talk about where we'll hit tomorrow.''

Rudy choked on a swallow of beer. When he had recovered, he protested, ''You said it was just this one time, for kicks.''

"Don't be such a wimp!" Steve emptied the brown paper bag lying on the floor between them. "Look at the money we picked up! We can get more next time."

"No, I'm scared. We might get caught!"

"You think I'm stupid? That's why I told that old geezer we were Japanese Ninja. They aren't going to be looking for a couple of white kids, are they?"

Rudy eyed the money at his feet. "One more time?"

"Sure, one more time, maybe two, depending how it goes. We'll have a blast shakin' everybody up just like real Ninja, and we'll pick up enough money to really do something! Now listen up. I've got a couple of places in mind . . ."

Ohara brought Peggy and Susie to the hospital, where they stayed for some time until reassured that young Jim's condition was improving. Peggy, unlike her usual calm self, seemed to have gone to pieces.

They stopped for a meal on the way home. Then, after Susie had gone upstairs to bed, Ohara sat on the sofa with Peggy, just talking, her head against his shoulder. It was something they'd done too seldom of late. He could feel the tenseness go out of her body as he gently massaged the back of her neck. Eventually he persuaded her to go to bed, promising he'd be up soon.

Ohara had too much on his mind to fall asleep, so he turned on the news.

The account of the Ninja attacks shocked him. "That's not possible," he said aloud. If he could see the *shuriken,* he'd know more. The report called them pointed stars, which was at least a description. He didn't buy the Ninja story, but the average person fed on a diet of kung fu and karate movies would. He'd not been happy about the vigilante patrols, but this was far worse. Who was behind it, some Asian hothead? It was possible in a world where terrorist

144

tactics were a fact of life. Still, from what he had heard so far, he didn't think so. It smacked of amateurs. Whoever it was, racial tensions would be heated to boiling.

His guess was confirmed when he switched to another channel, where they were reporting the growing panic and disturbances in the Maple Street neighborhood. He decided to go down to the station and see what he could do to defuse it.

He was on his way out when the phone rang. He picked it up on the first ring, hoping Peggy hadn't heard; it might be the hospital. Instead, Captain Gerhard Krauss's rasping voice shouted in his ear. "Ohara, have you seen the TV news?"

"Yes. I'm on my way in now. I think I can . . ."

Krauss snorted. "Forget that. Get your ass down to Channel Two right now. The TV people want a police officer for some bullshit interview show in half an hour. Public Relations here says your good-looking Japanese face is just the ticket."

"Yes, sir," Ohara said, wishing he hadn't picked up the phone.

"And what the hell is going on in that damn Maple Street neighborhood, anyway? Two killings down there, one of them yours. What have you been doing about it?"

Ohara cleared his throat, trying to think of something to say. He could picture Krauss's cherubic face, which belied his irascible temper, growing redder by the second. But the captain was in full spate and didn't wait for a reply.

"I need results," Krauss went on, "but all I get is reports of vandalism, protest meetings, teenage vigilantes. The mayor's office has been on the phone, not to mention the media. Now there's this Japanese Ninja panic! You know anything about Ninja?"

"Yes." Ohara's answer was carefully brief. "It's not possible that they are real Ninja!"

"They're real enough to scare hell out of people. So get on that TV program and cool it down! And Ohara, be in my office first thing tomorrow." Krauss banged down the phone, mission accomplished.

Ohara was impatient to get on to the Ninja investigation, but now he was saddled with a TV show. He would have very little progress to report to Krauss in the morning, but he put all thought of it out of his mind. Krauss was a shrewd old man and a good cop. He'd be more reasonable when he'd calmed down.

To his relief, Ohara found there were two other hastily called guests for the talk show. One was a phychiatrist, gray-haired and fatherly with a mellow voice and love-everybody smile. The other, a black woman with impressive degrees in sociology, represented the mayor's Committee on Human Relations.

They were seated casually in comfortable chairs around a coffee table, like good friends having a chat. But Ohara felt anything but comfortable. He was perspiring under the lights and wished he had a tall, cool glass of water.

He let the others bat the issue around, joining in only when asked something directly. He wasn't here as a personality. He did his best to cool the situation, as Krauss had demanded, feeling as he urged calm and gave assurances of police protection that he'd be of more use doing something about the Ninja. That he could and would do.

The talk-show host drew Ohara into the conversation. "I thought Ninja were a thing of the past. There aren't any real ones today, are there?

"There are real Ninja, yes."

"Tell us how . . ." the psychiatrist began, but the producer was signaling and the interviewer interrupted to bring the show to a close.

Ohara made his escape as soon as he could and headed for the station to get an accurate report on the attacks and examine the *shuriken*. He smiled when he saw them. These silver pointed stars were imitations, probably turned out by the factory in the United States that advertised in the martial-arts fan magazines. He spoke at length with Jack Bailey, who was in charge of the case. Bailey listened carefully, then said, "Irish, we sure can use you. If you've got any ideas to put a stop to this, let's have them."

Ohara outlined what he had in mind. Together they went over to the Maple Street business district and checked possible targets. Since the intruders would likely use the same M.O., hitting a small business through an out-of-sight window, they selected a small café, whose storeroom windows backed on an alley, as bait. Bailey would speak to the owner in the morning, and at night would have conspicuous patrols around to discourage their villains from choosing another target. Ohara volunteered to wait inside the diner with his partner; he did not say what else he had in mind. Tomorrow Ohara would talk to Murray Feinbaum. There were certain important questions he had to ask. Of course, there was no assurance that the Ninja would strike again, but he had a feeling they would. Their performance had been too good for a one-night stand.

Benny Polser had stayed in all day on the pretense of being sick. He'd checked all the newscasts for mention of Bill Stack. There had been nothing until the six-o'clock news, and then only a brief mention of a man found shot in his apartment on Chestnut Street. He'd been identified as Bill Stack, unemployed autoworker. Then came the words that made Benny breathe easier: "The victim's widow feels her husband may have been murdered because of his out-spoken dislike of Japanese."

When Benny checked the late news, his optimism blossomed. The reports of the Ninja attacks excited him. He watched the talk show, memorizing the face of the Jap cop. He only half listened to what was said. He was fantasizing the most daring strike of all: over and over he aimed the little black gun at the Jap cop and pulled the trigger. He remembered how he'd felt when he'd thrown the rock; this would be better, much better.

Chapter Eighteen

Ted Washington parked his car and looked around him. Venice, California, he thought, was a far cry from its romantic namesake. It was just another seashore community clinging to the coattails of the Los Angeles sprawl. Still, he'd always liked its quaint, funky atmosphere. It had bloomed in recent years. Once-gray, discouraged buildings were adorned with bright murals done by local artists. Boutiques, cafés, and restaurants of every sort now festooned its main street and beachfront.

Being a weekday morning, it was quiet, almost lethargic, as if waiting for the weekend when a visiting population of pleasure-seekers would create a buzz of excitement, filling the shops and stores, seeing and being seen, enjoying the strolling mimes, musicians, and sidewalk artists. On weekends Venice sparkled as a fun place for tourists, bikers, skaters, drifters, kids, and tanned musclemen bodybuilding on the beach. Still, a star attraction was the ocean, more affordable here than in Malibu.

Washington had come down to check out Joe Flynn's alibi for the night Shimizu was killed. He'd secured an old photograph of him from a sports editor he knew at the *Times*. It was good enough for an ID.

Joe had said he'd stopped for coffee at a stand where Venice Boulevard met the ocean. The one Washington found was closed, so he decided to see if Flynn had stopped anywhere else.

Washington had an idea that Flynn might have been looking for his son, so he took to the back alleys and side streets to see if he could get anything from the hypes and winos. He showed the photographs to anyone who would look, but it seemed hopeless. Then a young Chicano with a pale face and shaking hands recognized Mike's picture. "I know him; that's Mike. That's what I told the big guy who come lookin' for him a couple of nights ago."

"Was it this man?" Washington showed Joe's picture.

"Could be, but older. Looked like muscle to me. If I hadn't of been so hard up I wouldn't have said anything."

"What did you tell him?"

"Hey, man, it's not easy to remember." There was a sly calculation in the Chicano's voice.

Washington took out a bill and kept it folded in his hand. "Try," he said.

The boy's eyes shone. "I told him where Mike was. Later I heard the guy took him away."

Washington held out the bill. He hoped the kid would use it for food, but he doubted it. Watching the boy shuffle off, his emaciated body hunched and shaking, Ted had a sudden flash of sympathy for what Joe Flynn must have felt. Young Mike wouldn't have looked much different.

As he walked back to the beachfront, Washington thought about Flynn's alibi. If the guy at the coffee stand recognized him, too, he was in the clear. Why had he been unwilling to tell them he was searching for his son? Was it because he was afraid they'd put the narcs onto young Mike? Where had he taken the kid?

Suddenly the aroma and sizzle coming from a hot dog stand reminded him that he was hungry. He bought himself a "dog with everything" and a fruit drink, then walked down to sit on the sand and look at the ocean.

As he ate, his mind sniffed around the problem of Joe Flynn. If he could find young Mike, he might get Flynn off the hook. That was something that appealed to Washington. He'd rather prove Joe innocent than guilty.

The stand Joe had said he'd stopped at was now open. The counterman said he thought he remembered Flynn, but wasn't positive. Washington realized he'd better find young Mike. Before he left the stand he bought himself another hot dog, redolent of pickle and onion, eating it as he walked back to his car.

Flynn was probably trying to bring his kid back cold turkey, but he'd need help for that. He couldn't take him home, and wouldn't take him to a drug center, because they'd ask questions. Then it came to him. Flynn's brother-in-law, the broken-down wrestler, owed him. He also owned a motel. Muldoon, that was his name. Now he'd have to find the motel.

After a tussle on the phone with City Hall Records, an annoyed clerk told him there was absolutely no motel business license in the name of Muldoon or Flynn. So that was a bust. Or was it? Maybe Muldoon was only a wrestling name. Suppose he used his real name, the same as Joe Flynn's wife?

There was nothing more to do in Venice, so Washington drove to City Hall and checked the marriage-license bureau. There he found that Joe Flynn had married a Mary Dugan over thirty years ago.

Back at the business-license bureau, his welcome was less than cordial. The same annoyed clerk looked pointedly at the clock, which was almost at closing time, checked for Dugan, motel owner, and found him. Washington took down the address, smiled at the uncivil civil servant, and left.

He called the station to talk to Ohara. Sergeant Reagan took the call and told him that his partner was at Burbank General Hospital, where his son had been taken in serious condition.

Washington got over to Burbank General as fast as he could, arriving just as Ohara came out of Jim's room to call Peggy.

"I came as soon as I heard, Sam. How is he?"

"The doctor says his condition is improving, but he looks half dead."

"What happened?"

Ohara told him, then said he had to call Peggy. When he came back from the phone, Washington put a cup of hot coffee in his hand. Actually Ohara disliked coffee, but he sipped at it, knowing it was intended as comfort. "Do you want me to go get Peggy?" Ted asked.

"I'd be grateful," Ohara said. "I don't like to leave Jim just yet."

"Go on back to him, Sam. I'll have Peggy here in no time."

When Washington had delivered Peggy and Susie, Ohara told him they'd probably stay at the hospital for a while. "There's nothing you can do, Ted. Go on home, and thanks." The firm grip of Ohara's hand and the look in his eyes said all that was necessary.

Since there was nothing more he could do for his friend, Washington left the hospital, but he did not go home. Instead he decided to go and talk to Joe Flynn's brother-in-law. The motel Dugan ran, named Shady Valley, was a short distance out on the freeway to Pomona.

When he found the motel it was not in a valley, but its eight white frame cottages were indeed shaded by a stand of green trees. It was a nice little place, enough off the freeway to be restful. It had lawn chairs and old-fashioned porch swings under the trees, a kid's sandbox, and a shuf-fleboard court.

He parked and went into the office, where a comfortable-looking middle-aged woman smiled a welcome. "Yes, sir?"

Her smile faded when he produced his ID. "We've no trouble here, Officer," she said nervously. "We're very careful."

"I'm sure you are, ma'am." Washington smiled reassuringly. "I want to talk to Mr. Dugan."

"I'm Mrs. Dugan," she said. "Terry isn't here. He won't be back until late tonight. Maybe I can help."

The expression in her blue eyes told him she was lying and not happy about it. He had already decided how to play it. "I just want to ask him some questions about his brother-in-law, Joe Flynn. Have you seen him lately?"

"No." She got the word out too quickly. "Why?"

Washington smiled. "I'll talk to Mr. Dugan another time. Pretty place you have here." He left her looking after him, got into his car, and drove back toward the highway. As soon as he was out of sight, he pulled his car over, then walked quickly back to the tree-shaded grounds of the motel. Under the dim porch lights he saw Mrs. Dugan at the door of one of the back cottages. She was talking to a heavyset man with a bald head. Dugan, a.k.a. Mike Muldoon, looked much as he did in the picture on Flynn's wall. Washington would have bet a month's pay that young Mike Flynn was in that cabin fighting it out cold turkey, and Muldoon, the tough old bastard, was seeing him through.

Ted was pretty sure he had what he wanted. Tomorrow he'd give it to Ohara. The Dugans would talk when they understood they'd be helping Joe and that he and Ohara were not working for the narcs. It was a satisfying day's work, even though it would knock out a major suspect.

As he drove back to Los Angeles, he tuned in the news and heard the brief announcement about Bill Stack. He

153

discounted the theory that it was a revenge racial killing, but the possibility that Stack had seen something he shouldn't was likely. He needed to talk to Ohara.

Well, it would have to wait until tomorrow. Ohara had enough on his hands. He pulled off for a meal, then decided that he would make a sweep down Hollywood Boulevard for Jody.

As he drove down the famous street, Ted thought how it had changed. Tourists still came to see the stars embedded in the sidewalk honoring their favorite entertainers. They could still walk around the outer lobby of Grauman's Chinese, now a must-see landmark, touch the hand- and footprints of movie greats, and trace the famous signatures carved into each cement block.

But now, at night especially, the street looked shabby, its corners and storefronts a rendezvous for drifters, junkies, pimps, and prostitutes. What sickened him, though, were the kids, male and female, dressed to showcase what they had to offer, selling their bodies for the price of a fix. He wondered if their parents guessed where they were, or if they even cared.

He searched the corner groups and scanned the shadowed storefronts for a sight of Jody. Every now and then he'd spot a curly head of blond hair or a face in a crowd and would pause, but it was never Jody. A black BMW was cruising just ahead of him. There appeared to be two people in it. Maybe they were looking for a kid.

Then, as they came to a crossing, the BMW suddenly speeded up and turned right, past a parking lot into a street of run-down stucco bungalows. Held up in the intersection, Washington saw the car had drawn level with a girl. He couldn't see her face, but suddenly she started walking faster. The black car followed closely. He didn't like the look of it.

Bullying his way between several outraged drivers, he managed to turn right into the street. A woman jumped back onto the curb, just clearing his wheels. By the shouts that followed him, Ted guessed the police would be along soon. But the maneuver had cost him precious seconds. The BMW was already turning into another street. He could not see the girl. Reaching the corner and peering down the dimly lit street on his right, he saw the taillights of the car. It had stopped halfway down the street, its door open. As he approached, a man got out, grabbed the girl, and began to force her back to the car. In the struggle, the little leather cap she was wearing fell off and blond hair tumbled loose. As Washington slid to a stop, there was no mistaking that face; it was Jody.

The man was holding her in front of him. Washington knew if he tried to use his weapon she could be hit. Instead he threw his two hundred plus pounds into a flying tackle that brought all three of them to the ground. If Jody had kept still, it would have been easier, but in her terror she was fighting both of them, using knees, feet, and fingernails like lethal weapons. The man underneath grunted in pain as she kicked at his shins. Her nails scratched at Washington's face.

Her captor, a slender Japanese pinned under their combined weight, let go of Jody, then brought his fist up like a club, hitting her on the side of the head. With a cry, she stopped struggling and slumped. The man shoved her body to one side, then aimed a chop at Washington's throat with one hand, clawing for his eyes with the other.

Washington blocked the chop and, using the heels of his hands like hammers, struck the man below the larynx. The Japanese fell back, gasping.

Then, as Washington started to rise, a foot caught him behind the ear, splitting his head with pain. He heard the slight movement of the second kick, and remembered too late the other man in the car. The kick landed in the middle of his back, and he fell forward, feeling his body go numb. As his sight faded, he felt the kicks pound into his side.

Suddenly, blessedly, the kicking stopped. He no longer knew or cared if the shouts in the distance and the sound of a car's engine were real. The numbness faded, and pain flooded his body. A bulky lump pushed against his abdomen, making its own small pain, but he was too weak even to move. Why was somebody dragging him by the arm, yelling at him?

Then the kicks came again. Fighting the numbness that seemed to extend to his brain, he tried to roll aside, but he seemed to be fading in and out of consciousness. The yelling became a girl's voice, shrill and angry. "Shit!" she shouted, kicking him again. "Get up, you black bastard, get up!"

The numbness from the karate kick to his spine was gone, so carefully Washington tried to move his arms and legs. Suddenly hands grabbed both his ears and smashed his head against the ground. Forgetting pain, he swung his arm back, knocked aside the hands, and rolled onto his back.

Jody glared down at him, then shoved against his chest. "Move over. You're lying on my bag." With both hands she began to tug at a lumpy bundle beneath him.

Washington grabbed both her wrists and hung on.

"Let go," she shouted. "You're hurting me."

"Hey, Jody!" He struggled to get the words out. "I just saved your ass. I'll help you if you give me a chance."

"The hell you will! You want to put me in jail!" She spat the words at him, her face distorted with rage.

Washington stared dumbfounded at the change in her. This foulmouthed little tiger cat was a different Jody from the helpless girl who'd clung to Ohara in tears. Before he

156

could answer her, three men came pounding up the street. One of them shouted, "Hey, what's going on here?"

In an instant Jody was screaming and crying, "He attacked me! He attacked me!"

Attracted by the shouts, people were turning on lights and coming out of their homes to see what was happening. Immediately Washington let go of Jody's wrists and sat up. "That's a lie," he said, and fumbled for his ID. "I'm a police officer." Nobody paid any attention; all eyes were on Jody, who was sobbing wildly.

A motherly-looking woman put an arm around her. "What kind of slime would try to rape a kid? Somebody should fix him good!"

"He won't do it again," one of the men shouted, and aimed a kick at Washington's groin that missed as Washington scrambled to his feet.

Jody shrugged off the woman's comforting arms. "My bag! He was trying to steal my bag! It's all I've got in the world."

Two men grabbed Washington's arms and twisted them behind him. "Somebody call the police!"

"I already did!" A woman with curlers in her hair stuck her head out of a second-story window. Everybody looked up at her. "I saw what happened, and that little bitch is lying. Two guys were muscling her into a car; the big black was trying to save her, until they got him down. So I hollered at 'em that I was calling the police. And I did."

As if on cue, a police car drew up to the curb. Two patrol officers pushed their way into the considerable crowd. No one but Washington noticed Jody easing herself away. Holding out his ID to the officers, he said, "Stop her. She's an escapee."

Jody, with no way to evade the people now closed in behind her, began to cry, pitiful heartbreaking sobs.

Murmurs of "poor little thing" and "picking on a kid" ran through the crowd. One officer, obviously a veteran, examined Washington's ID. The other took Jody by the arm.

"All right, miss, step over here and we'll get this sorted out. Now, what's your name?"

"Jody Baxter," she answered with a quick glance at Washington.

A woman's voice broke in on them. "You gonna hear what I got to say? I'm the one called the police." It was the same woman who'd looked out of her upstairs window earlier.

The curlers had disappeared, leaving sausagelike curls, and for her public appearance she'd used lipstick, rouge, and violet eyeshadow with a generous hand. Her heavy body was submerged in a caftan printed with large jungle flowers, beneath which her surprisingly small feet sported spike-heeled red pumps. The total effect was not what she'd imagined, but Washington smiled at her as if she'd been a beauty.

"Thank you, ma'am," he said. "You're one smart lady, and I owe you."

She nodded, and patted his hand. "Just doing my duty, big boy." She smiled. Then, at the officer's request she gave her name as Maggie Ryan, and told how she had called the police and rushed back to the window in time to see the girl kicking the big black who was collapsed on the ground.

"I was frightened," Jody sobbed. "I thought he was one of the men trying to kidnap me. I'm telling the truth."

Washington looked at her. "I don't think you know what it is," he said softly. Then he turned to the patrol officers. "Check your APB list. She escaped from custody and is a witness in a murder case."

"Let's go over to the patrol car." The older officer nodded at Washington. "You need an ambulance, Detective?"

"No." Washington rubbed his neck and watched the younger cop disperse the crowd. Reluctantly the people moved back, but not so far that they couldn't watch the group at the car. Maggie Ryan, enjoying status as a witness, followed over to the patrol car, where she took in everything that happened for later distribution.

The want on Jody was confirmed. "Shall we book her into Juvenile?" asked the young officer, who had her by the arm.

"Yes," Washington answered.

Jody glared at him, but without protest started to get into the patrol car.

"Just a minute," Washington said as he deftly pulled the cloth bag from her grasp.

"My things!" she shouted. "I've a right to have my things!"

In answer, Washington unzipped the bag, rummaged inside, then lifted out the plastic bag of white powder and a folding knife. "I don't think so," he said, putting them back and handing the bag to the officer. "Take this into the station. I'll follow in my car and help get her processed. Then I'll sign a receipt for this and take it with me. It's part of our case." He had a hunch Ohara would want to see that bag.

As he went to his car, Maggie followed, offering him a belt of rye in her apartment to help him recover. He thanked her and diplomatically refused. When he drove away, she watched him out of sight, waving as long as she could see the car.

At last the paperwork at the station was finished and Jody was on her way to Juvenile Hall. Washington started for home, looking forward to a hot bath to relieve his aches and pains. He was angry at his stupidity in not remembering the second man. If it hadn't been for Maggie, the guy might have finished him. He made a mental note to send her some flowers. She might get a kick out of that.

He pulled up in front of the small house he'd rented when he'd acquired his dog, Irish. The shaggy mutt had been a "witness" in the first case he'd been on with Ohara, and was named in honor of his partner. As he opened the gate of the wire fence, Irish came running and jumped all over him, making joyous little sounds in his throat. His big paws padded his master's chest in ecstatic welcome, finding all the tender spots. But Washington hadn't the heart to push him away. "OK, boy," he said finally. "Let's go in. I'll get you some chow."

As he let himself into the house, it seemed more dark and lonely than usual. There were times, and this was one, when Washington envied Ohara his Peggy, and the kids. Somebody to care meant a lot to any man, but especially, he thought, to a cop. He hadn't found that somebody yet.

Then, as if he'd sensed his master's mood, Irish rubbed his head against Washington's leg, his big brown eyes looking up with their silent message.

Washington bent down and pulled the dog's shaggy head close, rubbing gently behind his ears. "I know, Irish," he said. "I love you, too."

Chapter Nineteen

"You asked to see me, Captain."

Ohara stood in the doorway of Gerhard Krauss's office observing the frown with which the captain was surveying the four small chunks of apple before him. Krauss went on a new diet every few months in hopes of whipping his chubby proportions into compliance with police regulations. Until he gave it up, he was like a bear with a sore paw. The meeting was likely to be difficult.

"Sit down, Ohara," Krauss growled. "Just eating my breakfast, if you can call it that." He chomped angrily down on a chunk of apple. "I was sorry to hear about your boy. How is he?"

"A little better this morning."

"Glad to hear it." Krauss demolished another chunk of apple, then pushed the rest aside. "You did a good job on the TV last night, but not good enough. People are calling in predicting some kind of 'Oriental Watts' and demanding protection. The meetings and the vigilante patrols were understandable, but when Japanese strong-arm guys start hassling white citizens, that's something else. Then the widow of that white who was murdered claims that was done by Japanese, too. What's going on with you people?"

Ohara's face tightened. "I doubt if any of those crimes were committed by Japanese, or Japanese-Americans."

"You and I know that may be true," Krauss admitted, "but it's what people think that panics them. This Ninja business has everybody scared. I don't like citizens arming themselves, or afraid to come out of their homes. What are we going to do about it?"

"I have an idea about the so-called Ninja attacks," Ohara replied. "I think we can wrap it up tonight. That ought to cool things down a lot."

"Tell me."

Ohara outlined what he had in mind. Krauss listened intently. "I like it, and if it works, I'll see the word gets out."

It was a good thing, Ohara thought, that Krauss didn't know exactly how he planned to deal with the suspected Ninja if they showed up. It was a personal thing with him. He would handle it in his own way, but it would still be a good bust.

Krauss leaned back in his chair. "Now, what progress have you made on this Shimizu killing? That's another time bomb."

Ohara briefed him fully.

Krauss sighed. "So you're still convinced there were three separate attacks on Shimizu?"

"Yes, for the reasons I've given."

"Well, Stack accounts for one, but you say he must have left Shimizu alive. Another possible is this Yakuza professional. He may have made it look like separate attacks just to confuse the issue."

"He could have," Ohara admitted, "but the neck-twisting puzzles me. Shimizu was probably dead when that was done. A professional would do the job and get away. This is like giving a dead dog a kick, knowing it couldn't bite back."

"That's sick," Krauss said. "What about that guy who owns the bar, the wrestler? He'd have plenty of experience in beating guys up, and according to what you've told me, he may have had a motive."

162

"That's true," Ohara said, "but he may have an alibi. Ted Washington's checking now."

Krauss shifted restlessly in his chair. "You've got damn little, Sam."

"I know, but Washington called me last night to say he'd found Jody Baxter in Hollywood. She's in Juvenile Hall now. Maybe when we talk to her again we'll come up with something more."

Krauss snorted. "Maybe! Meantime, I'm supposed to stonewall the mayor and the press. If you think that's easy . . ."

"I don't," Ohara assured him, and suppressed the thought that stonewalling was something captains were supposed to be good at.

"Well, get a move on!" Krauss growled. "Let me know if I can help."

"Thanks," Ohara said, accepting the offer of help as the wishful thinking it was. He sympathized with the old war-horse, knowing Krauss would rather have been an active cop than stuck behind a desk. As he left, the captain was already frowning over a pile of papers awaiting his attention.

On the way back to Detectives, Ohara ran into Macklin, his old mentor, who had the Stack case. "Hey, Sam," he said, "I've got something for you. The bullet from Stack's body matches the one you dug out of the garage wall. They fit a thirty-eight caliber revolver. How do you like that?"

"It's like finding a life preserver in a shipwreck, Bert."

"Whoever used that gun on Stack has to know something about the Shimizu killing, if he didn't actually do it. So we both want him."

"It's possible that somebody discovered the body, picked up the gun, and got out of there," Ohara said. "Nowadays people don't want to be involved with somebody else's trouble."

"I'd say he just wanted a free gun." Macklin's smile was grim.

"Yes. But why use it on Stack?"

"Well, that's something we'd both better work on."

"Did anyone at Stack's place see or hear anything, or were they all struck blind, as usual?"

"As usual, except for one old lady who said somebody ran down the back stairs about the right time. She just got a glimpse of somebody running away. A short, skinny guy, she says, maybe a teenager. A bunch of punks have been bothering the tenants there lately."

"No other description?"

"Remember, it was dark by then. Cheer up, Sam, we'll get the bastard." Macklin, always the optimist, lumbered off down the corridor whistling cheerfully.

Ohara continued on his way back to Detectives, so absorbed in his thoughts that he walked past Washington without seeing him.

"Hey, Irish!" His partner's voice halted him. Ohara looked up, surprised.

"Ted, I've been wanting . . ." Ohara stopped and stared at Washington's bruised face. "What happened to you?"

"I forgot to watch my ass, that's what happened. Let's go in." As they went into the office and headed for their adjacent desks, Ohara saw that Ted walked gingerly, favoring his left side. When they had sat down, he said, "Tell me."

"In a minute, Sam. How's Jim?"

"He was better when I stopped at the hospital on the way in. You look worse than he does. Now, tell me what happened."

"All things in order, friend. First of all, Joe Flynn." Washington told Ohara what he'd discovered in Venice. "So even if the guy at the coffee stand couldn't make a positive ID, the hype did."

"It's thin, though, Ted. A hype will sometimes say what he thinks you want to hear."

"I know," Washington admitted, "but I think the Dugans can confirm that Joe brought his kid to them, and the time. All we have to do is convince them we're not going to turn Mike over to the narcs. That's why Joe won't tell us where he was."

"I'd like to know why Joe suddenly went out to find his boy after Shimizu put the blocks to him. After all, Shimizu still had the incriminating picture if he didn't pay up."

"Right. But what concerns us now is Joe's alibi. If he was in Venice and driving half the way to Pomona to Dugan's place, he wasn't killing Shimizu."

"Well, follow up on it, Ted."

"I'll do that. I can tell the Dugans we're interested in Joe as a witness and also let them know we don't want to turn the kid over to the narcs. They'll talk."

Ohara nodded. "I think we should get some more background on Stack's buddies, Erne Smith and Benny Polser. You might have better luck than I would. They don't like Japanese much."

"Will do," Washington promised.

"Now, tell me—what put you into the meat grinder?"

"I went looking for Jody. When I found her, I got creamed." Amused by the look on his partner's face, Washington told his story. "It was funny, you know. I went dashing in to the rescue, a proper hero, and Jody starts kicking and scratching me more than the guy who was trying to kidnap her. That's why I wasn't thinking about the other man in the car. He got the jump on me and nailed my ass." Washington winced as he eased his body into a more comfortable position. "The two guys beat it when the noise started attracting attention, but even then

165

Jody was like a wildcat. Kicking, punching, screaming at me to get up.''

"To get up?" Ohara looked surprised.

"I was lying on her damn bag. She was like a maniac over it. Then, when a crowd began to gather, she yelled and cried that I'd attacked her. I tried to get my ID out, but everybody was looking and listening to the poor little girl screaming rape. One of the guys tried to kick my balls off.'' Then Washington told him about Maggie Ryan's timely intervention and the arrival of the cops.

"Did you get the license of the car?"

"Yes, while I was following them. The cops checked it out.'' Washington got out his notebook. "It belongs to the Seiko Wakari Import Company.''

Ohara stared at him. "I was thinking it might. Wakari was probably one of the men at Jody's so-called screen test. He has a thing for young girls. I've more information on that, but go on with your story.''

Washington gave him the rest of it, then said, "And here's her damn bag. I signed it out. Thought you might like a look at it before we give it to Narcotics.'' He set the duffel bag on the desk.

Ohara looked at him in admiration. "Ted, you're one great cop.''

"Sure as hell am.'' Washington grinned. "Even rounded these up.'' He handed Ohara a set of photographs: the one of Joe Flynn, another of Duke Walker, and a third of Bill Stack in a morgue shot showing just the face. "Might get a more positive ID from Jody.'' He handed over two other photos. "We can mix these in just to make it fair.''

"Thanks, Ted. Smart of you to include Flynn.''

Washington nodded. "Can't hurt. Take a look at this.'' He began emptying Jody's duffel bag onto the desk. The

166

plastic bag of white powder came out first. "It's top-quality coke. Tested it at the station."

Ohara picked it up. "The bag's been opened. The girl at Harriet Takai's hostel said it was sealed. Did you open it to test?"

"No, that's the way I found it, secured with a couple of plastic ties."

"Then she's been selling small amounts on the street."

"Yes. I think so," Washington said. "There's a box of fresh plastic bags among her things."

Ohara put the bag aside. "Some of the dealers I've come across would have a heart attack. They measure the stuff grain by grain. She's been shaking it out like salt."

"That's Jody for you. She has a few smarts, but she's not bright."

Ohara nodded. "A one-track mind. Depending on where the track is going, that can be dangerous."

"As I found out," Washington admitted.

Ohara lifted out the rest of the things: the businesslike knife, underclothes, a few small plastic bags of a popular brand, some cosmetics, a pair of jeans and red T-shirt rolled together, a fringed and silver-studded red vest, small change in a coin purse, and a roll of tens and twenties held together with a rubber band.

"Those people who thought Jody might be their daughter are due today, aren't they?" Washington asked.

"Yes, any time now." Slowly Ohara put the things back in the duffel bag. "We'll need to see Jody, but first I'd like to talk to them. If they are her parents, it will make a difference. Meanwhile, I'll bring you up to date on what's been happening." He sat down and leaned back in his chair.

"First off, Macklin says the bullet that shot Bill Stack and the one we dug out of Shimizu's garage are a match."

Washington whistled in surprise. "Go on."

Ohara briefed him on the Stack killing, the Walkers, and Miyuki's identification of Kano as a Yakuza killer. "Spielberg says Kano's been in town for the last two weeks."

"So Shimizu's killing could be a professional hit, as you thought."

"He's one possibility. So is whoever took the gun and used it on Stack."

"And anyone else Shimizu might have put the screws to." Washington looked as discouraged as Ohara.

"Yes. We're going to have to do some homework on that file of Shimizu's. Maybe his boss, Takematsu, can fill in a few names for us, if we push him a little."

Washington shook his head. "I don't think so," he said, and handed over a folded newspaper lying on his desk.

Ohara read the marked paragraph, which stated that Roger Takematsu, General Manager of Guardian Insurance, had fallen to his death from a twentieth-floor window in Guardian's Beverly Hills office building. Friends said Takematsu had appeared depressed recently. The police were investigating.

"Somehow I don't think he fell by himself," Ohara said softly.

"You think he had Yakuza connections who didn't like him fumbling the ball with Shimizu?"

"Yes, that's what I think. It makes me afraid for Miyuki. I'd better give Beverly Hills what we've got."

"Kano might have done Takematsu, too. It's a bad break that he knows Miyuki by sight. If he's had access to Shimizu's file, he knows where she lives."

Ohara nodded, his face grim as he dialed the Beverly Hills police to tell them what he knew.

When he had finished talking to the detective in charge of the Takematsu investigation, Washington said at once,

"Sam, I think maybe we should get Miyuki under protection."

"Spielberg has put a man on it. She refuses to leave her home, but she's probably as safe there as anywhere, provided there are no leaks, and the Yakuza don't make the connection." He sat silent a moment, then said, "Have you read about the Ninja attacks?"

"Yes, in the paper this morning. It's like throwing gasoline on a fire, as far as the Maple Street community is concerned."

Then Ohara told him what he had planned for that night. "I'd hoped to have you with me, Ted, but you've been pounded enough. This could get rough."

"I'm in, or else you just lost a partner, Ohara."

"OK, you're in. Now, this is what I have in mind."

A short time later the phone rang and Washington picked it up. He listened, then said, "Have someone show Mr. and Mrs. Wallis up to the interrogation room. We'll meet them there." He turned to Ohara and said, "The people who think they recognized Jody's picture are here. I said we'd meet them in interrogation."

Ohara stood up. "You go ahead. I'll take the cocaine to Narcotics, brief them, and then join you."

Arthur and Edna Wallis were far from the glamourous socialite parents Jody had claimed for herself. He was a big, sandy-haired man who looked somewhat uncomfortable in his dark blue suit. He began apologizing for being late. "We're small-town folks," he said, "and I got myself turned around on the freeways. Wouldn't want to drive 'em everyday, I can tell you. The wife's a nervous wreck."

"You're not late at all," Washington assured them. "Can I get you some coffee while we're waiting for Detective Ohara?" He was trying to put them at their ease. The stark, green walls of the interrogation room intimidated most people, but there was nowhere else they could talk.

Mrs. Wallis shook her head. "No, thank you, Mr. Washington, we just want to know about . . . about our daughter." She was a small, pale woman with dark hair graying at the temples, faded blue eyes, and a nice smile. Her fingers worked restlessly at the large black handbag she held on her lap. "I brought some pictures of our Jane," she said.

Ohara came in and was introduced. "I know this is difficult for you." He smiled at Mrs. Wallis, hoping to make her less tense. "Did I hear you say your daughter's name was Jane?"

"Yes, Jane," she answered.

"The girl described in the bulletin calls herself Jody," he said gently. "Jody Baxter."

The woman looked over at the man, who sighed. "I told Mother it wasn't the right name, but she insisted on coming. It's Jane Wallis we're looking for. Why would she call herself Jody?"

"Our Jane never liked her name," the woman said timidly. "She was always trying to get us to call her something else. One time it was Gloria, another time it was Karen. Remember?"

"Yes, forgot that. Don't know why she didn't like the name Jane. That was my mother's name. We're not fancy folks; I'm a carpenter and Edna works in a supermarket. When we adopted our daughter, we named her Jane, after my mother."

"You're daughter is adopted?" Ohara was interested. He'd been having trouble accepting these people, nice as they were, as parents of the girl he knew as Jody.

"Yes. We were a bit old to adopt a kid, but Edna here, she wanted a little girl real bad. So I said, 'What the hell, why not?' And we did it."

170

"She was three years old when we got her from the orphanage," Mrs. Wallis said softly. "Such a pretty thing, like a little princess, even at that age."

"Pretty is as pretty does," Arthur Wallis said. "You spoiled her, Edna. That's what caused all the trouble."

"What trouble?" Washington asked.

"It wasn't too bad until she got into high school. Then she got snotty. Nothing we did suited her. Should have heard the way she talked to Mother here. Stole money from us, she did. Ran away from home a couple of times, started stealing things from the stores. Looked like an angel, that girl, but if she didn't get her way, she could be a devil."

Ohara and Washington exchanged a look. Mrs. Wallis was staring at her hands as a tear trickled down her pale cheek.

"We couldn't do anything with her," Art Wallis went on. "She finally shoplifted in a department store and was seen by the security police. They let her off with a warning, but told her never to come into the store again. You'd think she'd be grateful they let her go, but no, next day she snuck back and tried to start a fire in the washroom."

He stopped, took out a large white handkerchief, and blew his nose. "Just about did Mother in that time. It was lucky they caught the kid before she'd done any real damage. Court ordered us to put her in Merton School. That's a real strict school for kids with behavior problems. She escaped from there, and the wife's been frantic with worry. That's why we came."

Wallis sat back as if he'd said all he was going to on the matter.

"Please," Mrs. Wallis said in her soft voice. "I brought some pictures." She fumbled in her handbag and brought out a small leather album. "See what a pretty child she was?"

Washington and Ohara looked it over: pictures of a cute three-year-old, others of an older child on a bike, a youngster in a pink party dress, a child next to a Christmas tree, in a school play, and, lastly, a leggy teenager in blue jeans and plaid shirt. The girl, her face innocent of makeup, had curly blond hair, wide blue eyes, and a soft, sensuous mouth. It was Jody.

"Is this the girl you have, Officer?" Mrs. Wallis appealed to Ohara. "The girl who calls herself Jody?"

"I think so," Ohara said, his eyes on the last photograph.

"Then it's my Janey! Is she here? Can we see her?" Mrs. Wallis clutched his arm in excitement.

Ohara hated to cause this frail woman more pain, but he had no choice. "She's being held at Juvenile Hall. When we found her she was a witness to a crime, and, since she said her parents were dead, we placed her in a youth hostel."

Edna Wallis looked as if she'd been struck. Her hands began to tremble, and Art awkwardly patted her shoulder. "Take it easy, hon, maybe it isn't Jane."

"We'll take you to see her," Washington said. "If she is your daughter, you may want to get her a lawyer."

"A lawyer? I thought you said she was a witness?"

Washington looked at Ohara, who took up the awkward explanation. "I'm sorry to tell you," he said, "but Jody attacked another girl in the hostel and escaped. When she was picked up she was in possession of narcotics and quite a lot of money."

"Where'd she get that?" Art was bewildered and angry.

Ohara didn't answer, avoiding what he'd eventually have to tell these poor people. "Let's go over to Juvenile Hall and see if it is your daughter, first of all," he said. "Then we can talk about the rest of it."

Chapter Twenty

Ohara phoned ahead to Juvenile Hall and made arrangements to see Jody, with a legal counsel present. Washington would bring the Wallises with him, but Ohara wanted to talk to Jody first.

She was waiting for him in an interview room with one of the Juvenile Hall matrons and a retired lawyer who donated several hours a week to young people in trouble. The matron let Ohara in, then left to wait just outside the door. At once Jody jumped up and ran to him. "Oh, Sam, I'm so glad you've come. Please, please, get me out of here!" She flung her arms around him, but he made no move to comfort her. At last she stood back and looked up at him with a rueful smile. "You're angry at me, aren't you? Please don't be." There was a hint of tears in her eyes. "I'm in so much trouble!"

"Yes," Ohara said, "you are. Your counsel can tell you just how serious charges of assault and possession of narcotics can be." He left her looking stunned and walked over to the lawyer. "I'm Detective Ohara," he said, holding out his hand. The lawyer shook it, introducing himself as Jacob Myerson.

"Are you familiar with the case so far?" Ohara asked.

"My client doesn't seem to want to talk to me, but I've been briefed," Myerson answered.

"She's a witness in a murder case I'm handling. I'd like to ask her a few questions. Any objection?"

"I'll reserve my opinion on that until I hear what you want to ask."

"Hey!" Jody's shout made both men turn to look at her. "What am I here, a piece of furniture? Sam, listen to me; I can explain everything."

Myerson started to object.

"You keep quiet," she flung at him. "Don't tell me what I can say, or what I can't!"

"I'd listen to Mr. Myerson if I were you, Jody." Ohara looked at her dispassionately. "He's here to help you, and right now he's the only one who can."

"Oh, Sam, don't be like that. You can help me." The whining little-girl tone was back. "I liked your friend Harriet, I really did. But you don't know what happened. That Lisa tried to rob me. Then she attacked me, so I had to defend myself."

"With a heavy bookend? Hitting a girl smaller than you?"

"Don't answer that," Myerson interrupted.

Jody glared at him, but took his advice. "Anyway, I was so frightened that I lost my head and ran away. It's been so terrible for me! Men chased me in a car, and that black bastard Washington tried to rape me and steal my bag. Look!" She was close to sobbing. "See the bruises on my arm."

"Cut it out, Jody." Ohara's voice was cold. "That's a lie, and you know it. There's a witness who saw Detective Washington save you from being kidnapped. Then, when he'd been knocked down, helpless, you kicked and pounded him."

She stared back at him defiantly. "Well, if you want to believe that old bitch. Anyway, I *thought* he was attacking me."

Then Jody grabbed Ohara's hands. 'You've got to help me, Sam," she pleaded. "Make them understand I just made

174

a mistake because I was so frightened. Then they'll let me go."

"I'm afraid not, Jody. When you were picked up you had a large amount of cocaine on you."

"Somebody must have put it in my bag!" she said. Two spots of red colored her cheeks, but her wide blue eyes stared innocently up at Ohara.

Ohara was unimpressed. "You can tell that to the officer from Narcotics who'll be talking to you."

"Why don't you believe me?" Jody sobbed. "Why won't you help me?" Timidly she reached out and laid her fingers on his arm.

Despite what he knew of her, Ohara felt a twinge of pity. He imagined how he'd feel if it was his daughter Susie. No matter what she'd done, he'd help her. Would Art and Edna Wallis help this girl?

Relenting, he said, "I'll do what I can for you. Now, tell me again everything you saw the night Tak Shimizu was killed."

She repeated her story from the beginning, but, beyond eliciting a few new details, Ohara discovered nothing helpful. Then he asked her about the robbery, and what was taken.

"Tak's good watch and some money," she said. "He seemed more upset that they'd gone through his file."

Ohara could well imagine that he had been. It might have cost him his life, as well as that of his boss, Roger Takematsu. He could only hope that Miyuki's picture had been overlooked in a hasty inspection of the file.

"I've some pictures I'd like you to look at, Jody." He opened a large envelope he'd laid on the table and took out the pictures Washington had secured. "See if any of these men were the ones you noticed from the window."

Jody made no move to take them. Her mouth had a sullen look. "I'm always helping you. But what about me?"

175

She turned to Myerson. "He can't make me talk anymore, or look at any pictures, can he, Mr. Lawyer?"

"No," Myerson answered. "But it might help you in court if the judge finds you've been cooperative."

"Oh, all right." She took the pictures and looked through them. "Didn't see him." She handed one of them back. Then, handing over the second picture, she said, "He's the man I saw in the alley carrying something. He had on a jacket with a patch."

Ohara took the picture. It was of Duke Walker.

She pointed to the morgue photo of Bill Stack. "He's the one I saw running away. That's a funny picture. Is he dead?"

Far from being shocked, Jody seemed fascinated. She stared down at the dead man's face, her tongue sliding across her lip. Silently Ohara took the photograph from her hands.

Jody tossed back the next one. "Didn't see him." Then, looking thoughtfully at the last picture, she said, "I saw him." It was the picture of Joe Flynn.

"You're sure?" Ohara asked.

"Well, he was older than this picture, but I was looking right at him. I thought he was sort of cute, with that big dimple in his chin."

"When did you see him? Where?"

"Sometime after the big guy ran out. I don't remember." Losing interest, she handed back the picture.

"Where was he, in the alley?"

She shrugged and looked away. "Where else?"

"What did he do?"

"I don't know. I went away from the window for a minute, and when I came back he was gone."

"Why didn't you mention him before?" Ohara tried to hold on to his patience. If she was telling the truth, Joe Flynn's alibi wasn't worth much.

Jody shrugged. "I forgot."

Ohara was aware that Washington was probably already behind the two-way window with Art and Edna Wallis. "I have some news for you, Jody," he said.

Her face brightened. "Tell me! Is it something good?" Again, with that chameleon change of personality, she was like a youngster looking forward to a treat.

As Ohara had expected, Washington and the Wallises were behind the two-way window. They had arrived just as he'd begun showing the pictures. The moment Edna Wallis saw Jody, she grabbed Art's arm. "It's Janey, our Janey, Art! We've found her!"

"That's her, all right." Art's voice sounded less delighted than his wife's. "What are they talkin' about?"

"My partner is questioning her about people she may have seen at a crime scene . . ."

"She witnessed a crime, my little girl?" Mrs. Wallis was very distressed.

"No, ma'am, she didn't witness the crime, but she saw some people who may know something about it." He did not tell them of Jody's presence in Shimizu's apartment. "I can turn on the sound if you'd like to hear what's going on. That older man is a lawyer." He turned a switch so the voices from the other room came in clearly.

Jody was just then identifying the picture of Joe Flynn. Surprised, Washington drew in his breath.

"Anything wrong?" Art Wallis glanced at him, full of curiosity.

"No. She may have made an important identification."

Edna Wallis smiled proudly.

When Ohara began to tell Jody about them, Edna Wallis leaned close to the glass. "My baby," she murmured, "my little girl!"

"My news is about your parents, Jody. A Mr. and Mrs. Wallis identified a description of you that we sent to Missing Persons. They say you're their daughter, and they're waiting to see you now."

Jody's face was a frozen blankness. "I told you my parents are dead. I don't know anybody named Wallis."

Inside the booth, Mrs. Wallis began to tremble. "Oh, no, you don't mean it, Janey, you don't mean it."

"Come off it, Jody," Ohara said roughly. "We checked your story, and it's all lies. The Baxters never existed. Neither did the aunt you said you lived with in Evanston."

"They did! They did!" Jody shouted. "Those people are lying. I don't want to see them. I won't see them!"

"Why not?" Ohara empathized with Art and Edna Wallis listening behind the window. "They've come a long way to find you. They've shown us pictures of you from the time you were a little child. They are your parents."

"They're not. I hate them!" Jody was trembling now. "They stole me from the place my real parents left me until they could come and get me. I hate them."

Her face was flushed and her voice shrill. "Those people kept me from my parents. They were mean and cruel to me. Wouldn't let me do anything. She made me wear crummy, homemade dresses that I hated. And she was always fussing over me, telling me what to do."

Jody's eyes narrowed. "And him! All he could do was talk about going hunting. If I did the least little thing, he'd beat me, and when she wasn't looking he was all over me. That's why I ran away from them."

Ohara was reminded of how she'd used that story before, and how she'd tried to accuse Washington of rape.

"Do you know what else they did?" she shouted. "They said I was bad, and had me locked up in a prison. I'll

178

never forgive them for that. I hate them! Do you understand that? I hate them!"

"Calm down, Jody," Ohara said, but she paid no attention. "I escaped from that place, and I'll never go back to those lousy, fucking bastards! Keep them away from me. Keep them away!" She whirled and started to run for the door, but Ohara caught her and pulled her back. She flailed at his head and chest with her fists until he pinned her arms to her sides.

"That's enough, Jody!" He shook her and stared down into her contorted face. Suddenly she slumped and fell against him, panting.

Mercifully Washington had turned down the speaker. Art Wallis was holding his wife, his big hand stroking her hair, trying to soothe her heartbroken sobs. "I never," the words dragged out of him, "I never touched that girl, never."

"I know," Washington replied, his face full of compassion.

Art Wallis seemed not to hear him, or know he was there. He kept on stroking Edna's hair, but his eyes were on the hysterical girl pinned like a wild thing in Ohara's grip.

Washington had to look away from the naked pain he saw in Art Wallis's face.

Chapter Twenty-one

It was a painful half hour before the Wallises could be persuaded to leave, since Jody still refused to see them. Tearfully Edna had pleaded that if she could just talk to her daughter, everything would be all right. Art knew better.

The matron took Jody to the infirmary. She would not be permitted to talk to anyone until her condition had been evaluated by a physician. For that, Ohara was profoundly grateful.

Art Wallis, having been informed of the charges against Jody, asked to see the lawyer who'd been with her. Myerson talked briefly with him and agreed to continue as Jody's counsel. Art thanked him. "We aren't rich, but we'll stand by her as best we can." He gave Myerson their address and wrote a check for a small retainer.

As they were leaving, Edna caught hold of Ohara's arm. "Please let us know about her," she began, then broke down into tears. Her husband quickly said their good-byes, got her into the car, and drove off.

Ohara turned to Washington. "You heard what Jody said about Flynn being on the scene?"

"I heard, Sam, and how she just forgot to tell us about it. She changes her story too much to suit me."

"Me, too," Ohara said, "but we can't ignore it."

"No," Washington agreed, "but even if Flynn did show at Shimizu's, as she claims, I don't think he'd have had time to commit a messy killing, get cleaned up, drive to

Venice, search around, and meet the junkie by nine o'clock. Even without his testimony, I can check the Dugans as to what time Joe brought young Mike to the motel."

"I think you're right about the timing, Ted. Maybe the report of the neighborhood check the patrol officers did at the scene will give us some more."

Washington sighed. "I don't know about you, partner, but I think we need a break before the caper tonight."

"I'm with you on that," Ohara said. "I want to go to the hospital to see Jim, then home until it's time to take on the Ninja."

Washington had something else in mind. Her name was Mindy; she was a bunny at the Playboy Club and crazy about him. After what had gone down the past few days, he realized how much he wanted to see her. Just being with her made him feel good. "I'm heading home, too," he said. "Got to feed Irish and catch up on some neglected business. See you at eleven."

Ohara grinned as he watched Washington walk off whistling. He'd met Mindy, and by the look on his partner's face he guessed exactly what it was he would be catching up on.

By midnight the tiger trap was baited and waiting. There were still some ifs about its success: *if* the Ninja would strike that night; *if* they would take the bait.

There was little Ohara could do about the first uncertainty, but it was likely that they would want to follow up their first easy success. The bait, a small café, had been made attractive. The partially curtained front window showed the cook-owner sitting at the counter going over his books. The real owner had turned his café over to the police for the operation. It was Washington, who looked quite convincing in a stained white apron and T-shirt, sitting behind the

181

counter checking cash and noting figures in a book. A back window was left slightly open.

They had worked things out with Jack Brady, who was handling the Ninja case, to make the café a tempting target. Uniformed officers made themselves visible in the general business area. On orders, the drive-by patrol cars barely glanced at the café, which was more or less isolated between a vacant lot and an empty building.

Following Ohara's instructions, Washington would play it dumb and scared, letting the wire he wore pick up whatever the Ninja had to say. Brady's men would be ready to make the pickup when he gave the signal that a break-in had gone down. His gun was hidden under the counter. Ohara had insisted on a flashlight as well.

Washington had whistled in surprise when his partner had taken off his gray-and-white sports jacket to reveal the tight-fitting black clothes he wore underneath. "All the better to be invisible in," Ohara had quipped. Then he'd removed his shoes and donned a pair of black *tabi,* the Japanese soft-soled socks with a separate space for the big toe. Then he drew on black hand coverings and pulled a black wrap-around headpiece from his pocket. When it was in place, only his eyes showed.

"You look like a refugee from a kung fu movie, Sam."

Ohara winked. "If our friends want to play Ninja, why not? Except this time it won't be a frightened old man waiting for them. Or, forgive me, Ted, a worn-out cook."

"I look pretty good, huh?" Washington was proud of his histrionic abilities.

"Too many muscles showing," Ohara said, "but you'll do."

Then the waiting began, with Washington at the counter and Ohara just another shadow in the back storeroom. He stood next to the light switches facing away from the lighted front room, his eyes adjusting to the darkness.

Time passed slowly. It was beginning to look as if no one was coming. Washington stretched his shoulders and looked at his watch. Suddenly Ohara, who had been staring at the slightly open window, saw it begin to inch upward. A black shadow seemed to glide through it and drop to the floor, followed by another shadow to be swallowed up in the greater darkness of the room.

Steve and Rudy remained motionless until they could get their bearings. Their Ninja outfits made them crouching blobs of darkness in the scant light from the window. Then Steve touched Rudy's arm. Together they ran to the lighted doorway and burst into the small dining room, where a black man pored over an account book.

"Ninja!" Steve shouted as he threw a pointed silver star. It barely missed the man's cheek as he ducked and covered his head with his arms. "Hey, what's happenin'? Who are you guys?" He stared at them, terrified.

The two black-clad figures moved toward him, the shorter one twirling a spiked ball on a chain. "We're Ninja," the tall one repeated. "We've come to avenge the wrongs done the Japanese."

It was like dialogue from a bad play. If these two were Japanese, Washington thought, he was a Mongol. Mindful of the recorder, he took his cue. "What you talking 'bout, man? I ain't done nothin' to nobody. Some of my best friends is Japanese."

"Lies!" A black-clad arm swept salt and pepper shakers, napkin holders, and sugar bowls from the counter.

The shorter figure drew up a leg to kick, but, seeing only solid padded booths, put it down again and settled for swinging the ball against the counter.

"Look, man," Washington said, "I'm oppressed, too. What you wanna do me like this for?"

183

"We'll do more," he was told, "unless you hand over that money!"

Washington cowered as the short one began to whirl the metal ball and chain nearer and nearer his head. "Shit, man! You got it!" He grabbed the bills on the counter. "Take the money, but please, man, don't hit me with that thing." Suddenly the lights went out.

Rudy gasped and jerked in surprise, which made the chain reverse. The ball hit him on the cheek and the chain began to wind around his head. The heavy ball thumped his head and shoulders as he clawed at the chain. Then he felt an arm close around his neck, and a pressure behind his ear. Without a sound, he slipped to the floor, unconscious.

"Rudy!" Steve shouted, his voice skidding high in fear. He stretched his arms out in the blackness like a blind man. "Rudy, help me!"

There was a soft shush of sound behind him, then two human legs fastened themselves around his waist like a vise. His body seemed to twist in the air, then crashed to the ground facedown. He had no breath even to scream as he was lifted like a rag doll and his arms were folded behind him. Then he was turned onto his back, and two heavy weights pinned his shoulders flat. He was so terrified that he pissed in his pants; a warm wetness ran down his legs.

Suddenly the beam of a flashlight searched the room and found him. What Steve saw then frightened him more than anything else. A figure shrouded in black, with only the eyes visible, was kneeling on him. A hand ripped off his head covering. All he could see was a pair of terrible eyes staring down at him.

"You dare call yourself Ninja?" a voice hissed. "Ninja do not harm the weak and old. You will be punished."

"No . . . please . . ." Steve screamed.

"Then confess what you have done to the police and you may live," the voice went on. "If you lie, you will learn what Ninja punishment is. You cannot escape."

"I'll confess. I'll tell them," Steve babbled. "Please . . . don't hurt me . . ."

A hand came up under his throat, and the voice was close to his ear. "You will speak of me to no one. I come from the shadows; I will know what you do."

Then Steve felt a slight pressure behind his ear, and plunged into oblivion.

The lights flashed on, and Washington stared at the bodies on the floor. "My God, Sam. Have you killed them?"

Ohara stood up and removed his black headpiece, "No. They're unharmed; they'll come around in a few minutes. But they'll remember this more than a tap on the wrist from some sympathetic juvenile judge." He went over and stood looking down at the figure with the iron ball and chain around its neck. Then he bent and peeled the mask from Rudy's pimply face.

"That little bastard meant to hit me," Washington said.

"Yes," Ohara agreed. "They're only boys, but already well practiced in fear and cruelty."

There was a banging on the door. Washington grinned at Ohara. "Sam, the recorder caught only what they said in the beginning. Wires got tangled or something. Didn't get any of your act at all. How about that?"

Ohara smiled knowingly. "Too bad. Nothing unusual for a defense attorney to play with. But I think they'll talk, don't you?" He walked into the back room.

Washington opened the door for Brady, who walked over and looked down at the culprits, who were beginning to stir. "I'll be damned," he said. "They're just a couple of kids."

185

Ohara came in from the back room, his jacket and shoes on again. "All secure back there," he said. "I've closed the window."

"How'd it go?" Brady asked.

"About as we expected," Ohara answered. "You guys herded them here; they climbed in the back window; my partner kept them occupied until I came in from behind and stopped the game."

"We had a little trouble with the lights," Washington said. "They banged themselves up trying to get away."

Brady looked at him straight-faced, then nodded. "Those things happen."

Two patrolmen had pulled Steve and Rudy to their feet. The boys seemed almost glad to see them, and went out without a word. As they were being put into the patrol car, Steve kept jerking his head around to look into the shadows.

At the station the two of them were read their Miranda rights and their parents notified. When they were questioned, Steve admitted to everything and Rudy followed suit. Asked what happened at the café, all they seemed to remember was that the lights went out and they must have fallen in the dark.

Steve said nothing about the real Ninja who'd come in like a shadow and told him he deserved to die. He was too afraid. The Ninja could be anywhere; they knew everything. He might come back.

When it was all over and a tired Washington and Ohara were heading for their cars, Washington said, "You sure looked like the real thing, Sam."

Ohara looked at him, his expression unreadable. "Yes," he said, and smiled.

"Well, this should calm things down on Maple Street a little." Washington stretched his shoulders and yawned.

Just about then, not far from Maple Street, the owner of the Maruchan grocery, Niko Watanabe, was locking the door of his shop. Someone fired two shots at him, missing him by inches as the bullets slammed into the door above his head.

Chapter Twenty-two

Hiding behind a parked car on the dark and almost deserted street, Benny Polser had simply pointed the small black gun and fired. His intention has been merely to shoot up the window of the grocery store that had once been his, but when its present owner, Watanabe, had come out, an urge to punish the Japanese who had made a success of his failed enterprise overwhelmed him.

Now he was running away. He slowed as he reached the back of Flynn's Pub, walked around the side, and went in the door. The jukebox was playing, which probably accounted for the fact that the shots hadn't been heard. For once he was glad that nobody ever seemed to notice him.

He slid into an empty stool at the bar and ordered a beer. By the time he had finished it, he was glowing at the thought of his own cleverness. Nobody but Joe had greeted him, but he didn't care. Before long he heard the siren of a police car approaching. It passed the pub, no doubt on its way to check out the shooting at the Maruchan grocery.

On impulse he called Joe over and asked for a whiskey. Even though he preferred beer, whiskey seemed more appropriate to his new status; the new Benny Polser was a dangerous man. He wished he could tell these wimps what he'd done. They'd respect him then, all right.

He stayed until closing time, every now and then pressing his arm close to his pocket, enjoying the hard feel of the gun against his body. He wondered if the Jap cop would come in tonight; then he began to fantasize how he would follow him out into the darkness, slip up behind him, and shoot the little gun. The thought scared him some, but like last time when he'd thrown the rock, he would be gone long before anyone guessed what had happened. No one knew the side streets and back alleys like he did.

He asked for another whiskey. Surprised, Joe poured it for him. Benny drank it slowly, reliving the night of Shimizu's killing. He remembered how careful he'd been to park the van well down the street when he'd seen Bill Stack run up into the driveway. He wished he hadn't crawled in behind that prickly hedge by the building; it had been uncomfortable, and he couldn't see much. He'd just caught a glimpse now and then of Bill messing around Shimizu's car. Then the Jap had come running across the alley, shouting. When the gun had gone off, he'd almost jumped out of his skin.

He'd tried to back out of the hedge, but then Bill had run past, his arm hanging down, dripping blood, so he'd decided to stay put. And that was a good thing! Because it was then he'd spotted the tall Japanese in the shadows of the garage across from Shimizu's.

Benny still wondered what the guy had been looking at. It had really spooked him the way the Jap had stared across at Shimizu's garage with that funny look on his face. That was when he'd tried again to back away from the hedge and it had caught on his hair and clothes.

"What's on your mind, Benny?" Joe's voice startled him, and he looked up, dazed.

"Nothin', Joe," he said, and took another sip of his drink.

Joe took the hint and went to talk to a guy farther down the bar.

Benny smiled to himself; if Joe knew what he'd really been thinking about, it would have rocked him. He took another drink and was back again under the hedge, trying to make it all come clear. He'd heard somebody run down the alley, but because of the way he was pinned all he could see was a flash of legs.

After a long wait he'd managed to free himself enough to look over to where the Jap had been. He was gone.

Benny gulped at his drink. Would the Jap pay him to keep quiet about what he had seen? For a moment the thought danced in his mind, but with sudden certainty he knew what such a man would do. Even in the safety of the bar, Benny shivered, and was glad the Jap did not know where to find him.

His feeling of well-being was shattered. The whiskey tasted foul. He shoved it aside, then remembered why he'd ordered it. He thought about how he'd finally stood over Shimizu's body and what he'd dared to do. His hand tightened around the gun. Having it had changed his life. He was still smiling happily to himself when Joe told him it was time to go home.

He walked the short distance to where he lived, lost in his new daydream. As he climbed up the drainpipe to his room, he wondered what the papers would say about the shooting at the Maruchan grocery.

The next day the story of the phony Ninja was on the news. Ohara listened to it on the car radio as he drove to work. Detectives, no names given, were credited with cracking the case in record time. It was hoped this would relieve the recent tensions in the Maple Street neighborhood.

Ohara knew the papers would make the most of the story later on. It was good PR, and Krauss would be happy.

Unfortunately the next item of news, which was the shooting at the owner of the Maruchan grocery, was, in its way, worse than that of the Ninja. A man had almost been

190

shot to death, though according to the news report there was no explanation for the assault.

When he reached the station, Ohara checked the reports on the incident. They gave him little except that the two bullets that had been recovered were from a small handgun. Watanabe, the victim, had seen nothing and could think of no one who would want to kill him.

Ohara knew that Bert Macklin would be interested in those bullets, too. He went looking for him, and found him just coming out of Krauss's office. His face was red and his lips tight. "If you're thinking of going in to see the old man, don't," Macklin warned. "He chewed my ass good because we've had another shooting. I don't have the ballistics report yet, but I bet they're the same caliber as the one that killed Stack."

Prudently they began to walk back down the hall. "That's four bullets fired," Ohara said, "including the one in Shimizu's garage, two sure matches, and two more, likely. It's not good."

"Yeah, we got a crazy running around with a small gun he likes to shoot. I wonder where he'll put the next two bullets." For once, Bert wasn't his cheerful self. His big shoulders slumped despondently and his eyes showed he was worried.

"Any results from your canvass of the neighborhood around Bill Stack's apartment?" Ohara asked.

Bert sighed. "No. The only nibble we got was a guy walking his dog, who saw a kid jogging across the street. Kid wore a two-tone jacket. Not much help. It seems like every kid in sight has a two-tone jacket."

Ohara shrugged in sympathy.

"Seen the paper, Sam?"

"No."

"There's a story in it about how Bill Stack may have been killed in revenge for what he said about the Japanese. That's going to make a lot of people edgy."

"Yes, it will," Ohara said. "I thought getting rid of the Ninja threat would help the racial climate, but a story like that and the Watanabe shooting will have everybody up in arms again. By the way, what background do you have on Stack's friends?"

"He hung around with a couple of guys named Erne Smith and Benny Polser. Erne was home with his wife and brother-in-law watching TV when Stack was killed. I found Polser at the drugstore where he does deliveries. He claims he was in bed asleep. Says he got up about ten to check on his invalid mother."

"Sounds a little pat."

"I thought so, too, so I went to see the old lady, and she verified it. Mad as hell, too, that we dared suspect her darling boy of anything. There was another old biddy there, and she said she was visiting that night when Polser came out of his bedroom and asked them to turn the TV down because he was trying to sleep."

"That's lucky for Polser, isn't it?"

"Yep. Erne Smith, too. So where do we go from here, Sam? You better go try some of that meditating you do. We gotta get something fast."

When Ohara went back to his desk he called Joe Spielberg's office. What Spielberg had to say was disquieting. "We can't find Kano. He hasn't returned to his hotel or been seen with Wakari. We have a man on Wakari, and one working in the warehouse, but all they come up with is that he's planning to return to Japan shortly. His Beverly Hills house is closed and the servants dismissed. He's staying at the Biltmore."

192

"Too bad you can't get a look in the house," Ohara said.

"Forget it. We'd never get a warrant on what we've got so far."

"I'm worried about Miyuki."

"I know, Sam. I've had a man on her, too, but I can't justify it much longer."

"Justify it or not, you've got to keep him on until you find Kano!" The intensity of Ohara's feeling was evident even over the telephone.

"OK, Sam, keep your shirt on. Nothing's going to happen to her. She's part of our case, too."

Ohara hung up, thinking that Miyuki was more than just a case. Maybe if he tried some of his own contacts in Little Tokyo, he could come up with something. He'd check it out that night.

While waiting for Washington to return from interviewing the Dugans, Ohara checked the patrol report on what the neighbors had observed at the scene. It wasn't helpful.

He took out Shimizu's files and the photographs, and concentrated on them with a one-pointedness that blotted out everything else. These were Shimizu's victims; all had reason to kill him.

After two hours of work checking the developed negatives against Shimizu's notes and his legitimate insurance files, Ohara uncovered a few solid leads. From the license number of a car in one photograph he located the name of an owner to interview. Immigration would have to be checked on two others. Another looked like a make for Narcotics.

Shimizu's notes appeared to be places—many of them out of state, some in Japan—dates, and amounts of money. The records he was able to match up with Miyuki and Joe Flynn gave him a few clues about Shimizu's cryptic shorthand. He wondered why the man had kept such notes. Maybe they were an accounting for a partner, possibly Roger Ta-kematsu. Most likely, careful bookkeeping was necessary when blackmail was a volume business.

When Washington got back, Ohara was still at it. "How did it go with the Dugans?" Ohara asked, stretching his arms above his head to relieve the stiffness in his shoulders.

"They didn't want to talk at first," Ted replied. "So I laid it out for them. I told them we weren't narcs and not interested in young Mike, but we needed to confirm Joe Flynn's alibi for all of Wednesday evening.

"After a little more persuasion Dugan admitted that Joe had called him that night a little before seven. He said he thought young Mike was in Venice, and as soon as he'd given his wife her dinner he was going to look for him. Once he found the kid, he was going to bring him to the motel, so Dugan could pull him through cold turkey."

Ohara thought about that. "It tentatively places Joe at home at seven o'clock, maybe for half an hour. Jody said it was already dark when she heard the shot, which puts it around seven-thirty that Stack ran out of there. She saw Flynn shortly after that."

"Timewise, Joe's boxed in," Washington admitted, "but I still don't think he could have done it and made it to Venice. Have you checked the patrol report on what the neighbors saw?"

Ohara smiled, dug out the report, and handed it to him. "No joy here. Just about what we heard verbatim. We'll have to dig it out ourselves."

"Well, let's get at it."

"Hold it, Ted. We've a few things to check." Ohara filled his partner in on what he had dug out of Shimizu's files. "We've got to talk to those people. Today."

"My feet ache already." Washington sighed. "Let's have a Code Seven first, I'm starved. I could go for a bowl of noodles."

"No hamburger with onions?" Ohara stood up, grinning, and put on his jacket.

"What's with you, man? Ain't you got no Japanese solidarity?"

Ohara patted his stomach thoughtfully. "You are right, honorable partner." He smiled. "After noodles, we'll have much more solidarity. Let's go!"

At Takemura's little restaurant they had not only noodles, but sushi, yakatori, vegetables, and rice, all topped off with a mountain-grown green tea.

They then plunged into an exhausting round of investigation, checking leads with Motor Vehicles, Immigration, and Narcotics. When this yielded a name or an address to match someone in one of the photographs, they tracked down the individual, or, if that wasn't possible, talked to neighbors and friends. One man had died, two others had been deported, another was in jail. All of them held policies with Guardian Insurance. The three possible victims they managed to track down and talk to all had verifiable alibis for the night of the killing.

The address for Carmelita Flores turned out to be a run-down stucco bungalow with peeling paint and broken steps. Mrs. Flores came to the door with two little ones hanging on to her skirts. Four older kids stood silently behind her. She seemed terrified to see them. "Please," she begged, "don't take my babies. Tell Mr. Shimizu I will have the money next week."

They produced their IDs, which seemed to frighten her just as much. "What you want?" she asked. "Did he send you here?"

When they finally made her understand that Mr. Shimizu had been killed and they had not come to collect her payment, tears rolled down her cheeks. "Mother of God," she whispered, "thank you!"

"Don't worry," Ohara said. "No one will come to ask you for money again. If anyone bothers you, call me." He gave her his card, which she looked at, then clutched to her chest. She watched silently as they walked back and drove away.

Washington looked down at the list in his hand, and with his pen scratched out the name of Carmelita Flores. "Where to now?"

"It's already late. Let's go over to Shimizu's apartment building and do some checking with the neighbors. It's just past dinnertime, so they should be home."

For once they got a break. The neighbor on the right of Shimizu's apartment had been expecting company the night Shimizu had been killed, and had been watching out the window. He looked at Joe Flynn's picture and said at once, "Yeah, I saw a guy something like him that night. He drove up, parked his car across the street, but didn't get out. Just sat there looking over at the apartments. I thought that was funny, so I called my wife and we both watched him. Pretty soon he got out of the car and stood in the driveway."

"Did he go down the alley?" Ohara asked.

"No. He walked up the driveway and right over to Shimizu's door. He rang the bell, waited, rang again. No one answered, so he went back to his car and drove away."

"About what time was that?"

"I'm not sure. A little before quarter of eight, I think."

The two detectives thanked the man and left. "That seems to clear Joe, doesn't it?" Washington said. "He was in sight of the neighbors from the time he got to Shimizu's until the time he left."

"Yes, it looks like he's clear," Ohara agreed, "but I still want to talk to him."

It was a short drive over to the pub. When they entered, Joe was at the bar. He froze when he saw them. "Take over, Barry," he said, and with a resigned look motioned them over to a booth. "I've been expecting you," he said as they sat down.

The big man looked almost haggard. "I heard you went to see my brother-in-law. He called and told me what you said about Mike. Thanks for that. I'll tell you what you want to know. Just don't go talking to my wife."

"Tell us, then, Joe," Ohara said quietly.

Joe took a breath, then looked him in the eye. "I didn't kill Shimizu. Oh, I wanted to. I even thought of ways to do it. But I couldn't because of Mary and Mike. They haven't anybody but me."

"Why did you go to Shimizu's apartment the night he was killed?"

"You know about that, too?" Flynn was obviously shaken. "I wanted to plead with him not to hurt my son. When I'd told him earlier that I couldn't pay the extra money, he said he had some friends who would take it out on Mike. I don't know what I thought I could say to him, but when I got to his apartment he wasn't there. So I went to Venice to try to find Mike and put him somewhere safe."

"Dugan's place," Washington said softly. "You should have told us."

"I was afraid you'd turn Mike in. I couldn't let that happen again. Maybe this . . ." He let the forlorn hope remain unspoken. Then he looked from Washington to Ohara. "That's it. I've told you all the truth now, whether you believe it or not. I didn't kill Shimizu."

"We believe you," Ohara said. He didn't mention the witness who had had Flynn in sight from the time he arrived at Shimizu's until the time he left.

197

Joe slumped back against the leather booth. "I thought you'd come to take me in." The nightmare he'd been living showed in his face. "I had to help Mike, and I couldn't let Mary know. She thinks he's away in the Peace Corps."

Tactfully, Ohara changed the subject and began questioning him about the night Shimizu was in the bar. "Tell me what happened from the time Erne and Stack came in."

"Actually Stack came in with Erne and Benny Polser. They were drinking and listening to the story of the Victor Chin case on TV. You know the one?"

Ohara nodded.

"Stack was going on about the Japs ruining the country and costing him his job. Then Benny chimed in about how they took away his father's grocery."

"A grocery?" Washington asked.

"Yeah, Benny's folks owned a little grocery store near here. When his dad died, Benny took over and ran it into the ground. He was lucky a Japanese couple bought it. It killed Benny that they made a go of it. It's called the Maruchan grocery now."

Ohara looked at Washington and stood up. "Thanks, Joe. Benny should be home now. I think we'll go have a talk with him." Then he got directions to Polser's house.

It wasn't far. As they drove down the ill-lit street where Benny lived, Washington said, "He looks good for it, Sam."

"Trouble is, Macklin checked his alibi for the Stack killing and his mother and another woman say he was home in bed asleep. Whoever killed Stack had Shimizu's gun."

"Won't hurt to talk to them again," Washington said as they parked and got out of the car. A small van with faded lettering on the side pulled up halfway down the block behind them. They didn't even see it.

The Polser house was an old two-story building set back among some trees. The house on one side of it was vacant.

From its look of neglect, Benny didn't spend much time on it. When no one answered the bell, Ohara told Washington to keep trying and he would go around to the back.

As he went around the side he stumbled over a piece of wood. Reaching out a hand to catch his balance, he grabbed hold of a drainpipe running up to the roof. When he looked up he saw that it was within two feet of an open window. He stared at it, studying its possibilities.

The first shot caught him completely off guard. He dropped to the ground as the bullet hit the drainpipe and ricocheted into the darkness.

Chapter Twenty-three

As Ohara dropped to the ground, he rolled to the left into a patch of darkness formed by the branches of an old elm tree. Lying motionless, he scanned the dark bulk of an overgrown hedge, the only possible concealment for his hidden enemy. The sound of the shot, which had missed him by inches, had brought no inquiring lights in Polser's house or the one next door. Ohara carefully withdrew his gun from a shoulder holster and waited.

He tensed at a faint rustle of sound from a few feet away, then relaxed as he heard Washington whisper, "Sam?"

Ohara snapped his fingers twice, a small cricket-sound signal that answered without betraying his position. With the unforgotten skill of a combat veteran, Washington slithered up beside him. They waited, breath stilled, until at last they heard a whisper of sound behind them in the direction of the street.

"Cover me," Ohara said. Gun in hand, he ran silently to the front of the yard. A man, short and slight, was climbing over the fence. Ohara's shout of "Police, freeze!" had no effect. The man fled down the street.

Leaping the fence, Ohara ran in pursuit; he could hear Washington pounding along behind him. The sniper was quick, darting into a side street. By the time Ohara turned the corner, he had disappeared.

Washington caught up to Ohara as he stood checking both sides of the street into which the sniper had fled. "Cut him off around the block, Ted.'' Ohara's voice was soft but urgent. "Try to get some backup. I'll go this way."

Washington nodded and ran back the way they had come. Then Ohara began walking slowly forward. He was grateful that no one was around to be in the line of fire. Two houses farther along the right side, he saw an alley and turned into it, pressing close to a backyard fence. At the end of the alley on the opposite side stood a row of large trash cans. If there was to be an ambush, it would be there.

As he moved carefully in the shadow of the fence, Ohara tried to guess the mind of the man he was pursuing. The sniper could have finished him in Polser's yard, but instead he had run away. Whoever had shot Watanabe had done the same thing. So had the person who had thrown the rock at him from the dark back lot of Flynn's Pub.

Thinking of that, he remembered the hate-filled men who had surrounded him that night in the pub. One of them, Erne Smith, had put his hate into words. His companion's weak, pinched face had smiled ingratiatingly, the smile of a man wanting no trouble.

The impact of his mental image held Ohara motionless. He was remembering Benny Polser looking up at him with his sly little eyes, one hand smoothing the rumpled two-tone jacket on the seat beside him. Benny Polser! Anybody's dog for a bone, whose idol, Bill Stack, had publicly shamed him once too often, who hated Watanabe for succeeding where he'd failed, who'd back off from a fight, but would throw a rock from the safety of darkness . . . Benny Polser, whose alibi had been broken.

Everything pointed to the probability that it was Polser waiting for him at the end of the alley. He wanted to take him now, before he had a chance to slip away again. Ohara had a hunch Polser wasn't the type to have much experience with guns. Assuming he hadn't bothered to reload, there should be only one bullet left in Shimizu's revolver. Besides which, it would take a better marksman than Polser to make a hit in a dark alley. The odds wouldn't get much better.

Through the years, Ohara had learned to trust his hunches, so he decided to go for it. He took a deep breath and let it out slowly, releasing all the tension from his body. Then he began to walk toward the trash cans, his gun drawn but held out by his side. "All right, Polser," he shouted. "It's all over. Throw out your gun and stand up." The sound of his footsteps was deliberately loud in the alley; he was the perfect target. Sweat bloomed on his body, cold and clammy.

Every sense focused on the trash cans at the end of the alley, Ohara saw a small, dark shadow rise up from behind them. "Keep away from me, you Jap bastard," it shouted. "I'll shoot!"

Ohara kept on walking, his eyes on Polser's raised arm stiffly pointing the gun. When he saw the slight, lifting movement of the amateur, he dropped to his knee, a hairsbreadth of a second before the muzzle flash of the gun. The bullet went harmlessly over his head.

Washington loomed up behind Polser, his weapon raised. "Hold it!" Ohara shouted, then leapt at his would-be assailant.

Benny Polser didn't even look around. He was still pointing his little black gun at Ohara, pulling uselessly at the trigger. When Ohara grabbed the gun from his hand, he was crying like a child whose toy was broken.

Benny seemed in a daze as he was cuffed, but he went docilely to where the car was waiting. As Washington put a hand on his head to guide him into the back seat, Benny seemed to register what was happening, and suddenly looked up at him. "My ma," he said, his tearstained face worried, "what'll she do?"

As Washington radioed in a Code Four, "No further assistance required," Ohara chalked one up for Benny Polser. It was strange what seemed to concern people at a moment of personal crisis. Once, he'd taken a brutal ax murderer whose only worry was about who would feed his cat.

"Only friend Ma's got is Mrs. Reilly next door," Benny told them.

"We'll notify her." Washington spoke evenly. "Your mother will be looked after."

Benny clutched at his arm. "Do you have to tell her?"

Ohara let his partner handle it. He knew Benny could never relate to him. As he got into the front seat of the car he heard Washington say, "She'll find out one way or another, Polser. What else can you expect? It's the best way."

As Benny was being booked at the station, Ohara got hold of Macklin and told him what they had. He was elated, and thumped Ohara on the shoulder. "You're good, Sam. Couldn't have done it better myself." He said he would take the gun to ballistics, then join them in interrogation.

Benny had been read his rights, but he had refused a lawyer. "Don't trust no lawyers," he said, then asked for a bathroom. An officer took him there, then to an interrogation room.

While waiting for Macklin to join them, Washington said, "That was a hell of chance you took, Sam. The little creep shot at you point-blank. I was ready to take him out."

Ohara shrugged. "I had a hunch it was the only way we'd nail him alive. He's good at getting away. Besides, I knew he was a poor shot; the only thing he could hit in that dark alley was a garbage truck."

"That's not what they teach in Officer Survival," Washington remarked, knowing as he did so that survival had never come first with Ohara. Getting the job done was what mattered.

When Macklin arrived, they went in to interrogate Benny.

"Who's he?" Benny asked at once, looking at the older man.

After Macklin introduced himself, they began the questioning. Benny was so nervous his voice had a tendency to squeak as he was led through the formalities of his name and address.

Then Macklin said, "We want to talk to you about your friend Bill Stack, son. Some folks saw somebody a lot like you near his place the night he was killed."

"No!" Benny looked as if he might collapse.

"No, what?" Washington asked.

"No, I didn't kill Bill! I didn't hurt nobody. I just did stuff to scare people. I didn't mean no harm."

"You didn't mean any harm?" Washington's disbelief was withering. "Did you ever see what a thirty-eight-caliber slug can do to a man's body? Suppose you start by telling us where you got the piece."

With many stops and starts Benny told them how he's followed Stack to Shimizu's apartment in his van, then hid behind the hedge to see what was going on.

"That wasn't such a good idea," he admitted. "I couldn't really see from there, but I heard Bill messing around in the garage and figured he was doing something to the Jap's car. I was going to crawl out and help him when the Jap comes out of the apartment shouting and swearing. Then I heard a sort of 'plop' sound, and real quick the gun goes off. In a minute Bill runs out, his arm all bloody, gets in his car, and drives away."

"What happened then?" Washington prompted.

"I started to crawl out, but got caught on the hedge. Then I spotted this Jap guy standing in a garage across the alley, and I was afraid to move."

"Describe the man." There was an intensity in Ohara's look that made Benny uncomfortable.

"Big guy, dressed in a black suit and white shirt, like an undertaker. He looked like one mean son of a bitch." Benny was beginning to like being the center of attention.

"What did he do?" Ohara asked.

"Just stood watchin'. Don't know what he was lookin' at, but it spooked me. I lay real still, even though the hedge was stickin' me all over."

"Did you hear anything?"

"Not right away. Then somebody ran down the driveway and around to the right."

"Did you see who that was?"

"Nope. It was too dark."

"Well, go on." Washington sounded impatient.

"I waited some more, then peeked out. The Jap was gone. Nobody was there."

"Then what? Get on with the story," Macklin said. He knew Benny was spinning things out, playing for time.

"I crawled out from behind the hedge, looked in the alley, and saw the Jap who'd yelled at Bill, lying on the ground all beat up. And his head was twisted to one side, sort of funny. I saw Bill's wrench lying beside him, all bloody. Then I saw what he done to the Jap's car. Man, that was somethin'."

"Did you pick it up?"

"No."

"How did you know it was Bill's wrench?" Washington took over.

"I seen it lots of times."

"Did you touch the body?" Washington continued.

205

"No!" Benny looked revolted. "I wouldn't touch a dead guy."

"Where was the gun?"

"Beside him. I stepped on it when I was lookin'."

"So you just picked it up and took it with you?" Macklin wanted to know.

"Why not? He sure as hell didn't need it no more."

"Why did you want it?" Washington asked sharply.

Benny shrugged. "Don't know. Just thought it might come in handy. Look, ain't I been straight with you? I didn't do nothin' bad." Benny's ingratiating smile faded as he looked at them.

"Did you empty the dead man's wallet?"

Benny swore that he hadn't touched the wallet.

Finally Macklin said, "What did you mean when you said you just did stuff to scare people?"

"Just jokes on the Japs," Benny said. "I got the idea from Bill about the tires. But I did better stuff than he did." Even in his miserable situation Benny clung to his little puff of pride. However, no one seemed to be appreciating his cleverness. Nervously, Benny glanced at Ohara. The look on the Jap detective's face made him squirm.

"Just a joke on the Japs, was it?" Ohara said bitterly. "You slashed people's tires, painted 'Fuck the Japs' on the cars and sidewalk. That was for laughs? To frighten some helpless, elderly people? Tell us about the garden you destroyed with acid. A man spent twenty years of his life on that garden!"

Ohara, playing his "bad cop" role to the hilt, stood up as if he couldn't sit at the same table with Benny any longer. He walked a couple of steps away, then turned back. "It was no gag, Polser. You did it because you've been a loser all your life, and you've become so screwed up with hate and anger that you had to take it out on somebody. Especially somebody who couldn't find you to strike back.''

Benny licked his lips and swallowed nervously. He could not look away from the cold contempt of the Jap cop's eyes when he bent over and said, "You'll always be a loser, Polser, because you can't see beyond your own warped little mind. You're a disgusting little wimp.''

Ohara walked away from the table and stood looking out the window. Washington and Macklin had never seen him like this. They wouldn't soon forget the look on his face.

In the silence that followed, Benny shrank back into his chair. The Jap cop had stripped him bare; he felt a terrible sense of loss. Nothing seemed to matter anymore, not even being safe.

He answered their questions in a monotone, only showing some animation when he talked about Bill Stack. "He didn't treat me so good, but he let me hang around. I didn't have anybody else. That night I went to see him I thought everything would be different. I had the gun in my pocket to show him. I was going to tell him what I'd done; he'd of liked that.'' Benny's eyes flicked toward Ohara, whose back was toward them, then went on.

"I told him I knew he had slugged the Jap, but I wouldn't tell the cops long as we was buddies and he gave me respect.'' Benny seemed lost in the memory of how he'd thought it was going to be.

"Go on,'' Macklin said softly.

Benny looked at him, startled. "He just got mad, terrible mad, and grabbed me by the throat. He was gonna kill me! I tried to get the gun out of my pocket to scare him, but it went off, and Bill fell down dead.'' Benny shook his head, still not understanding. "It wasn't supposed to happen like it did.''

Macklin supposed that with a guy like Polser, it could have happened just like that. At least he was talking. Ohara had played his part well. A good lawyer would probably plead self-defense, but they could still nail him on the Watanabe shooting.

When questioned about that, Benny seemed unconcerned, almost proud. "He took my dad's store. He had to be punished." It was a statement of fact, as far as Benny was concerned. He'd chosen to forget that the Watanabes had purchased the run-down store from him in good faith, for cash.

He sat back, resigned. He had stopped hoping, stopped daydreaming. Though he wasn't aware of it, he had a kind of dignity to him for the first time in his life.

When it was all over, and Benny was on his way to County Jail, Macklin went in to tell Krauss that the Stack and Watanabe shootings had been solved.

Ohara and Washington had lost one more suspect for Shimizu's killing. But the tall Japanese Benny had described could be Kano. Now all they had to do was find him.

Benny sat in his cell at County Jail. The admitting procedures had been humiliating and exhausting. Finally he'd been locked into a cell with two big blacks and an even bigger Chicano.

The only bunk left was an upper. He climbed up, feeling them watching him, and sat hunched with his back against the wall. Slowly he looked around the barred cage that was now his home. If only he could see his pictures, he thought. Then he realized that his heroes had betrayed him, like everything else in his damned life.

He closed his eyes, and the tears streamed down his face. Worst of all was when the Jap cop had called him a disgusting little wimp.

All he'd wanted in his entire life was for somebody to like him and show him some respect. Why couldn't anybody understand?

Chapter Twenty-four

It was Sunday, and a day off for Ohara. After the late-night session with Benny Polser, he needed it. Normally he worked straight through on a case, but the way things were there was nothing that couldn't wait until Monday morning. He was glad to have the time with his family, especially since his son Jim had come home from the hospital.

Washington was glad because he wanted to drive Ethel, his antique Ford, in Sunday's rally. Maybe he'd be able to persuade Mindy, the latest love of his life, to ride with him. If she and Ethel got along, prospects for the future would be bright.

Peggy made all the family favorites for brunch. It was one way of expressing her joy in having her son home again. They ate to bursting, laughed a lot, and reveled in the closeness that comes to families who have brushed elbows with tragedy.

Susie seemed to be seeing Jim with new eyes. He had suddenly been transformed from a bossy older brother to some kind of folk hero. Ohara knew the awed respect would not last. Jim, wolfing down his seventh popover with honey, lapped up the adulation and TLC as though it were no more than his due.

Later, at Peggy's not too subtle urging, Ohara gave some needed attention to the grape arbor. Jim watched lazily from the hammock.

Already sweating in the hot sun, Ohara grinned enviously. "Pretty soft, Jim, no yard work for a month, even if you did escape it the hard way."

"Yeah," Jim answered, "lucky me." He was silent for a time, then said, "Dad, we didn't accomplish much with our Asian Defense League, did we? People just got mad, and a lot of kids were hurt. I guess it was a dumb idea. Still, somebody had to do something. You understand?"

Ohara gave careful attention to his pruning, and to his son's words. "I know, Jim. It's always easy to be wise after something happens. The idea wasn't bad, but when you throw down a challenge, you can be sure somebody is going to pick it up. The 'us against them' theory wins some of the time, but it doesn't solve anything."

"It sure didn't solve things around here, or on Maple Street," Jim agreed. "Why can't people understand that whether a guy's white, black, Chicano, Asian, or anything else, he just wants a fair shake and a chance to be happy? Why do we have to fight about that?"

Squatting down on his heels, Ohara looked at him, understanding his mental turmoil. "I don't have an answer, Jim. In my job I try to stop trouble before it starts, or pick up the pieces after it happens. But from what I've seen I know that behind every killing, or assault, whatever the motive seems to be, is some kind of fear. Sometimes the fear is small, even ridiculous, or imaginary. Sometimes it's life-threatening. It comes in all shapes and sizes. The recent Ninja scare was a good example."

"Yeah, I heard. And the Ninja turned out to be a couple of white punks. You did a great job on that, Dad."

Ohara got up and started again on the vine. "It was Jack Bailey's operation."

"Come off it, Dad. Ted Washington came by the hospital yesterday morning and told me all about it. He said you

210

were fantastic. You scared the pants off of those punks. Do you think I could learn to do that stuff?"

"How hard do you want to work?" Ohara asked.

Jim sat up, his eyes bright with enthusiasm. "Hard, Dad."

Ohara smiled at him. "Then you can learn. When you're well again, I'll have a word with Ojiisan."

Jim's face fell at the mention of learning from Ojiisan, who was his mother's grandfather and at age eighty still taught aikido. Long, hard workouts at the dojo were not to his liking. "You mean I've got to practice aikido and judo, all that stuff? I want to learn the real tough moves."

"And where do you think they came from?" Ohara replied. "You have to start at the beginning."

He knew perfectly well what Jim was thinking. He wanted to be what Ojiisan called "a leaping acrobat," like those in the kung fu movies. It would take considerable maturity to get beyond that concept to the reality. The tough moves Jim spoke of were far beyond, down a long, hard road— a way of discipline, pain, and dedication. At the end of it a man attained great physical and mental power. He also learned humility and respect.

It was a way Ohara had learned many years ago as a young man, when his skills in the major martial arts were already polished. One day Ojiisan, who had watched his progress, told him, "Isamu, you have done well, but what I see in your mind and heart is of greater value. It is time for you to learn more."

Then came the long hours of training at Ojiisan's quiet mountain retreat. Every minute he was free from work Ohara spent with the old man. His mind and body were pushed to the limit, but when the training was over, Ojiisan had passed on to him the rare knowledge of a Ninja master.

Bound by custom and teaching, Ohara never spoke of what he knew, even to his wife. It amused him sometimes

211

to think how often Ojiisan had been mistaken for a frail, old man, busy with his garden and his *koi*. Even the students in the dojo, like young Jim, perceived no more than a strict, demanding elder. Only Ohara had been given the chance to know Ojiisan for what he really was.

"Jim!" Peggy's voice broke in on their thoughts. "You've got company."

Jim got up from the hammock and went into the house to greet his friends, leaving Ohara to cope with the arbor. Soon the sounds of the record player were spilling out the open window of his bedroom.

Presently Peggy came out carrying a cold drink. "Some juice, Isamu?"

Ohara accepted it gratefully. "Keep me company," he said as he finished the juice. "I'm almost done."

She did, sitting companionably beside him, and eventually the arbor was finished.

With a sigh of relief, Ohara took Peggy by the hand, drew her over to the oversize hammock, and flopped down, pulling her with him.

"Isamu!" Peggy squealed as the hammock swayed wildly, almost upsetting the two of them. Then, as it steadied, she looked belatedly toward the house. "The children . . ."

Ohara didn't move, except to hold her tighter. "Let them learn something," he said. "I'm showing admirable restraint. If I can't kiss my own wife in my own backyard . . ." He did so, thoroughly, then his hand moved caressingly over her hip.

The music stopped and Jim stuck his head out of an upstairs window. "We're going over to Ben's place," he shouted, "but Susie and I will be back in time for dinner. OK?"

Peggy jumped up, smoothing her dress. "Take care, Jim! Don't tire yourself," she called anxiously.

Jim nodded, and disappeared from the window.

Then Peggy turned to Ohara, her eyes teasing. "You were saying, Isamu?"

Ohara grinned, stood up, and followed her into the house.

The next morning Ohara rose early and went to the dojo for a workout. Then he had a light breakfast with Ojiisan, telling him about the pseudo-Ninja. The old man was distressed that young boys should have done such cruel things in the name of Ninja. Then his lips twitched into a smile. "But perhaps you have taught them a new lesson, Isamu. Of that I approve."

The hard workout had been a good antidote for the problems on his mind, and Ohara was at the station well before the other detectives on the day shift arrived. In the relative quiet, he settled down to study the forensic and other reports on Shimizu's killing. So much had been happening, he hadn't been able to give them the attention he should have.

As he read through them, he noted some small discrepancies. The only explanation so far for the sticky prints on Shimizu's wallet was that Miyuki had left them when she handled it after icing her chocolate cake. Yet somehow he couldn't imagine her going outside to greet her husband with sticky fingers. Everything about her appearance was clean and well groomed.

Nor was there a satisfactory accounting for the bits of silvered metal found near the trash bin.

Ohara's training had ingrained in him a meticulous attention to details; they were part of the truth, and sometimes made the difference between life and death. It wasn't good enough, either, to assume that the small shred of material caught in the window of Shimizu's apartment had come from a cleaner's cloth.

According to the report, it was fairly new, the dye unfaded. He made a note to check with the manager of the building as to when the windows had last been cleaned. Also, to ask him if he had seen the tall Japanese Benny Polser had described.

Things seemed to be narrowing down to Kano, although Ohara wouldn't have thought the neck-twisting was his style. Maybe Joe Spielberg had something new.

When he put in a call to Spielberg's office, Joe did have something. "I was going to call you, Sam," he said. "I talked to my opposite number in Tokyo. Kano's on their list, all right, though they haven't been able to pin anything on him. But get this. There have been a number of killings in the Tokyo area in the past couple of years with one similarity: the neck of every victim had been twisted, regardless of how they'd been killed. Talk on the street says it's Kano's trademark, but no one will testify against him."

"In other words," Ohara said thoughtfully, "it's more a signature than a killing method." It was beginning to make sense to him. "Any trace of Kano?" he asked.

"None. But we're working on it. I'll let you know."

Next, Ohara called the Beverly Hills police. He asked for Tony Gallardi, the detective he'd talked to earlier about Takematsu's death. After the usual greetings were over, Ohara said, "Have you got the autopsy reports on Takematsu handy?"

"Sure, just a sec." In a moment Gallardi was back on the line. "What do you want to know?"

"Will you read me about the injuries to the body?"

Gallardi laughed. "Are you kidding? He fell twenty stories."

"Just see what it says about his neck."

After a moment the Beverly Hills detective spoke again. "Funny you should ask. His neck was twisted. The injuries

214

from the fall were so massive they can't tell for sure when it happened."

"I don't think it was in the fall," Ohara said, and told him what he had learned about Kano.

"Yeah, you mentioned something about him before. We checked with Takematsu's secretary, but she doesn't remember anybody of his description visiting Takematsu before he was killed."

"What's her name?"

"Uh," there was a pause, "Betty Miyamoto."

"I'd bypass her," Ohara said, "and circulate Kano's description in the building. It's possible she's working for the Yakuza."

"Well, thanks for the information." Gallardi sounded pleased. "If you get anything more, give me a ring."

"Will do," Ohara replied. "And give my regards to Masuto when you see him."

When he put down the phone, Ohara sat staring at his desk, wondering if Jody might have seen Kano. She'd come up with new details each time he'd interviewed her. Maybe he should do it again. He only wished he had a better insight into the girl's erratic mind. The Wallises obviously didn't understand her.

The school she'd been sent to was his best bet. He remembered that Art Wallis had mentioned the name. In a moment he had it: Merton School. Checking, he found it was in Fresno, and in a few moments he had the head of Merton School on the phone.

Ohara remembered to ask about Jane Wallis, Jody's real name, and the head, a Mr. Jacobi, remembered her well. "Yes, Jane had problems," he said. "Too bad about the drugs. I suppose now she'll be sent to a correctional institution. Actually we'd come to the conclusion that we couldn't help her here."

215

"Why was that?" Ohara asked.

"Our school is for problem children referred to us by the court. We try to help the youngsters adjust more positively to society. But Jane refused to cooperate. She rejected every overture of friendship and was extremely antagonistic to both the staff and the other children."

"I can see your difficulty," Ohara sympathized.

"What's more," Jacobi went on, "she would go out of her way to pay back anyone who opposed her wishes. We had some nasty incidents. Also, she was a congenital liar, but so convincing that her most fantastic stories had the solid ring of truth."

"I suspected as much," Ohara said. "Unfortunately, she's a prime witness in an investigation here."

"Well," Jacobi said slowly, "in something that didn't affect her directly, she might tell a straight story. In her way she's smart, or maybe I should say clever. She's the only one to escape from the school so far. We're very security-conscious."

"How did she do it?" Ohara asked.

"In the middle of the night, after the last room check, she managed to take apart a louvered window high up on the wall of her room. She did it with a steel ruler, stolen from one of the staff, and a nail file. It was quite a jump to the ground, but not impossible."

When Ohara didn't say anything, Jacobi chuckled. "Surprised you? It just about bowled us over. She was originally in a dormitory, but she caused so much disruption that we temporarily put her in a single room. We won't make that mistake again." Ohara thanked Jacobi and concluded the conversation. This new information gave him a lot to think about. He leaned back in his chair and began doodling intertwined circles on his notepad as his mind searched for inspiration. He didn't even look up when Washington came in.

Ted knew the signs, and sat down without speaking. In a moment Ohara looked up at him. "Did you pick up a record from Property when you turned in Jody's bag?"

"Yes, it's here somewhere." Washington searched in a small file of papers, then handed one across the desk.

Ohara scanned it and read aloud, "One red silver-studded vest, torn, dirty."

"So?" Washington queried.

Ohara handed him the forensic report he'd been studying, and pointed to the item about the scraps of red cloth.

"That's reaching, Sam. Unless you know something I don't."

Ohara told him about his talk with Mr. Jacobi.

When he had finished, Washington looked stunned. "That's hard to believe. You think she might have done that here, too? But you found her inside Shimizu's apartment in a locked room."

"Let's go over there, Ted, and have a look at that window."

They drove over to Shimizu's apartment building and looked up the manager. His cold had improved, but not his disposition. He said a professional crew did Shimizu's cleaning, including the windows, but they weren't due for another week. He didn't know about any tall Japanese asking for the dead man.

That disposed of, he grudgingly took them over to the apartment and unlocked the door. He did not take kindly to being asked to leave.

Examining the louvered window of the room where Jody had been found, Ohara discovered that three of the louvers were slightly crooked in the frame, which showed evidence of being bent. Also, the edges of three of the louvers were splintered. Using his pocketknife, Ohara was able to loosen the metal frame that held them enough so that they could have been taken out. It was a cheap installation for such an elegant-looking building, perhaps because this window was facing an alley. "She could have done it with a kitchen knife," he said.

"No workman with proper tools would have replaced them like that," Washington observed. "That's what I don't understand. Why did she come back in once she was out? Why lock herself in and replace the louvers?"

"I have to guess at that," Ohara answered. "Suppose she had just barely made it out the window and was going down the alley when a car drove in. She could have recognized it as Shimizu's and ducked into one of the garages farther down to hide."

"Yes," Washington continued, "then, when Shimizu went into Miyuki's apartment, Stack arrived. She must have seen the whole thing, including Kano!"

"She must have."

"Then why didn't she say so? You don't think she was protecting him?"

Ohara shrugged. "Why? More likely she was protecting herself. How else could she play the innocent locked-in prisoner?"

"But she didn't need to do that, just for running away."

"She would have to," Ohara said, "if she'd done something more than that."

"Such as?"

"Take the money out of Shimizu's wallet," Ohara replied.

"Why didn't she just take it and get the hell out of there?"

"She didn't need to settle just for what was in the wallet if she found his keys."

Washington stared at him. "So she let herself in the apartment and had a look around for whatever she could pick up." Washington's mind was racing ahead. "The stains on the wallet, Sam. Jody made them."

"Why do you think so?" Ohara realized Ted had picked up something he hadn't considered.

Washington turned and pointed to the rumpled bed in the corner. "Remember Jody sitting on that bed munching cookies while we talked to her? She even offered you one. I saw the bag; they were chocolate chip."

Ohara smiled. "And the report said the stains contained traces of sugar and chocolate. Go on, you're doing fine."

"Maybe she knew about the cocaine, and when she found the keys decided to get it. She had time to search. But why put back the window? She could just have walked out."

"No. Someone rang the bell."

"Flynn!" Washington said. "Then, later, Midori was in the alley, followed by Duke, so Jody was trapped."

"Yes, when Flynn rang the bell she went to the door and looked through the peephole. How else would she have recognized his picture from the dimple in his chin? She couldn't have seen that from the window."

"So she puts back the window and locks herself in the room to wait for the police." Washington shook his head in reluctant admiration. "That kid's got street smarts, and then some."

"It worked, didn't it?" Ohara said. "I never gave a thought to the possibility of Jody robbing Shimizu."

"Well, let's go talk to Jody again," Washington said. "Maybe this time she'll tell us what she saw from the alley."

Ohara was silent for so long that Washington was curious. "What is it, Sam? What are you thinking?"

Ohara began putting back the window. "First, I want to go over to Properties and have another look at Jody's bag."

219

It didn't take them long to go over to Properties. When they signed for Jody's bag and the sergeant in charge handed it over, Ohara opened it and searched among the clothes until he found a red silver-studded vest. Some of the silver studs had been torn off.

"The bits of silvered metal," Washington noted. Then he pointed to the ragged tear in the vest.

"Yes," Ohara said. "It will probably match up with the piece of red cloth Forensics has."

Then he held the wrinkled vest under a light. It had been washed, but several reddish-brown spots had not disappeared.

Ohara looked at Washington, who put their common thought into words. "That sure as hell looks like blood."

"We should have suspected it sooner, Ted, with her lying, her instability, the violent episodes." Even now it was hard to accept. Yet, in his mind Ohara could picture Jody standing over the helpless Shimizu, then calmly picking up the wrench and pounding the hated face to pieces, punishing the man who had wronged her.

"Jody killed Shimizu," he said, "though we may never be able to prove enough to convict her."

Taking the bag with them, they got into the car and drove to Juvenile Hall. When they went into the matron's office and asked to see Jody, she looked at them, surprised. "Didn't you know?"

"Know what?" Ohara almost bit off the words, dreading to hear the answer.

"She's been released to the custody of her parents."

Chapter Twenty-five

"Who granted the release?" Ohara's calm face gave no indication of his angry frustration.

"Judge Margery Whitaker," the matron replied.

Washington and Ohara looked at each other. Judge Whitaker was a softhearted, some said softheaded, juvenile judge. Her record for putting hard-core juvenile offenders on the street rivaled that of a colleague who had once performed a similar service for adult felons, and who'd come to be know among law-enforcement officers as "Turn-'em-Loose Bruce."

"It figures." Washington sighed.

"Who approached Judge Whitaker?" Ohara asked.

"Oh, there was quite a row. Jody became hysterical, sobbing and beating her head against the wall. The doctor tried to calm her, even gave her a sedative, but the poor child only kept crying for her parents."

"What?" Washington exploded the word. "Last time I saw her she was screaming and shouting that she hated her parents and didn't want to see them."

"Well, I heard it, too," replied the matron, "and mentioned it to the doctor. Jody assured us it wasn't true. She'd only said it because she was ashamed of what she'd done and couldn't bear to face them. Why are you here?"

Ohara felt it would be useless to enlighten her. "Nothing for you to be concerned about. Please go on with your story."

"Well, the doctor felt Jody might suffer irreparable damage if she was kept here. He saw no reason why she couldn't be released in the custody of her parents. So we got in touch with Jody's lawyer, who spoke to Mr. and Mrs. Wallis. They said they'd be glad to take her home."

Ohara could imagine how happy Edna Wallis must have been at the news.

"It was really touching," the matron continued. "When Judge Whitaker was approached, she scheduled an immediate hearing. She was very sympathetic, and impressed with what a sweet, well-mannered child Jody was. She authorized her release immediately. The parents took custody this noon."

"Why weren't we informed?" Ohara asked.

"The notification was sent over. That's policy." But by the red seeping into the matron's face, Ohara judged she hadn't been in a hurry to do it. Jody must have given an Academy Award performance to fool this usually hard-nosed woman. Sympathetic Judge Whitaker wouldn't have had a chance. The matron frowned. "Is anything wrong?"

"Nothing we can't handle," Ohara said. After thanking her, he and Washington left. She looked after them, definitely uneasy, hoping there would be no repercussions about delaying the notice of the release.

As they walked to their car, Washington muttered, "Nobody can make me believe Jody was crying for her parents. Not after what we saw."

"I agree. But it got her out of Juvenile Hall." Ohara began walking faster. "Let's go talk to Krauss."

When they entered Captain Krauss's office, he was busy working on a report to the Commissioner and didn't welcome the interruption.

"We have to talk to you," Ohara said.

Krauss leaned back in his chair, studying Ohara's face. "Shoot." He pushed his papers aside and sat back to listen.

They told him what had developed in the Shimizu case, which left little doubt that Jody had murdered the Japanese. "Apart from the case against her," Ohara concluded, "she's unbalanced and dangerous. For the safety of others, she should be in police custody."

"From what you've said, I'm inclined to agree." Krauss chewed his lower lip thoughtfully. "You'll have to get the judge's order rescinded if you want to bring the girl back, or else charge her with murder."

"That would be premature," Washington interjected.

"Right. I suppose you know Whitaker has a reputation of never reversing a decision."

"Yes," Ohara admitted. "But this time she must."

"She'll probably refuse to see you," Krauss commented.

"I know," Ohara said. "It would help if you'd put on a little pressure."

Krauss began to smile. "She'll see you if I have to go all the way to the Commissioner." Like most cops, his opinion of the judicial system was somewhat soured, thanks to judges like Whitaker who frequently laid a heavy thumb on the scales of justice. "Give me twenty minutes," he said. "I'll let you know."

It took thirty minutes, but at last Krauss was able to tell Ohara and Washington that Judge Whitaker would see them at her home in an hour.

Judge Whitaker lived in Brentwood. Knowing her penchant for punctuality, Ohara rang the doorbell right on time, and was admitted by a maid. "Judge Whitaker is expecting you in the library," she said, and led the way.

The library, with one discreet wall of books, was furnished with French antiques and looked like a layout for *Better Homes and Gardens*. Judge Whitaker, seated behind a delicately carved desk, looked up from a brief she was reading and gestured the two detectives to chairs nearby.

She was a tall, slender woman with silver-blond hair, elegantly styled. Her gray eyes studied them as they seated themselves, Washington somewhat dubiously, on the thin-legged chairs she had indicated. She was dressed for the evening in a long-sleeved, peacock-blue silk dress that did a lot for her. In an icy sort of way, she was a handsome woman.

"Gentlemen," she said. "I have an important dinner engagement. So please be brief. What is so urgent that you must talk to me at this hour?" Her voice was unexpectedly deep, and she clipped her words precisely.

"I'll come to the point, Judge Whitaker," Ohara replied, mentally gearing for battle. "We want you to rescind your order releasing Jane Wallis, a.k.a. Jody Baxter."

The gray eyes surveyed him, assessing him as a man, and an opponent. The trace of a smile touched the judge's lips, a tribute to Ohara the man. "Detective Ohara, I see no reason to reverse my decision in this case. I have examined the girl thoroughly, and in my judgment she's been more sinned against than sinning. I have degrees in child psychology as well as law, and I have served ten years on the juvenile bench. Wouldn't you say my experience is adequate to render judgment?"

Washington made a sound in his throat, hastily turning it into a cough, and left his partner to answer.

Ohara was tempted to say that what the judge needed was a crash course in gang control and a few years on patrol, but he opted for courtesy. Judge Whitaker's stubborn chin warned him she would balk like a mule at any hint of criticism. "Your Honor is certainly well qualified in those fields, but this is a special case. Additional evidence has been found that might alter your opinion."

"I doubt it," the judge said.

Ohara called on his reserves of calm, and smiled. "I'd like to present the evidence."

The judge found herself thinking that the Japanese detective had a lot of charm, but she had no intention of being swayed. She looked at Washington. "I take it your partner agrees?"

Washington straightened and, following Ohara's example, put honey in his deep voice. "I do indeed, Your Honor."

Judge Whitaker nodded, satisfied that she had established her dominance. Besides, she couldn't ignore the blunt instruction of the president of the Bar Association, who called her. She had to give them a hearing. "Very well, I'll listen."

Given his chance, Ohara made the most of it and laid out Jody's true history from the moment he'd met her. Step by step he led Judge Whitaker through the evidence showing that Jody had killed Shimizu. "It's no longer a case of possession and assault, Your Honor, but of murder. The girl is dangerous."

Judge Whitaker merely stared at him when he'd finished. "I can't believe that the sweet child I interviewed could be as you say."

"You can believe it," Washington said. "If you've read her arrest report, you know she tried to claim I was attacking her, when I'd just saved her from kidnapping. She beat the hell out of me, too." The judge's expression froze Washington into silence. Lamely, he said, "Excuse me, ma'am. I mean she was physically abusive to me."

"Oh, come now, Mr. Washington. A big man like you?"

"It's in the arrest report," Washington said stubbornly, and clamped his jaws shut in case he found himself in further difficulties.

"I pay little attention to arrest reports beyond the charge," the judge said. "I find the officers are frequently biased."

Ohara did not contest the implied rebuke. The Japanese in him expected some such face-saving gesture before she conceded to unwelcome demands.

"I doubt you can prove your murder charges against the girl, but if she is unbalanced, as you seem to think, she should be under professional care. Therefore," she pulled over a court order and began to sign it, "I will authorize you to return her to the custody of the juvenile authority."

Ohara took the paper she held out to him. "Thank you, Your Honor." He rose, ready to leave.

"One moment." The judge's voice sharpened. "You must be accompanied by a female officer, and the girl must be returned to Juvenile Hall. I do not accept that she is a criminal. She is a minor currently under suspicion. When do you intend to pick her up?"

Resenting her unnecessary instructions, Ohara nevertheless said quietly, "Tonight, Your Honor."

"Tonight? You could give the child until tomorrow, couldn't you?"

"No, Your Honor."

There was a small silence. The contest of wills almost vibrated in the room, but there was something in Ohara's face that made the judge give it up with an annoyed sigh. "Very well, Detective Ohara, Mr. Washington. That should conclude our discussion. I am already late for my appointment."

They left Judge Whitaker's a little after six. By the time they had returned to the station and picked up a female officer, it was seven. Ohara made a quick call to his home before they left, but they did not stop to eat. It was a three-hour drive to Juniper, where the Wallises lived; they could pick up a burger when they gassed the car.

The female officer, a good-looking black woman named Sarah Martin, who had been with the force for some time, was pleasant and had an air of calm competence that Ohara liked. As Washington drove, the three of them shared brief interludes of conversation, but for the most part they sat silently absorbed in their thoughts. Ohara's were not pleasant; he knew that taking Jody—he still couldn't think of her as Jane—would devastate Mrs. Wallis. He was uneasy about the whole situation; he'd be glad when they were on their way back to Los Angeles.

As they neared their destination, Ohara briefed Officer Martin on the case, and the nature of their young prisoner. "Don't worry," she said. "I can handle it."

Juniper was a typical small town. They asked directions to the street where the Wallis couple lived, and were directed to the outskirts of town. As they found the street and started to turn up it, Ohara's stomach tightened. In front of a modest house in the middle of the block stood an ambulance and two police cars. The number on the slightly askew mailbox was the number of the Wallis home.

As they got out of the car, a body wrapped in black plastic was being loaded into the ambulance. Ohara identified himself, Washington, and Sarah Martin to the officer in charge, who turned out to be the small town's police chief.

"I'm Chief Bowen," he said, and shook their hands.

Ohara guessed that in a town like Juniper the chief and a couple of officers probably made up the force. "What happened?" he asked.

"Double homicide. Teenage girl took the father's hunting rifle, shot both parents, and took off in the family car. A neighbor working in his garden saw her through the window with the gun. He was scared she'd look out and see him, so he hunkered down and crawled around to his back door. Soon as he got inside, he called us. Said a few minutes after the shooting the kid drove north to the highway." Chief Bowen looked at the Los Angeles officer curiously. "What are you doing in this neck of the woods?"

Ohara didn't seem to hear him. His face grim, he began walking up the path to the small white house.

227

Chief Bowen stared after him in surprise, then turned to Washington. "He know the family?"

Washington spoke quickly. "Yes, we did. My partner's taking it hard, Chief. He did everything he could to prevent something like this happening."

"What are you talking about?"

"The girl, Jane Wallis, is involved in a murder case in Los Angeles," Washington said, filling him in. "We had picked her up on another charge, but unfortunately she was released in care of her parents. It wasn't until late today that we could get a court order to take her back into custody under suspicion. We busted our ass to get here, because she's extremely unstable. We were afraid of what she might do."

"Too bad you were so long about it," Bowen snapped, then walked to the house, where Ohara was standing in the open doorway staring into the living room.

"Hey, you!" an officer shooting pictures shouted at him. "You're not allowed on a crime scene."

"It's OK," Bowen said from the doorway. "He's an L.A. cop."

Ohara had seen many crime scenes, but this one hit him hard. An old leather recliner chair facing the TV was stained with blood. At about where a man's head would rest, the leather was scarred by two deep holes. A rifle lay on the floor by the chair.

Another officer was working across the room, where an ugly red patch stained the carpet. The small taped outline on the floor marked the spot where Edna Wallis had died. Ohara pictured the bullets plowing into her frail body. Then the memory of how she'd smiled so proudly as she'd shown him the pictures of her little girl came to mind. It too was painful, like salt in a wound.

Used as he was to such things, still a sadness and sense of personal loss filled him. It was almost a shock to hear Bowen's voice at his elbow.

"Rotten shame!" the chief said. "Shouldn't have happened to good folks like Art and Edna Wallis."

Ohara looked at him, the careful blankness of his expression concealing the rage inside him. "It needn't have happened," he said.

He walked away from the house, knowing he would never forget why it had.

Chapter Twenty-six

Chief Bowen escorted his Los Angeles colleagues back to his plain but comfortable office next to the city jail. He had already alerted Highway Patrol to look for the Wallis car; it was a matter now of waiting.

With true small-town hospitality, he sent out for some Chinese food. "The chop suey place is usually open late," he explained as he laid his cap on his desk and ran his fingers through wiry iron-gray hair.

Ohara wasn't very hungry, but he suspected the Chinese food was for his benefit, so when the assorted cartons arrived, he ate with every evidence of enjoyment. Bowen talked police talk until they had finished, then looked at Ohara. "So the Wallis girl is suspected of killing someone in L.A. Tell me about it."

Ohara outlined the case, including how Jody had managed to get herself released, and the subsequent confrontation with Judge Whitaker.

"That's why I like being a cop in Juniper," Bowen said when they had finished. "None of that crap here; no agencies, no criminal-psychology stuff, either. We've just got Judge Harmon, and he's good. Nothing much gets by him; he gives everybody a fair shake according to the law. A cop knows where he is with Judge Harmon."

"Right now," Ohara said, "I'm tempted to ask if you would have any future openings for an ex-L.A. cop."

"I asked the same question of the Juniper police chief twenty years ago, when I was a cop in Sacramento. I'll be retiring next year, if you're interested."

Bowen's phone rang. He picked it up and listened. "Don't you worry, Miss Mason. The patrol car should be out near your place pretty quick. You put your light on, and Fred'll take a look, like always."

He hung up and smiled at Ohara. "Poor old girl's over eighty and lives alone. Thinks she sees a prowler about three times a week. Keeps her happy just to call in and talk to somebody."

"Down our way," Washington said, "there aren't enough cars to roll on prowlers. They're too busy with hard-core crime."

Bowen, who'd been balancing on the two back legs of his chair, came down on all four and picked up the phone. "I'll give Highway Patrol a jingle. See if they've got anything yet on the Wallis car."

He frowned as he took the Highway Patrol report and jotted a name on a piece of paper. Ohara and Washington tensed, waiting.

Bowen hung up and said, "They were about to call. Found the Wallis car abandoned with a flat tire about fifty miles north of here. She's probably hitched a ride. They've put in a roadblock at the interchange for San Francisco. Hell of it is, she may already be past it." He did not say what they were all thinking, that San Francisco was the perfect hiding place. Who'd notice one more kid among the hundreds of runaways already there?

Washington mentioned the Missing Persons descriptions they'd sent out to all major towns as far as San Francisco. "We can update them through the computer. They may pick her up."

231

Bowen straightened. "You make sure to include a Juniper murder warrant on them."

"Sure," Washington agreed, surprised at the suddenly tough look on the chief's face.

"I don't want any jurisdiction hassle with you guys," Bowen said. "You've got a good case, Ohara, but without a confession. And with that Kano guy, who's your only likely witness, missing, you've got troubles. If you drew a judge like Whitaker, the little bitch could get a year on a health farm. Then she's out to do it again."

Ohara nodded. He knew what Bowen said was probably true.

"Here in Juniper," Bowen went on, "I've got a witness who heard the shots and saw the girl with the gun through the window. I want her tried as an adult and put away for good, so no more innocent folks get killed. You understand what I'm saying?" There was nothing genial about Bowen now.

"We understand." Ohara looked at his partner.

"You're coming through loud and clear, Chief," Washington said, "and I like what I'm hearing."

Ohara stood up and held out his hand. "You'll have no jurisdiction problem with us, Bowen."

The chief stood up and took Ohara's hand in a firm grip. "I appreciate that. I'll keep in touch."

They said their good-byes and started the long drive back to Los Angeles.

The next day, Ohara and Washington reported to Krauss. "Damn it to hell!" the captain said. In his agitation he took out one of the large cigars he was trying to cut down on, and lit up. "About the jurisdiction, I'd have done the same thing. It'll piss off Judge Whitaker, though."

"So be it," Ohara said quietly.

"Well, I guess that wraps it up." Krauss had simmered down, and was beginning to look pleased. Then a thought struck him. "Tell me, Sam, do you think that girl wrung Shimizu's neck, too?"

"No. I can see her in a sudden rage, picking up the wrench that was handy and beating his head in. She always got back at anyone who did her a wrong. It took stronger hands than hers to wring his neck. I'd say Kano did it. According to what the Tokyo police told me, that's his signature when he does a killing."

"Beats me why he'd sign a murder he didn't commit, though."

Ohara shrugged. "Maybe he did it because he'd been paid for the killing. After all, a man in his profession has a reputation to maintain."

Krauss looked at him. "Sam, you have the damndest sense of humor sometimes, but I like it." He was already turning over in his mind the statement he would give the press. "Looks like the news should help Maple Street settle down again. The Ninja scare is over. Stack was shot by a white, not an Oriental, and the Japanese guy was killed for personal motives not related to race. That's going to relieve a lot of people's fears, and make us look good."

Ohara was sure the scars left by the events on Maple Street would take longer to heal than the captain thought, but he said nothing.

Krauss leaned back and beamed at them. "You did a good job, both of you!" An "attaboy" like that from him was like receiving a knighthood. Ohara and Washington basked in the unaccustomed praise, but not for long.

"Well?" Krauss put out his cigar in an ashtray. "What are you sitting around here for? I want all the paperwork on file by tonight."

The endless details of the paperwork took all day. They had hoped there would be some word from Bowen that Jody had been found, but nothing came through.

It was late when they finally finished the reports and were ready to go home. They had made it as far as the office door when Ohara's phone rang. Ohara turned back to answer; Washington waited, cursing his luck.

It was Duke Walker. "How much longer are you and Spielberg going to keep my wife?"

"Miyuki isn't here, Duke. Why did you think so?"

"She left me a note," Duke said. "She said Spielberg had sent his assistant, Eddie, to pick her up. That he and Detective Ohara wanted her help with something."

Ohara tried to keep the worry out of his voice. "Did you call Mr. Spielberg?"

"Sure, but they say he isn't there. That's why I called you, Ohara."

"I'll call Spielberg's home," Ohara told him, "and get back to you, Duke."

"You don't think . . ." Duke began, but Ohara had already hung up, and was dialing Joe Spielberg. As the phone rang, he looked at Washington. "Did you get all that? Miyuki's missing."

"I got it." Washington looked as worried as Ohara.

Spielberg answered the phone himself. "No, Miyuki hasn't been with me. Why did her husband think so?"

Ohara told him.

"Miyuki's note said Eddie picked her up?" Spielberg asked.

"Yes."

"Eddie didn't come in today. He said he had personal business to attend to, so I gave him the day off. My God, Sam, you don't think he's a plant? He came to me with a high civil-service clearance. Could they have got at her?"

"It's almost certain," Ohara said. "Remember, Eddie saw her looking at the pictures in your office. If he is a Yakuza plant, he would report it, and if he overheard her decision to testify, they'll know that, too."

"But I've had a man watching her," Spielberg said. "His orders were to follow her when she left the apartment. He'd have reported in."

"Not if she left with your assistant. Eddie may even have talked to your man, told him the witness would be with you."

Spielberg swore. "That little shit—"

"Forget that!" Ohara cut in. "They've got Miyuki. Now, how do we get her back?"

Chapter Twenty-seven

Joe Spielberg wasted no time. "I got a warrant for Wakari's warehouse in Japanese town. We'll use it now. That's the most likely place for Miyuki to be hidden." Like Ohara, he would not admit, even to himself, that she might already be dead.

"I'm going with you," Ohara said. "Tell me where and when."

"Be at the office in forty-five minutes; it'll take me that long to get the personnel organized. We'll leave from there."

Ohara hung up, quickly briefed Washington, then said, "Joe will have plenty of people, Ted. You don't have to come on this."

"The hell I don't, Sam. If those two goons in the black BMW are on Wakari's team, I've got a big score to settle."

"Ted, when you checked the BMW with Motor Vehicles, it was listed to Wakari. What was the address?"

"Some office building in Little Tokyo. What have you got in mind, Sam?"

"I was trying to figure out where they'd take her, if she isn't at the warehouse. Miyuki told us Wakari was a Yakuza boss; Kano was only muscle. She said Wakari liked to watch the girls being punished. He made it last a long time, as a lesson to others."

"That son of a bitch!"

"Miyuki not only ran away, but she gave him up to the police. He'll have something special in mind for her. He may be smarter than we've thought."

"How, Sam?"

"He could have hidden her in his Beverly Hills home."

Washington looked dubious. "Then he'd have to be crazier than we've thought."

"No. Spielberg told me the house had been closed and the servants dismissed. There's a For Sale sign posted. Wakari's living in the Beverly Hilton."

"You might have something, Sam. Do you know the address?"

"I saw it on the report Spielberg showed me. Give me a minute." Ohara shut his eyes, sending every ounce of energy to his brain in one-pointed concentration. Slowly the numbers and street name appeared in his mind like a picture on a screen. "I've got it," he said. "Let's go."

The phone rang again. It was Duke Walker. "We're leaving now to search for her," Ohara told him. "Stay by the phone. We'll be in touch."

An hour later, Ohara and Washington stood with Joe and five muscular officers on the darkened street half a block away from Wakari's warehouse.

The warehouse was a large, concrete-block building. Its small high windows, protected by iron bars, showed only reduced night lighting. A small single bulb glowed in front of the service door.

Joe sent two of his men to cover the loading entrance on the side. "According to our information, they have a night watchman and an armed guard," he said. "So first we'll bang on the door and try to get in nice and legal, waving our warrant." Joe grinned. "If that doesn't work, we'll get in any way we can."

He thumped loudly on the service door, keeping it up until at last the door was opened by a tubby middle-aged Japanese in khaki work clothes. Behind him stood the guard, his hand on his gun.

"Police!" Joe said, shoving the warrant at the watchman. The guard let go of his gun and looked on stolidly as the watchman took his time reading the warrant in the light of the overhead bulb. Then he shrugged, flipped the light switches on the wall near the door, and stood aside. The look on his fat face was complacent.

Ohara glanced at Washington, who read his thought: it was almost as if the man had been expecting them. If that was so, then Miyuki wasn't there.

Nevertheless, they folowed Joe inside and watched the beginning of the search, which was thorough and efficient. The watchman and the armed guard merely observed the proceeding, saying nothing.

After a few minutes of this, Ohara tapped Joe on the shoulder. "I think we should double our chances," he said, "and search Wakari's Beverly Hills house."

"I can't do that without a warrant, Sam. Why do you think she's there?"

"Well, Kano can't just have disappeared. What better place could he hole up in than a closed and supposedly empty house? Why shouldn't they hide Miyuki there?"

"You're making sense, Sam," Joe admitted, looking unhappy, "but it'll take time to get the papers."

"I'm going in now, Joe," Ohara said. "I think you know why."

One of Joe's men shouted to him from behind a pile of crates.

"Is it the girl?" Joe asked, going over at once.

Ohara and Washington followed, but it was something about gun oil.

"We're wasting time," Ohara muttered. "Let's get over to Beverly Hills."

Wakari's house was set back from the street behind a low stone wall. A ten-foot-high iron gate across the driveway bore a sign that read "For Sale," with a telephone number. The house, a stately colonial, gleamed white in the moonlight, remote and sheltered by lovely old trees. Not a light showed.

"Looks empty." Washington had thought they were on the right track.

"That remains to be seen," Ohara said as he grabbed a small gym bag that was tucked behind the driver's seat. From it he pulled out a long-sleeved, high-necked black sweater. Then, taking off his jacket, he put the sweater on, shoving his gun into the waistband of his dark trousers. After removing his shoes, he extracted a pair of black *tabi* socks and put them on.

"Socks?" Washington remarked doubtfully.

"All the better to be quiet in," Ohara answered.

They slipped silently out of the car, ran to the wall, and jumped over it. Using the shelter of bushes and foliage, they approached the house from the side and knelt behind a bush to study it. Every window in the front and side appeared dark. They moved along the driveway to the back. Here, although the shutters were drawn on the outside, a chink of light showed in a lower window. "Probably the kitchen," Washington said.

Ohara studied the scene. The patio on the back of the house led to a pool and changing cabana farther on. "They may have an alarm. We'll have to get them to turn it off and come out, so I can get in there."

"Leave it to me." Washington looked toward the area beyond the back patio. "I'll give them something to investigate that will get them off your back."

Ohara touched his shoulder. "Thanks, Ted. After you take care of whoever you manage to smoke out, better keep an eye out for any new arrivals."

Washington grinned. "Will do. Give me a minute," he said, then disappeared into the shadows around the pool. Ohara moved close to the back door and waited, invisible in the darkness.

Soon a loud clang broke the silence from somewhere near the pool, where Washington had overturned a metal table. A small flow of light told him the back door was opening. Slowly a man emerged, gun in hand. He stood a moment looking around until the sound of someone moving behind the pool house galvanized him. He shouted over his shoulder and began running in the direction of the sound.

A second guard appeared, carrying a shotgun, and called out to the first. When there was no response, he ran toward the darkness behind the pool. Ohara looked quickly around the open door, then slipped into the empty kitchen.

As he had been trained to do, he surveyed the room for information. The table told its own story. Three hands of cards lay on the table, two apparently thrown down, the third neatly folded. Beside the folded hand, a lighted cigar smoldered in an ashtray. That meant three men. Two had run out at Washington's alarm, but one had left the table earlier. Ohara strained his ears for the man's whereabouts. Then he heard the flush of a toilet not too far away and smiled. He slipped out of the kitchen through the open swing door into the darkness of the dining room, reaching it just before the third man came back down the hall to the kitchen. He would undoubtedly follow the others outside and into Washington's waiting hands.

Ohara listened to the intimate sounds of the house. His eyes followed the arch of the dining room that led to a tile hallway. The hallway was dimly lit. A flight of stairs curved to a second story. Ohara crossed the hall to the stairs, and seemed to fly up them to the sheltering darkness above.

A corridor stretched to the right and left, with a smaller corridor leading toward the front of the house. He explored that first, and found it led to a master suite, which was empty. Then he came back and surveyed the corridor to the left. The faintest glimmer of light showed beneath one door, and he heard the sound of a television.

Then suddenly the next door down opened. Ohara flattened himself against the wall. A man looked out, listening, then shrugged and went back inside. The man was Eddie, Spielberg's supposed assistant. He went back in, but left the door open. Ohara slipped over beside the open door and stood motionless, stopping his breath in a way he knew. His sensitive hearing told him Eddie was standing on the far side of the room toward his left. Reaching into his pocket, he took out a dime and with a flick of his wrist threw it into the room toward the window on the right.

It was an old trick, but it worked. Eddie may have sensed the movement of the small missile or heard its faint click against the window glass. In any event, he went to the window to investigate, unable to find anything amiss. When he did, Ohara crossed the pool of light from the open door and moved on to another closed door at the end of the corridor. There was no sound of any search, so Washington must have been successful. It was a good feeling to know he was still on watch outside the house.

Gently Ohara tried the doorknob of the last door. It turned easily. Inch by inch he opened the door onto a darkened room, then stood listening. The room was occupied, judging from the faint, irregular breathing he heard. His nostrils quivering, he tried for more information. The occupant was female, not male: he caught a faint whiff of fragrance. He also detected the acrid smell of sweat and fear.

Slipping into the room, he closed the door quietly behind him. By the tiny light of the palm flashlight he carried, he

241

surveyed the room. A large bed stood in the center of one wall; he went toward it. Suddenly the faint breathing stopped, and he smelt the fear again. He turned the light onto the bed. A woman lay on it, gagged, naked, and spread-eagled, her arms and legs tied to its four brass posts. It was Miyuki. She gave a muffled whimper, deep in her throat. Instantly Ohara bent over her, putting a hand across her mouth. He turned the flash up into his own face for a moment, then back at hers.

Her black hair was a tangled mass against the mattress, her face bruised and smeared with blood. She looked up at him, helpless tears flowing down her cheeks.

"It's all right, Miyuki," Ohara whispered. "I'll have you out of here in no time." He laid the small flash on the pillow and began to remove the gag.

He froze at the sound of footsteps outside the door and, shutting off the flash, dropped down beside the bed. The door opened, and the beam of a large torch shone into the room.

Ohara was surprised that the lights were not flicked on, then realized the guards had been given orders not to use the overheads where they could be seen from the street. The figure behind the torch moved into the room and laid the light on a table facing the bed.

"Lonesome, sweetheart?" For a moment the torch illumined his face as he stood next to it. It was Eddie. He grinned and began to unfasten his pants as he moved toward the bed.

Chapter Twenty-eight

Eddie pulled off his pants and shirt, and approached the bed with such eagerness that he banged his shin noisily against the brass footboard. Angrily he cursed the darkness and kicked the bed in retaliation. Ohara wondered if the commotion had been heard down the hall; then he heard someone call out in Japanese. He knew he would have only seconds to deal with Eddie and face whoever came.

Eddie forgot his discomfort as he eyed the helpless girl and began to crawl up on the bed. Suddenly his head was jerked back by the hair and a strong, relentless hand squeezed his neck. That was all he knew.

As Ohara heard the footsteps coming down the hall, he let Eddie's unconscious body fall and turned his back to the door, bending over Miyuki. A squat, powerful-looking Japanese stuck his head into the room. When he spotted Eddie's lantern, he laughed and said in Japanese, "My turn with the bitch next!" and began to walk toward the shadowy figure bending over the girl. Before he could register that it was not Eddie, the figure whirled and hit both his ears with cupped hands. His head seemed to explode; he knew he was screaming, but could hear nothing. Then a hand like a blade pierced between his ribs and he dropped to the floor. He scarcely felt the thumbpress that rendered him unconscious.

Ohara listened. There was no other sound in the house. He again leaned over Miyuki, removed the punishing gag, and began to untie the ropes that held her.

At the warehouse, thanks to traces of gun oil an alert agent had spotted, they found the first cache of arms hidden in the cleverly designed false bottom of a carton of bicycle parts. The discovery justified the warrant, but there was no trace of Miyuki Walker.

Joe Spielberg was beginning to think that Ohara had been right. Miyuki could be in Wakari's home in Beverly Hills. He decided that, warrant or no warrant, he was going there. But he had walked the tightrope of bureaucratic red tape too long not to watch where he put his feet. Beverly Hills police would not take kindly to another unit barging into their jurisdiction.

As an Organized Crime officer, he could probably weather that storm, but Ohara and Washington couldn't. What they were doing broke all the rules in the book. For their sake, as well as his, he'd better take precautions.

He got the watch commander of Beverly Hills police on the phone. "Two of my detectives," he said, "are entering your jurisdiction. I'm following. We have every reason to believe a female informant is being held in danger of her life." The thought crossed Spielberg's mind that if Ohara had been wrong, his neck was out a mile. But what the hell!

Protocol was protocol. Beverly Hills immediately agreed to assist. "We'll send a car," the commander said.

Joe countered quickly. "The situation is volatile. If you're spotted, the woman will be killed instantly. Do nothing until I get there. OK?"

That attended to, Spielberg grabbed one of his detectives and started for Beverly Hills.

Washington was growing uneasy. He'd taken care of the two guards, plus a third man who'd come out of the house to look for them. The three of them now lay in the cabana, trussed up with the Venetian-blind cords from the windows. He was just about to follow Ohara inside when he heard a car coming up the front drive. It paused a moment with the engine running, then the doors slammed and the car lights began to follow the driveway to the back of the house.

Washington ran over behind the garage and worked his way toward the front. The garage doors began to lift to admit the car. There were two Japanese in the front seat.

The garage door came down slowly, so he knew they'd be using the small door that faced the house. The first man came out and walked a few steps, stretching; he never knew what hit him, and went down without a sound. Then the chauffeur came out and locked the door. When he turned around, he looked into the barrel of a gun.

"Not a sound," Washington said, and laid his finger across his lips to be sure the man understood. "Speak English?" he asked.

"Some I speak." The man looked terrified.

Washington gestured to the man on the ground. "Pick him up and carry him behind the pool." He gestured again, and the man obeyed at once. Soon, the two of them were trussed neatly beside the others.

It took Ohara longer than he liked to untie Miyuki. Her wrists and ankles were rubbed raw by the coarse rope. They had been tied so tightly she could scarcely move her arms or legs. He looked around for something to put on her, but there was nothing except Eddie's discarded shirt. After putting it around her shoulders, he tried to get her on her feet. Her knees buckled under her and she started to fall.

"So sorry," she whispered. "I can't."

He gave her a minute to rest as he dragged Eddie and the other man into the closet. Then he picked her up in his arms and started for the door. They had reached the balcony when Ohara stopped, listening to new sounds from below. He heard a key turn in the lock of the front door. It was opened, and the voices of two men came up to him. Walking swiftly despite his burden, he made his way through the shadows and pressed against the wall at the top of the stairs. He and Miyuki could just see the two men talking below.

Miyuki clutched at him. "It's them," she whispered. "Wakari and Kano." Ohara would have recognized Kano, but Wakari's picture had not done him justice; he had the huge belly and massive chest of a sumo wrestler.

Ohara ran to a walk-in linen closet he'd discovered when he'd first explored the upstairs. Kano and Wakari's voices were loud as they argued about the guards. Then heavy footsteps headed for the kitchen.

Setting Miyuki on the floor of the closet, Ohara reassured her. "You'll be all right here for the moment. Try to get your strength back; we may have to run for it."

She nodded, but there was terror in her face.

Ohara closed the closet door silently and ran for the back room. Now he could hear one set of footsteps returning from the kitchen, ponderous and slow-moving. Not Kano's; he was probably checking outside the back door. Then the heavy footsteps climbed the stairs. Wakari was coming to check on his prisoner.

Ohara pulled the door of the room closed behind him, turned off Eddie's light, and waited, pressed against the wall beside the light switch.

In a few seconds the door opened slowly. Ohara controlled his breath so there was no sound to betray him, but Wakari was wary, standing well back from the open door as he peered into the darkness. "Kano!" he shouted. "Get up here!" Then his plump fingers reached around the doorjamb, fumbled for the light switch, and flicked it on.

Grasping the huge hairy wrist, and turning his body in one swift movement, Ohara jerked Wakari into the room. The fat man fell to his knees and screamed in pain as his arm was pulled up behind his back. The heavy body suddenly slumped forward. Ohara, pulled off balance, had to brace himself to take the tremendous weight and not let go of the arm.

Then, with unexpected swiftness, Wakari threw his immense bulk backward. The maneuver forced Ohara to give ground, but he managed to maintain his one-point balance and hold on to Wakari's arm.

Though the pain must have been agonizing, the big man managed to turn his body and get up on one knee, his free hand clawing for his tormentor's groin. Then the years of painful *yubi* training that had given Ohara's fingers extraordinary strength paid off, as he leaned over and sank a rigid thumb like a spike into Wakari's right side, above the kidneys.

Wakari shrieked once and collapsed, his great weight almost pulling his arm out of its socket. A second too late, Ohara sensed another presence in the doorway.

"Let go of him," Kano said, "and put your hands up." The gun in his hand was pointed at Ohara's belly.

Letting go of Wakari, who fell to the floor half-conscious and groaning with pain, Ohara raised his hands.

In that moment Kano leapt at him and whipped the gun across his head, forcing him off balance. Then he pulled Ohara's gun from his waistband and tossed it under the bed. "Lock your hands behind your head," Kano said, stepping back.

Ohara obeyed. Closing his mind against the pain in his head, he studied Kano's face with care. Anything one could learn about an opponent was valuable in defeating him. This man's handsome face showed vanity, arrogance, and

247

self-confidence, qualities that could be used to goad him into a fatal mistake.

Kano's next words confirmed it. "You're pretty good, whoever you are, but I'd have finished him in half the time." He nodded toward Wakari's prostrate form.

Ohara smiled with contempt. "Perhaps, as long as you had a gun." Imperceptibly he tensed his leg muscles as he watched the spark of rage flare in Kano's eyes. For that split second, he'd broken the man's concentration. It was enough. His body responding as he had trained it, he jumped, at the same time shooting both feet out to hit the gun in Kano's hand, sending it flying over the balcony rail.

Even as Ohara rebalanced himself, Kano recovered and began to ease himself out onto the balcony, braced and ready. Aware that his lapse of concentration had cost him an advantage, he now focused fully on his opponent with a new respect.

Each man watched the other for a betraying eye movement or telltale change in breathing that would signal an attack.

Ohara strung out the tension, moving after him onto the balcony, straining Kano to the limit. If he could force the attack, it might give him the opening he needed.

Neither man saw Washington on the first floor looking up at them. He had his gun in hand, but he well knew that in a close, swift combat like this, he might hit the wrong man. He could only watch and wait.

Kano moved first, and came in with a kick aimed at the throat. Ohara blocked it, caught Kano's ankle, and with a twisting jerk threw Kano to the floor. But the man was a professional. Without pause he threw a ramrod kick from the floor at Ohara's chest, powerful enough to break the sternum. Ohara turned, but Kano's heel crashed against his arm. The blow made it numb from elbow to wrist.

248

Kano jumped to his feet as Ohara dropped back, expecting a lightning follow-up, which didn't come. In a moment he saw why.

From his pocket Kano was pulling a *numchuck*, a short length of chain with weights on the end. Ohara knew that if a man was good at the chain technique, it could be deadly.

Kano smiled, as if he could read Ohara's thoughts. The two men seemed scarcely to breathe as their eyes and minds locked, Kano looking for the advantage, Ohara trying to guess how he would make his throw: the legs, the arms, the head?

Then, like a snake, the chain slithered through the air and wrapped around Ohara's neck. One of the lead weights swung up and hit just below the temple. The pain stunned him so that he rocked backward and tried to grab at the chain. Swiftly Kano was behind him and, grasping the weighted ends of the chain, began to pull it tighter.

As it bit into his neck, Ohara felt as if his eyes were popping out of his head. His brain dimmed, and he felt his strength going. Then instinct, some lesson learned long ago, gave him one last chance to survive. He let his knees drop slightly, then, forcing his last bit of strength into his legs, he shoved his body upward, ramming the back of his head against Kano's jaw. At the same time, fingers rigid, he thrust his good arm upward, trying for whatever he could reach, and felt his fingers sink deeply into an eye socket.

Kano screamed, let go of the chain, and clutched his eye. Ohara, gasping for breath, found his own eyes clouded with a red haze. He staggered away from Kano, trying to pull the choking chain from around his neck, until his legs refused to support him and he dropped to his knees at the head of the stairs.

With a cry of agonized rage, Kano came for him in a stumbling, weaving run. The end of the chain was in Ohara's hands as Kano loomed above him and aimed a kick at his head. Ohara whipped the chain around his foot and jerked. Kano pitched headfirst down the stairs, his own momentum throwing his body up and over in a giant somersault, the chain weights banging and bouncing on the stairs.

Washington ran over to where Kano's body lay, stared down at him a moment, then looked up at Ohara. "You all right, Sam?"

He bounded up the stairs as Ohara wearily pulled himself to his feet. There was an ugly red ring around his throat and a cut on his temple.

"Any others still around?" Ohara whispered, unable as yet to control his voice properly.

Washington grinned. "They're all trussed up and accounted for outside."

Ohara smiled and touched Washington's arm in acknowledgment. Painfully he swallowed, then said, "Wakari's in the back room with two others. Not dead."

"I'll take care of them," Washington said. "Did you find Miyuki?"

Ohara pointed to the door of the linen closet. Washington went over and opened it. Miyuki, crouched in the far corner clutching a pink blanket around herself, looked up at him.

"Hello, Miyuki," Washington said gently. "It's all over; you can come out now." When he held out his hand, she took it with the most beautiful smile he'd ever seen on a girl.

"Washington-san," she said as she stood up. "So thanks you come."

"Thank him," he said, and pointed to Ohara.

She looked at Ohara, leaning against the wall by the stairs. "I know," she said simply, "save life." Clumsy blanket trailing, Miyuki ran to Ohara and threw her arms around him. Then, in a moment she stood back, the blanket a crumpled heap on the floor, and bowed low, her hands on her knees.

Washington could not understand what she said to Ohara in Japanese, but he would never forget the picture of Miyuki in her formal bow of gratitude, long black hair tumbling over her shoulders, Eddie's shirt barely covering her. Somehow it seemed exactly right to him.

Ohara smiled and, speaking softly in Japanese, put a hand under her chin and raised her head. Then, picking up the pink blanket, he wrapped it around her.

As if on cue there was a banging on the front door and shouts of "Police! Open up!"

Washington was already running down the stairs. He opened the door to let in Joe Spielberg, his detective, and a king-size sergeant of the Beverly Hills police.

"Did you find the girl?" Spielberg asked at once.

"Sure did!" Washington pointed up the stairs.

Ohara put his arm around Miyuki and began leading her down the stairs. She shuddered as she passed Kano's sprawled body.

Spielberg was reaching for her hands. "Miyuki, Mrs. Walker, are you all right? We'll get you to a hospital right away."

"No, please," she said. "Not much hurt, just want go home. My husband so worry."

"Don't you worry! We'll send you home just as soon as a doctor checks you out." Spielberg took out a handkerchief and blew his nose, hoping his colleagues wouldn't guess what a softhearted man he was.

"I'd better call Duke," Washington said. "He must be dying by now."

"I come, talk," Miyuki said, and followed him out of the room to find a phone.

Spielberg turned back to Ohara, thinking that this wasn't the man he knew. He took in the black clothes, the *tabi*, and the abrasion circling Ohara's neck. Recognizing a garrote mark when he saw it, he decided not to ask too many questions just yet. The facts would do for now, and for the Beverly Hills sergeant.

"You and Washington got things under control, have you?"

"Yes." Ohara's voice was still whispery. He was grateful to see Washington returning, and gestured to him to do the talking.

"That's Kano," Washington said, nodding toward the body on the stairs.

Spielberg frowned. "Too bad you had to kill him."

"He fell down the stairs," Washington replied with a straight face. "But Wakari's upstairs with two others. A bit battered, but they'll live."

Joe Spielberg brightened. "Let's go up and get him. I've been waiting for this."

Washington shook his head. "Better call an ambulance. Wakari's so big, they may need a derrick."

"Any others?"

"Four," Washington replied. "I've got them trussed up in the pool house."

"These two guys did all this?" the Beverly Hills sergeant asked. "They must be something else."

"They are," Spielberg said. "I'd appreciate it if you'd take care of the ambulance. Also, we'll need transport for the other prisoners, and Mrs. Walker. Where is she?" He looked around.

Washington grinned. "Talking on the phone to her husband."

"I'll take care of things right away," the sergeant said.

"Now," Spielberg looked at Ohara and Washington, "let's go up and see Wakari." He turned to his detective. "Bob, go check on the guys in the pool house."

Wakari was unconscious and breathing heavily. The two in the closet were conscious, but refused to say anything. Spielberg had to resign himself to wait for that.

However, he would not wait to hear the story from Washington and Ohara.

They gave him the bare bones of what had happened. When they'd finished, he shook his head. "I've heard what you did, and I've seen it, but I still don't believe it." The sounds of the ambulance and police cars arriving put an end to questions, so he let them go.

As they left Spielberg staring down at Wakari and his two thugs, Washington grinned at Ohara. "I don't believe it myself." On the way downstairs, they paused beside Kano's body. His head was twisted crookedly against the stair tread.

A paramedic who'd been checking the body looked up. "He's dead," he said, making it official. "Weird the way his neck's twisted, isn't it?"

Washington looked at Ohara and gave a short laugh. "Oh, I don't know," he said. "On him, it's appropriate."

"Something like a signature," Ohara agreed gravely.

Miyuki was just being taken out to a car by the sergeant. They followed her outside, then paused a moment on the steps, grateful just to breathe in the cold night air.

Chapter Twenty-nine

The following week gave Ohara and Washington no time for self-congratulation, had they been so inclined. It was filled with paperwork, depositions, interviews with Organized Crime brass, and an official reprimand from Captain Krauss. Breaking and entering, for whatever the reason, had to be frowned upon, but his heart wasn't in it. Duty done, Krauss dismissed them.

As they started for the door, he stopped them. "Off the record, if you guys had stood around sucking your thumbs when there was a chance to get that girl out, I'd have blasted you. I only wish to hell I'd been there, too. That's all."

Despite all the fallout of work on the Wakari case, they still had their normal routine. "Normal" that week included a domestic homicide. Fortunately it was a "smoking gun" case where a man shot up his wife and mother-in-law, then called the police. More paperwork.

Maple Street had disappeared from the news except for one item, which Ohara read with relish. It was a story of how a gang of boys had picked on a Japanese gardener, named Fred Hata, just outside the victory garden he'd made for senior citizens. The older people working in the garden at the time, mostly non-Japanese, saw what was happening and rushed out armed with rakes and hoes to drive Hata's tormentors away. Police action had not been necessary. Maple Street was taking care of its own problems.

Despite the pressure of work, Ohara's mind was occupied with the problem of Jody. There was still no word about her. It didn't seem possible that a youngster with little or no money could survive in San Francisco without being picked up by the police. All the search reports had come back negative. In a way it didn't surprise him. Jody could take care of herself.

He knew only too well that she wasn't the only murderer walking the streets. Still, she was in the national police computers, and the search had been extended throughout the country. Ohara hoped they'd find her before someone else got in her way. He knew he would never again walk past a blond, sweet-faced teenager without remembering Jody.

His moody thoughts were interrupted by a phone call from Duke Walker with an invitation to dinner at a noted Japanese restaurant. After consulting his partner, Ohara accepted for them both, for the following Saturday evening.

Neither Ohara nor Washington had been to the famous establishment before, and were surprised to find that the entrance was up a winding drive into the hills. After parking, they were directed through the ordered perfection of a Japanese garden. Its uncluttered patterns of green planting, rocks, small pools, and gray stone tori lanterns filled them with a sense of serenity and peace. Seeing it, Washington thought that the streets they had left behind seemed like something from a lesser world.

A hostess in kimono met them at the main building and led them to a private tatami room. After they had removed their shoes, she slid open the *fusuma* door to the room, where Duke and Joe Spielberg were already seated at a large black lacquer table surrounded by silk cushions.

Duke welcomed them enthusiastically. He looked as if he felt a bit out of place, but was enjoying things just the same. He explained that Miyuki would join them later.

Ohara knew this was simply an old-fashioned Japanese custom, which he regretted, but he assumed it had been Miyuki's idea to do things in correct Japanese style.

The small dining room had a beautiful painted scroll on the wall and beneath it an exquisite arrangement of chrysanthemums. When Duke saw him looking at it, he said, "Miyuki did that," and his voice was full of pride.

Much to Washington's relief, they did not have to sit cross-legged, for beneath the table was a low pit that comfortably accommodated his long legs. Pretty waitresses in kimonos brought hot towels, sake, beer, and a parade of dishes in lovely lacquer plates and bowls that were as beautiful to look at as the food was delicious to eat.

Joe Spielberg was in his element, since he loved anything Japanese. Encouraged by several cups of sake, he began to talk entertainingly about Japanese history and art. It was a side of him Ohara had never seen before. Duke and Washington listened, fascinated.

After the last course of the superb dinner had been served, the *fusuma* door slid open once more. Ohara and the others fell silent in delight and pleasure. Framed in the doorway was Miyuki in an exquisite kimono of peach silk. Its sleeves and hem were deeply bordered in pale wisteria flowers. The obi around her waist was of silver and lavender brocade. Her long hair was piled high on her head and caught with ivory and silver combs.

Her dark eyes shining, she knelt and bowed first to Duke, then to each of the guests. "Good evening, my husband and honored guests," she said in English.

A waitress, who was standing outside the open door, handed in a rosewood *shamisen,* then reluctantly slid the door closed. Washington eyed the long-necked stringed instrument with its brocade-covered bottom curiously. Spielberg saw at once that it was old and valuable. Taking a large ivory pick from its silk case, Miyuki began to play.

For a little while they were transported to old Japan. Miyuki did more than justice to her geisha training. She played the *shamisen* with skill, and sang to them in a sweet, soft voice. It was beautiful and moving, her gift to them all. It was not the music so much that enchanted, but her presence, the turn of her head, the delicate movements of her hands across the strings.

When she had finished and bowed, there was silence; no one seemed to want to break the spell.

Duke was the first to speak. "Thank you, Miyuki," he said with a new dignity. "I never knew what a geisha was until now."

Then, her silk kimono rustling softly, Miyuki went round the table, pouring more sake and spending some time with each man—enjoying a joke with Washington and teaching Joe an old-fashioned Japanese hand game. Ohara remembered playing it as a child. It was called "Rock, Paper, Scissors," and the loser had to drink a cup of sake. Before long they were all playing, enjoying themselves and accusing Washington of losing on purpose.

After it was over, Miyuki smiled at them. "I no words have to thank good friends. Just try to please best way I know."

Duke looked around the table. "That goes for me, too."

Then the evening was over and the little party broke up. As Washington and Joe followed Duke to put on their shoes outside the room, Miyuki came up to Ohara. She took his hands in hers and began to speak quietly in Japanese. "There is so much I want to say, but I cannot find words. You risked your life . . ."

Ohara stopped her by laying one finger against her lips. Then he said, "It was worth it, just to see you as you are tonight."

Then Miyuki did something very un-Japanese. Putting her hands on his shoulders and standing on tiptoe, she reached up and kissed Ohara good night.

Once more on the noisy city streets, Ohara and Washington drove in companionable silence, keeping the magic of the evening close for a little longer.

Ohara found his thoughts turning to the people in the case whose lives they had touched. Nothing could ever be as it had been for them. He knew Miyuki and Duke would be all right, but what about Joe Flynn and his boy, or old Mrs. Polser? And then there was Jody.

He knew Washington would say such thoughts were best filed away with the paperwork. He was probably right. Deliberately, Ohara closed his mind to the problems that were no longer his. Instead he thought about Peggy, and the promise he'd made to her at the beginning of the case. It was time to keep it. He'd take his overdue long weekend so they could go away together, just the two of them. Maybe they'd drive up to their favorite haunt near Monterey. He smiled and stepped on the gas.

"Where's the fire, Sam?" Washington asked, drowsily comfortable on several cups of sake.

"No fire." Ohara laughed. "I just want to get home."

As Joe Flynn closed the pub that Saturday night, he found himself whistling while he polished the big mahogany bar to a shine. He hadn't felt like whistling for a long time, but tonight it seemed as if a load had been lifted from his shoulders. It looked as if young Mike was going to make it. When he did, Joe would take him home to Mary.

This time they'd tell her the truth. It would be rough, he knew, but it was going to be all right. He'd see to that.

On that same Saturday night, the lights of a car picked up a girl thumbing a ride just outside of Barstow. The car slowed and the girl ran to climb in.

She was a pretty kid, the driver thought, with that long blond hair, prettier than the others. Excitement grabbed him and he picked up speed. As he turned onto the highway, his palms grew damp on the wheel. He hadn't been caught the other times; he wouldn't be caught this time, either. The desert beyond Barstow was made to order for what he had in mind.

"What's your name, sweetheart?" He turned to the girl and smiled, reaching to pat her knee.

Imperceptibly she moved away from him, but her eyes were wide and innocent as she said, "My name's Jody."

"We're going to get along just fine, honey." The driver grinned.

The girl didn't answer. Quietly she put her hand in her pocket, grasped the switchblade she hid there, and waited.